A Time to Die

A Time to Die

Mickey Zucker Reichert

Five Star • Waterville, Maine

Copyright © 2004 by Miriam S. Zucker

All rights reserved.

This novel is a work of fiction. Names, characters, places and incidents are either the product of the author's imagination, or, if real, used fictitiously.

No part of this book may be reproduced or transmitted in any form or by any electronic or mechanical means, including photocopying, recording or by any information storage and retrieval system, without the express written permission of the publisher, except where permitted by law.

First Edition
First Printing: February 2004

Published in 2004 in conjunction with Tekno Books and Ed Gorman.

Set in 11 pt. Plantin by Ramona Watson.

Printed in the United States on permanent paper.

Library of Congress Cataloging-in-Publication Data

Reichert, Mickey Zucker.
    A time to die / by Mickey Zucker Reichert.—1st ed.
      p. cm.—(Five Star first edition titles)
    ISBN 1-4104-0197-9 (hc : alk. paper)
    I. Title. II. Series.
PS3568.E476334T56 2004
  813'.54—dc22   2003064226

ACKNOWLEDGEMENTS

To Cindy & Melissa Mosko, Mark Moore, Gary Reichert, Mike "Overconfident" Batista (who probably thinks he should be listed first), Mike Giudici, and a host of colorful attendings, residents, and patients: some of whom are gypped by confidentiality and others by my faulty memory.

"To everything there is a season, and a time to every purpose under heaven:
A time to be born, and a time to die; a time to plant, and a time to pluck up that which is planted;
A time to kill, and a time to heal; a time to break down, and a time to build up;
A time to weep, and a time to laugh; a time to mourn, and a time to dance . . ."

—Ecclesiastes, 3:1–4

Prologue

March 18, 2021

Perched on Dean Stanley Schober's patterned couch, Patricia Jewett hugged her skinny knees, her gaze fixed on the television. On the screen, presidential candidate Benjamin Nash harangued a cheering crowd, inspiring an awe Jewett could not wholly understand. The televangelist-turned-politician sported shoulder-length, white locks that made him look saint-like; and his long-lashed, dark eyes inspired trust. Nash's figure allowed no sharp edges. Every feature, from his moon-shaped face to his thick hands, was gently smooth. Only his movements remained crisp. His gestures punctuated his speeches at all the right places, and he struck poses appropriate for stained glass windows and Renaissance paintings. His was an act worthy of attention, even from this roomful of graduating doctors, and Jewett focused on Nash's booming promise: ". . . an end to death by 2030!"

An end to death? Jewett's hands slid to her sides in surprise. She cast a surreptitious glance around Doctor Schober's family room. At the opposite end of the couch sat Jewett's classmate and boyfriend, Kaign Jones, his handsome jaw slack, revealing a row of straight, white teeth. Stanley Schober occupied a stuffed recliner catty-corner to Jones, his mouth set in the same grim line he assumed whenever his magnetic imaging machines detected abnormalities in a patient's fetus. Cross-legged on the floor in front of the television, frizzle-haired Zachary Janecek said nothing. Schober's wife, Elaine, stood frozen in the doorway between the kitchen and family room.

Moralist party candidate Benjamin Nash posed, his hands spread and his feet together, until the plaudits of the crowd beneath his podium faded low enough for him to continue his speech. "The Republican candidate claims to be pro-life, but I maintain he is only pro-fetus!" A smattering of television applause followed. "He opposes the very social programs that will allow the babies he saves to reach adulthood. He supports capital punishment and turning off ventilators. I ask those of you with moral fiber, is that pro-life?"

Jewett pursed her lips as Nash's supporters shouted, "No!" The Moralist Party had grown out of the inconsistencies in the standard bipartisan system. Its devotion to Christian principles and the ultimate sanctity of human life had swept it to victory in the last two presidential elections.

Nash's features twisted into a perfect mask of revulsion. "The Democratic candidate would have us reinstitute abortion, yet he opposes the death penalty. He would put the life of criminals over that of our future generations. *Gentle followers, we have to stop playing God with our children!*"

Stanley Schober's fist crashed to the arm of his chair. The fabric muffled the blow, but his shout of outrage broke the students' Nash-inspired trances. "Playing God! *Playing God,* he says."

Every eye in the room turned from the screen to their dean and host. For the moment, Nash was forgotten. Jewett craned her neck to gaze around Jones. Unnerved, as always, by shouting, she twined a strand of long, mouse-brown hair around her finger.

Schober's friendly, aging features assumed a reddish hue

that contrasted sharply with his salt-and-pepper hair. "Playing God," he repeated for emphasis. "The expression was stupid when I first heard it as a medical student, and it's even dumber now. For Christ's sake, we're doctors. Everything we do is playing God."

Janecek grunted noncommittally, trained, as all medical students and residents are, never to argue with the attending physicians. Since their names were alphabetically consecutive, Janecek, Jewett, and Jones had been teamed on every cadaver, microscope, and project since their first day of medical school. Knowing Kaign Jones, Jewett realized the same aggressive audacity that attracted her to him and made him the ideal candidate for a surgical residency would drive him to challenge Schober's assertion, despite the fact that some attendings would find such impudence grounds for dismissal. Jewett wished she had a tenth of his nerve and sometimes wondered how he had made it through four years of medical school without enraging some self-important professor into throwing him out of the program.

True to his calling, Jones straightened in his seat, drawing up his imposing, six-foot three-inch frame. He shook back his dark hair, though no strand ever fell out of position, and spoke through his square-cut, classic American features. "I happen to agree with Nash. True, our job is to thwart death, including the God-given afflictions like cancer and infectious diseases. But killing a microbe is not the same as killing a baby."

Janecek sucked in a sharp breath. Jewett turned her hazel eyes to her lap, clasped her hands, and feigned an inordinate interest in her fingers. Match Day had concluded yesterday, and the national computers had already determined the type and location of each graduating senior's residency. Jones, like Jewett, would be staying at the C. Everett Koop

Memorial Hospital and Medical School, Jewett specializing in chronic care, Jones in surgery. They would both have to interact with Schober for several more years, at least; and Jewett looked forward to his keen obstetrical advice and experience. It seemed rude and foolish to alienate their host.

Schober's features darkened. "But we're not talking about babies, Kaign." He emphasized the last two words, drawing out the double syllable word into three, "bay-bee-eez," and the young doctor's single-syllable name into two: "Kay-ayn." "We're talking about a fetus, a blob of pluripotential cells, and an abnormal blob at that." He leaned toward Jones. "If you don't know it yet, standard abortion's been illegal for years. What grates on me is the woman who walks in, discovers she's carrying a fetus with the body of a pulverized Buick and half the I.Q. I present the option of abortion, and she squeals . . ." Schober's voice jumped to falsetto. ". . . 'Oh, no, Doctor. I wouldn't want to play God.' " Schober's octave returned to normal. "Kaign, if not for the 'miracles' of modern hormonal manipulation, *God* would have seen to it that that blob of pluri-un-potential cells was miscarried. At the least, it would have died at birth. But we have the revised Baby Doe laws to thank for the fact that every baby born, no matter how unnatural, has the 'right to life,' too. Which is playing God? Letting this creature die or forcing it to live?"

Jones' strong hands tensed and loosened spasmodically at his sides. "You're using an extreme example. What about babies with cleft palate? Should we abort them? Where do we draw the line?"

Jewett exchanged wary glances with Janecek. Able to see the relative merits in both sides of the argument, she was embarrassed by her boyfriend's display.

Schober leaped to his feet. "Where do we draw the line?

A Time to Die

Somewhere! Anywhere! Damn it, Kaign, don't you see that's precisely the problem? Every day of our lives we have to make decisions and draw lines. That's how this Moralist party took hold in the first place. Human life is sacred. Period. It doesn't draw any lines, so it's easy for simple minds and politicians, if I'm not being too redundant, to grasp." Schober lowered himself into the cushions of his chair. "Now this idiot, Nash, wants to make it illegal to take anyone off life support equipment. Madness! He's not ending death; he's just creating a sort of living death. Brainless children surviving for eternity in the hospital because it's possible we may find a cure for their conditions before they die of old age? If Nash has his way, it won't even be possible to die of old age anymore. I, for one, would rather go to hell than live forever."

Jones shrugged, his calm exterior making Schober's screaming look foolish. "Most people don't agree. Why do you think the cryogenics labs have flourished? Why do you think the Moralists keep getting elected? The new generations do believe human life is sacred. Our ancestors promised us eternal life, or at least greatly prolonged lifespans. We grew up with that promise, and we're going to get it. This is the first step."

A brief silence ensued. Jewett peeked up from her hands in time to see Schober's lips moving, his words too soft to hear. He mumbled a bit louder. "Yeah, well, it's an unnatural attitude, in my opinion. I still remember when the military budget made the hospital monies look like peanuts instead of the other way." Schober's voice regained its resonance. "A lot of things have changed for the better, but this isn't one of them. Hell, everyone thought gene-washed organ transplants and stem cells would be the wave of the future. Now they're impossible. If choosing to sustain the braindead takes precedence over using their cells or organs to save quality lives in order not to play God, I'd rather play God."

As Jones gathered breath for a rebuttal, Jewett sank back into the couch. Schober was nicer and more understanding than most attendings, but even he must have limits to the amount of guff he would accept from an underling.

Elaine Schober's husky voice interrupted the discussion. "Time to eat! Over dinner, I'd like to hear what you new doctors will be doing next year. After all, this is supposed to be a Match Day party." Her tone was cheerful, the warning glare she turned her husband less so.

Grateful for Mrs. Schober's intervention, Jewett rose and took Jones' arm. From the television, Benjamin Nash's voice rose above the silence. "Conquer death by 2030!" Beneath his podium, his followers chanted in a steady, fanatical rhythm: "End Death! End Death! End Death!"

Stanley Schober groaned.

Chapter 1

April 20, 2030

By the eighth year of Benjamin Nash's presidency, the argument in the Schobers' living room had faded into dim memory. Dr. Patricia Jewett wandered between the aisles of the open life support bay, glancing across horizontal faces that seemed as gray and glazed as waxed fruit. One of four chronic care specialists at the C. Everett Koop Memorial Hospital, Jewett covered the ward duties for one-month periods only three times a year. But the patients rarely changed. The infants and children grew in length and breadth, nourished by calorie-laden liquids dripped through nasal tubes or infection-prone catheters in their great vessels. Occasionally, an aged heart crumpled beyond the redemption of even the most modern electrostimulation machines, and a body disappeared from its bed, finally truly dead.

Jewett stopped in front of Judson Payne, a six-year-old near-drowning victim who had required antibiotics the previous day. Glassy blue eyes seemed to stare back at her, unseeing. Despite daily physical therapy, the boy's legs had rotated from disuse, making his knees appear to bend backward, like a bird's. The feeding tube ran from his nose to a bag above his bed, its individualized formula, Nutristat, colored a tasteful tan. The standard, flexible ventilator tube jutted from his neck, running unobtrusively beneath the blankets to the briefcase-sized ventilator at the bedside to which the boy's family taped flowers and pictures of animals.

Now, a photograph of a panting, stub-tailed mongrel sat inside a wreath of wilting daisies. The blankets hid the portal of his great vein catheter, closed between antibiotic dosages, and the wires of the electrostimulation machine; but Jewett watched the ceaseless blips on the fist-sized monitor screen at the bedside. Scattered telemeters transmitted information about the gaseous, nutritional, drug, and electrolyte content of the boy's blood to the nurses' station.

Jewett sighed, feeling helpless and futile, wondering when medical science would catch up to the living death it had created. True, antibody manipulation had led to cures for most viruses and cancers, but the technology had only benefited the newly diagnosed. While the application had cleared up the underlying maladies of some chronic care patients, there was still no way to restore the neurological and organ damage which had occurred in the intervening years. Despite volumes of knowledge gleaned on the function of the brain and its related systems, science had barely uncovered the tip of that iceberg.

Jewett placed a hand on the boy's foot, feeling the warm life of his flesh beneath her fingers. The child did not seem to be suffering, and he brought joy to the parents who loved him. Every movement of his eyes, each attempt at facial expression was a sweet triumph to them, every bit as important as a normal infant's first word. Still, sometimes to Jewett it felt easier to justify her job in the name of experimentation. Because of these patients, the form of life support equipment had advanced in great leaps. The huge, clanking monsters that had served as ventilators a decade ago had become museum curiosities, and the patients temporarily dependent on life support devices benefited from the knowledge as well. Jewett recalled intensive care units filled with the ceaseless pound, whoosh, and electric snap of machines which now hummed almost imperceptibly. Now, Jewett had become so accustomed to the steady buzz, she no longer even heard that.

The sound of footsteps at the opposite entrance drew Jewett's attention. She glanced over the rows of patients to where the open bay resident physician, Curtis Maltorf, led five new, white-coated medical students into the room. Three women and two men in their early twenties edged into the bay, eyes darting nervously between the beds, noses twitching to catch the flowery, pleasant odor of the antimicrobial cleansers and air fresheners that had replaced the old, alcohol-based scrubs Jewett had known as a student. Like a mother hen, Maltorf herded his charges toward the first bed, his red-haired head bobbing between the patients.

The scene reminded Jewett of Ronald McDonald prancing through one of his fast food restaurants, surrounded by admiring kids. Smiling, she trotted around the rows of beds and met the group by the door. "Morning, Curt."

"Good morning, Dr. Jewett." Maltorf gestured at the students. "Since we've got a new group of studs, I thought we'd start—"

The beeper at Maltorf's hip shrilled, interrupting him and visibly startling the students. Maltorf thumbed the button silent, pulled the device from his belt loop, and freed the catch. It fell open to reveal the speaker. "Excuse me." He touched the inner button, and the cordless receiver automatically pulsed out the number the caller had programmed into it.

The students shifted uneasily, pocketed ophthalmo-otoscopes rattling against reflex hammers, tuning forks, and tape, a standard mixture of archaic and modern equipment. It was the students' job to see to it they carried anything a resident or staff physician might need.

Jewett grinned at the students, trying to put them at ease.

Apparently in response to an answer from the beeper-phone, Maltorf nodded. "Yes. Curt Maltorf, chronic care resident. What can I do for you?" Maltorf balanced the device between his shoulder and ear. Hands freed, he rooted through his pants pocket, emerging with a pad and pen. He scribbled. "Uh huh . . . no, that doesn't sound familiar to me . . . uh huh . . . uh huh." He wrote some more. "O.K. Send him to private room 163. We'll be expecting him." Maltorf snapped the beeper-phone closed and clipped it to his hip pocket.

"New admission?" Jewett asked.

"Yep." Maltorf studied his scrawled notes. "Seventy-eight-year-old white male MVA."

Jewett clarified for the students. "Motor vehicle accident." She frowned. Those had become rare since the electronic mapping and alerting road systems, especially in broad daylight on a weekday. Usually such mishaps occurred only as a suicide or after the driver had taken an unauthorized excess of drugs or alcohol.

Maltorf continued. "A bystander found him first and moved him from the car, resulting in a C-spine injury."

Jewett cringed. Despite television campaigns, untrained do-gooders still moved accident victims before calling the paramedics. A cervical spine injury could turn the patient into an instant quadriplegic, and the odds were even this patient would lose his ability to breathe without machinery as well.

"Luckily, the bystander knew CPR. He kept the patient

alive until help arrived, but the E.R. says he's a definite quad."

Jewett pulled at her lower lip. With advanced life support systems, it would have been possible to revitalize the heart even after an hour or more without beating, but the brain would die of oxygen deprivation within minutes. If the cardiopulmonary resuscitation was performed correctly, it was possible the bystander had averted brain death in the man he had paralyzed.

Maltorf closed his pad and shoved it back into his pants pocket. "The E.R. staff said the patient was a doctor here at Koop. An obstetrician."

Jewett's blood ran cold. Her vocal cords seemed to snap shut, and it was all she could do to ask the question in a high-pitched whisper. "Who?"

Maltorf studied Jewett, concern in his dark eyes. "A Stanley Schober."

Jewett loosed a sharp sound of pain and closed her eyes. Suddenly dizzy, she grabbed for the nearest cot. Her fingers closed over cold metal, her nails gouging into the padding.

Maltorf seized Jewett's skinny arm, inadvertently jerking a few strands of her straight, dark hair in the process. "Are you all right?"

Gathering her scattered wits, Jewett opened her lids. The dim lighting of the ward seemed to burn her eyes. "I'm . . . fine," she managed. "You . . . didn't go to med school here, did you?"

Maltorf shook his head. "No, Doctor. Harvard. Why?" He released his grip on Jewett's arm.

Now, Jewett shook her head. There was no way to explain to an outsider the improvements Stanley Schober had implemented since he took over the dean position at Koop. The former head had been a stuffy codger; a call from an attending to his office meant the complainee repeated a year, at best, or got expelled. Schober had brought an air of friendship to the position, mediating problems and smoothing the ruffled feathers that invariably resulted when powerful men and women accustomed to success and demanding near-perfection and obedience came together. Frequently, he and his wife, Elaine, had entertained medical students on special occasions or following rotations on his obstetrical service. "How? Why?"

Jewett's questions were rhetorical, but, since she spoke aloud, Maltorf apparently felt obligated to answer. "The E.R. docs think he had a vascular accident while driving, a C.V.A. or an M.I."

A stroke or heart attack. For reasons Jewett could not understand, it seemed necessary to put the description into layman's terms. Jargon seemed too distant, too incomprehensible to refer to Stanley Schober. *This can't be happening. I can't believe this is happening.* She forced composure. "Curt, why don't you introduce the students to their patients and the ward routine? We'll postpone attending rounds." She glanced at her watch. Discovering it was already 15:20, she added, "Until tomorrow."

Accustomed to talking to patients' families, Maltorf put just the right amount of comfort in his voice to soothe without patronizing. "Sounds good. The studs and I will see to it everything's taken care of." He made a vague gesture, turned on his heel, and the students followed him deeper into the room.

Patricia Jewett watched them leave through a blur of rising tears. She tried not to think about Stanley Schober, but the memories came in defiance. Her mind conjured images of a day thirteen years ago. Then, Schober's curly hair had been more brown than gray, splashed with silver mostly at the temples. Except for fewer creases, his face was the same: pudgy cheeks with permanent smile lines, a straight nose, and blue eyes that sparkled even in faint light.

Jewett had received a letter from Rudy Yates, her boyfriend since grade school, breaking off their relationship of fifteen years. They had grown up together, two scrawny, gawky kids, best friends and neighbors for as long as Jewett could recall. There was never any doubt they would marry; over the years they had planned their intertwined lives to eternity. She would become a doctor, he a medical researcher discovering the therapies she would effect. As older scientists beat them to the cures for the common cold, diabetes, and cystic fibrosis, they merely set their goals one step higher. But, where Jewett had matured from a skinny child to a skinny adult, Yates had blossomed into a sturdy, well-proportioned man. The same women who would snicker at him as a teenager fawned and purred over him at twenty. And Yates dropped the familiar to explore this new part of his life.

Crushed by Yates' rejection, Jewett had found concentration on medical school work impossible. The professors' voices droned by her. Computer-generated lecture notes scrawled across the screen, unread; and first-year medical student Patricia Jewett had decided it was time to see Dean Stanley Schober.

Jewett recalled how Schober had sat, speechless, behind an oaken desk covered with knickknacks, sports paraphernalia, and photographs, never taking his eyes from her throughout her tearful story and patient with the frequent interruptions to wipe her eyes or blow her nose until she delivered the *coup de grace*. "I'm quitting medical school."

Gaze still locked on Jewett, Schober had produced a pencil from beneath a ceramic elephant and tapped it thoughtfully. Just as the silence seemed to grow unbearable, he spoke. "So, the only reason you came to Koop was to make your boyfriend happy?"

Jewett lowered her head, saying nothing.

The eraser made muffled tapping sounds on the desktop. "And all that stuff you wrote on your application about wanting to help people and be challenged by the ever-changing field of medicine. That was a lie?"

Shocked Schober could remember her essay from thousands of applicants, Jewett glanced up suddenly.

"You lied to me? You don't really care about human suffering?" Schober sounded genuinely, personally hurt by her obvious deception.

A pang of guilt penetrated Jewett's grief. "Well, yes, sir. I mean no, sir." She paused, trying to remember how he had phrased the questions. "I care. I just think you should give my slot to someone more dedicated." Schober's reaction was not at all what she had expected. Most elder physicians would have given her a lecture on how doctors should be able to handle stress. She could almost hear the former dean saying, "If you can't hack it, get out. We'll find someone who can."

"Request denied!" Schober slapped the pencil to the desk with a hollow crack.

"Denied?" Had she felt less battered by circumstance, Jewett would have laughed. "You can't deny my request to quit. I'm not an inmate. I can just up and leave whenever I want to."

"True." Schober leaned across the desk, his smile conspiratorial, as though he and Jewett shared a secret. "And after you miss enough tests, you'll fail. But, in the meantime, as long as I don't sign any paperwork, you have two weeks to realize this guy Yates isn't worth depriving yourself of an education or the world of a damn fine doctor. Now go. Take a vacation. Come back in a week. If you still feel like quitting then, I'll talk you out of it again. I never met a person yet able to get this far without a strong dedication to medicine."

Flattered by Schober's notice of her essay and the powerful emotions her writing must have conveyed, Jewett took his advice.

Now, standing in the doorway of the chronic care ward, Jewett smiled at the memory. Only the knowledge of experience made her understand Schober probably had not known her essay from any other. Every medical student since time began had written the exact same sentiments, in different words.

Patricia Jewett unclenched her hand from the patient's bed, no longer able to hide behind remembrances. Too soon, the Emergency Room doctors would finish the preliminary work, the nurses would attach the necessary equipment, and Stanley Schober would become another glazed face on her chronic care ward.

This is morbid. Jewett shuddered, forcing the thought away. *Paralyzed, certainly, but I don't know for sure he's sustained brain injury.* She left the main bay and slipped into the straight, white corridor that opened onto the shared bays, private, and semiprivate rooms composing Koop's chronic care ward. Painted prints lined the walls in sterile, metallic frames. These were changed monthly; the families of long term patients appreciated the subtle difference this made. Currently, the theme was Cubists, and the multiple, malpositioned heads and detached limbs made Jewett uncomfortable. She passed two semi-privates on her left and another open bay to the right. Most of the patients there suffered from degenerative neurological diseases, such as amyotrophic lateral sclerosis, Lou Gehrig's disease, which stripped away bodily function but left the mind intact. She could hear the clicks of brain-, lip-, or eyelid-operated communication devices and computer-simulated voices.

Patricia Jewett passed two private rooms on the right side of the hall and the subacute open bay on the left. There, she had always found the ray of hope in an otherwise bleak specialty. This room housed patients dependent on technology for months or years but expected to eventually return to society: those with reversible conditions, coma, or the ability to operate wheelchairs and portable communications boards. Generally, Jewett spent as much time as possible with the subacute patients, but today she passed their bay without a glance. The last three rooms on either side of the hallway were privates or semiprivates, patients for whom their families donated money over the amount the government supplied for care. Jewett could hear movement and muffled voices emerging from the first door on the left, room 163. She drew a deep lungful of air and entered.

At the far end of the chamber, a team of male and female nurses in green chronic care uniforms plugged and fastened equipment, blocking Jewett's view of Stanley Schober. Closer to the door, one of the Emergency Room physicians spoke softly with Schober's wife. A retired sales manager for an appliance company, Elaine Schober had always seemed strong to Jewett, who still felt tense giving verbal orders to nurses. Now, the older woman looked frail despite being slightly overweight by the fitness standards the government employed since it took over health care payments. The whites of her eyes were tinged pink, etched with prominent vessels and hollowed into their sockets. Old tears filled the wrinkles on her cheeks. As Jewett entered the room, she was caught into a wild embrace.

For some time, the women clung amid the equipment rattle and gentle exchanges of the nurses. There was nothing to say, so they both said nothing, sharing a silent misery beyond words. The Emergency Room physician slipped quietly from the room, and Jewett glanced uneasily toward the brain wave monitors. As the nurses shuffled about, she caught intermittent glimpses of an abnormal wave pattern. She assessed it from habit. Schober obviously lay unconscious. There was evidence of a severe infarction involving the left middle cerebral artery, a particularly serious location for a stroke. It would rob Schober of neurological control of whatever few muscles below the diaphragm the spinal cord injury might have spared. Additionally, there would surely be deficits in communication, most likely a complete inability to construct or understand speech.

Under the circumstances, Jewett could only hope head injuries obtained during the crash had damaged the intelligent portions of his brain as well. She dared not imagine the frustrations of a fully conscious doctor, hearing but not understanding, wanting to speak, but unable to form words to fit the concepts. But distance would not allow Jewett to discern the subtleties of the brain wave pattern, and even her professional interpretation of the most modern technology would be flawed at best. There were still too many unknowns about the human mind: the abilities of some areas to take over the function of others in some brains, the collateral flow of emotion and ideas.

Gradually, the violence left Elaine's embrace, and her hands slid, limp, to Jewett's arms. Though surrounded by redness, her green eyes glimmered with purpose. "What should I expect?"

Jewett swallowed hard, believing honesty was the best

course but wanting to ease into the prognosis. "Hard to tell, yet. He's asleep and certainly not suffering. I'll have a better idea when he gains consciousness and I can get a look at his waking thought patterns." She added unnecessarily, "I'm sorry, Elaine. It doesn't look good."

Elaine nodded, apparently not surprised by Jewett's assessment.

"I'm sorry I didn't come down to see him in the E.R., Elaine. I wish I'd been there for both of you, but I didn't know until they contacted my resident that Stan was on his way."

Elaine barely acknowledged the apology for a lapse that clearly had never occurred to her. "How's Kaign, dear?"

Jewett's relationship with Kaign Jones was the last thing she wanted to talk about now, but she recognized Elaine's need to discuss matters more trivial than her husband's condition. "Better. Now that he's off the teaching service, we have more time together. His temper's better, too. You know surgeons. High-strung."

Elaine let her hands drop to her sides, managing a crooked smile. "When are you two kids getting married?"

Recognizing the same essential release of tension that causes parents to laugh when a terminally ill child dies after a prolonged illness, Jewett returned the smile. "You're starting to sound like my mother."

Undaunted, Elaine continued. "How long have you been together now? Ten years?"

"Nine, but who's counting? Before Kaign, I dated the same guy for fifteen years. Started when I was ten." Jewett chuckled. In the background of Schober's room, it sounded strained. "No one can accuse me of not being able to handle a long-term relationship." She glanced into Elaine's haggard face and saw a need to get away. "Come on.

There's nothing you or I can do here now. Let's get a cup of coffee." She seized Elaine's elbow and steered her toward the door.

Elaine allowed herself to be led. As they emerged into the hallway, she rambled. "You may not be a glamour queen, Pat, but you're a decent-looking young woman. Kind. Understanding. Kaign's okay, but he's loud and opinionated. Not at all right for you, dear. I hope you're not staying with him from habit."

From anyone else, Jewett would have found the words insulting; but she had become familiar with the various reactions of stunned relatives of seriously injured patients, from impenetrable despair to wild, violent hostility. "Deep down, Kaign's a good guy. You just have to get to know him."

Elaine made no direct reply. She stopped and glanced up and down the hallway. Assured no one could overhear her, she pressed her back against a copy of Picasso's *Guernica* and whispered. "Pat, I'm glad you're the one taking care of Stan. You know him and what he would want."

Patricia Jewett pursed her lips. More than once, Stanley Schober had made his position clear. He loved life. Even entering his eighth decade, he still kept active playing tennis and softball in the senior leagues. In a situation like this one, there was no question he would want the ventilation machines discontinued. "I'll respect his wishes." Even as she spoke, Jewett felt a sudden urge to kick herself.

"Thank you." Elaine Schober continued her walk toward the main hallway.

Sobered, Patricia Jewett trailed her, grimly, knowing there was no way the law or the government would allow her to keep that promise.

Chapter 2

Five o'clock had come sooner than expected. Unable to concentrate, Dr. Patricia Jewett had left her wards in the residents' hands and returned to her small, rented house. Now, slouched across the blue sofa that lined one wall of her living room, her feet propped on the coffee table, she felt as drained as if she had run for miles. The tears she had not allowed herself to shed in Elaine Schober's presence came and went, tightening on her cheeks before each new jag of crying began. She glanced around the familiar room as if seeing it for the first time. The oak table beneath her shoes held her white, plastic telephone and the latest issues of *The Journal of the American Medical Association* and *Chronic Care Annals*. Matching easy chairs of gold-flecked blue sandwiched the couch, all facing the television screen. Disinterested in cooking or cleaning, she grabbed the remote control from its holster on the arm of the couch and tried to distract herself with mindless entertainment.

The television flicked on. A flawless image of President Benjamin Nash appeared instantly on the screen. As usual, he addressed a crowd of cheering followers, and Jewett recognized the scene from his State of the Union address the previous month. A newscaster spoke from the background. "As the President begins his trip through the Midwest, the First Lady . . ." The cameras panned to Ashley Nash wearing the newest fashion, a salmon-colored, satiny garment that flattered her usually nonexistent curves. ". . . plans to . . ."

Jewett changed the channel. She knew about Nash's visit to the chronic care facilities of the Midwest. It bugged Kaign Jones to rants that the President had chosen to visit the larger university-affiliated hospital in Iowa City rather than Koop in Des Moines; but, for now, she was glad. It was not in her nature to become extreme in her devotion to a cause. Despite Jones' emphatic support for Nash, Jewett felt indifferent. Now, at least, with Nash's policies standing in the way of Stanley Schober's wishes, Jewett did not care to be reminded of the Moralist party.

All the major stations were carrying coverage of the President's visit. Jewett shifted through them quickly, then jumped to the minor stations and settled on an ancient rerun of a sci-fi situation comedy based on a classic movie from the 1970s.

At first, Patricia Jewett had difficulty concentrating, but the trite drivel the writers called a plot was so predictable, she picked it up at once and was soon laughing at the crude but glitzy special effects that had characterized turn-of-the-century television. Fuzzy, teddy bear-like aliens had just boarded the heroes' spaceship in a wild flash of light when Jewett's telephone buzzed.

Startled, Jewett stiffened, muted the television, and plucked the receiver from its recharging cradle. "Hello?"

Kaign Jones' familiar voice wafted to her, the clamor of the operating room muffled but recognizable behind it. "Pat, I heard about Stan." His tone went appropriately remorseful. "Too bad."

Jewett crossed her legs onto the couch cushion, wishing Jones had not reminded her of the tragedy she had finally managed to push to the back of her thoughts. She changed the subject. "You still at the hospital?"

"Just finished the last case. I'm done for the night."

Jewett glanced at her watch. It was 18:43, later than she expected.

Jones continued. "How did he look?"

The question was unexpected, and Jewett's frazzled nerves did not allow it to register. "Who?"

"Stan. How did he look?"

Jewett fought another wave of tears, voice quavering. "I—I didn't get a good look. I spent more time with Elaine." She knew Jones wanted Schober's medical condition, but it still seemed wrong to discuss her former dean in standard patient terminology.

"How's she taking it?"

Jewett swept mouse-colored hair from her face. "Pretty well, actually. In some ways, better than I am."

Jones paused, apparently processing Jewett's words and emotional state. "Have you eaten yet?"

"No. I really haven't felt up to it."

"Well don't. I'll come by, and we'll catch dinner at Webster's."

Jewett glanced at the rumpled shirt and pants she had not bothered to change since work. "I don't know, Kaign. I don't feel . . ."

Jones interrupted. "No arguments. It's just what you need. I'll be there in ten minutes." He disconnected before she could protest.

Jewett replaced the receiver with a sigh. Visiting a public place was the last thing she wanted to do, but it was too late to cancel now. Once Jones got an idea into his head, it was difficult to dislodge. Besides, Jewett knew he was probably right. *It'll do me good to get things off my mind.* She rolled to her feet as awkwardly as a pregnant woman and trotted into the adjoining bedroom to prepare.

A Time to Die

★ ★ ★ ★ ★

Webster's Convention occupied a prime location in Des Moines, beside one of the parking garages. A throwback to the previous decade, it sported walls of purple brick and numerous windows, a quaint oddity amid the older, bleak cinder block storefronts and the modern, heat-retaining plastics. Having purchased a locked compartment in the public garage for Jones' sports car, Jewett and Jones walked the single block to the restaurant.

Immaculate concrete steps and a black handrail led to the upper story of Webster's. Beside the stairs, a door led to the lower level, clearly labeled "Bar." It seemed an unusual combination. The restaurant attracted professional clientele—doctors, publishers, and businessmen—while the patrons of the bar formed a more mixed and lower-class crowd. Jones and Jewett climbed the steps. Opening the door, Jones ushered Jewett into Webster's Convention. As they stepped across the threshold into a plush interior decorated in shades of red, Jewett could feel the pounding bassline of the bar's rock music beneath the softer strains of the contemporary verses piped into the restaurant.

A hostess in a black skirt and buttoned red vest met them at the doorway with a portable body fat measuring device. Behind her, a regal man in a matching uniform waited beside a burnished menu stand. Beyond him, rows of tables were dimly visible, lit only by a single, electric candle centered on each scarlet tablecloth. This late on a Monday, Jewett could make out only a handful of patrons.

The hostess smiled. "Good evening. Welcome to Webster's Convention. Could I have an arm, please?"

Jewett slid up the sleeve of her dress without thinking, accustomed to the formality since the government took over medical payments in exchange for instituted measures to keep the population physically fit. The stepwise program began in restaurants. So far, it had mostly just discouraged overweight people from eating out, though the Congress expected better results when the laws were established for supermarkets.

The hostess poked the probe into Jewett's arm. The display lit, luminously yellow in the ruddy darkness. "Menu A."

Jewett accepted the unrestricted menu from the waiter and took a step toward the main dining room while Jones bared his arm. She stared out over the other patrons, idly, trying to count their shadowy forms.

"Menu C."

"C?" The annoyance in Jones' voice startled Jewett. She whirled back toward him.

Jones' face went as crimson as the decor. "There must be some mistake. I've never been worse than a B."

The hostess shifted from foot to foot. "I'm sorry, sir." She turned Jones an uncomfortable smile. "Would you like me to try again?"

"Yes, I'd like you to try again!" Jones was nearly shouting now.

Jewett studied Jones. His gray dress slacks did seem a little tighter than usual, his shirt tauter over a mild paunch. She knew his busy surgery schedule had kept him from his workouts. She elbowed him gently in the ribs. "Kaign, please."

The hostess touched the probe to Jones' arm. She shook her head apologetically. "I'm sorry, sir. It's close, but menu C."

"Damn it!" Jones yanked stiltedly at his pants' creases. "That's impossible." He pulled his wallet from his back pocket, riffled through identification, business cards, affiliations, and credit waivers and pulled his government-issue workout card from the pile. He thrust it beneath the hostess's nose. "Look. I've got a seventy-five percent fitness stamp."

Every head in the restaurant turned in their direction.

Jewett had become accustomed to Jones' abrasive manner. His good looks had served him well in the past, and the government's emphasis on fitness had made everyone sensitive. She could understand his offense, but she also realized arguing with the hostess could not change the situation. Knowing her boyfriend teetered at the edge of humiliating them all, Jewett plucked at Jones' sleeve. "Kaign, please, it's not that big a deal. If the probe's broken, there's nothing we can do about it now."

The waiter stood stiffly, the menu balanced in his hands. The hostess stared cross-eyed at Jones' fitness card.

Jones scowled.

"Please," Jewett repeated.

Jones' features softened. He replaced his card in his wallet and his wallet in his pants. Without a word, he snatched the menu from the waiter's hands and followed the hostess to a table in the near corner. Jewett trailed after them, accepting the chair the hostess indicated.

Once seated, Jones caught Jewett's hand. "I'm sorry. That was the last thing you needed. I'm a jerk."

Jewett took the bait. "Most of the time, but I love you anyway."

Jones gave Jewett's fingers a warning squeeze. He laughed. "I guess I deserved that. Too much time playing God in the surgery suite, and I forget I can't demand instant obedience from the outside world."

Jewett knew Jones meant "playing God" to refer to the power surgeons held over their staff in the operating room rather than the standard layman's interpretation, but she cringed at the phrase. "Would you mind if we talked about something other than the hospital?"

Jones opened his menu, frowning at the unfamiliar pages. "Not at all. That's why we're here, right, gorgeous?"

"Right, handsome." Jewett consulted her own menu.

Jones looked up. "Did you hear President Nash might come by Koop tomorrow after all? I just found out tonight."

Shit. Jewett buried her nose in her menu with a groan, imagining the corridors crammed with Nash's followers and television crews shoving cameras in her face. Jewett had always been shy, and the idea of interviews terrified her. *I just know I'll say something stupid.* "Kaign, right now I don't want to talk about Nash either."

Jones raised his hands as if in surrender to indicate he would respect her wishes. Unfortunately, the couple currently had few other topics to discuss.

After an unusually quiet dinner, Patricia Jewett had to admit she felt better. Jones' dark eyes danced in the flickering light of the electric candle. In the semi-darkness, his sharp features seemed ivory-colored beneath settled black curls, like a statue of a Greek god. Jewett whipped strands of her straight hair behind her ears, feeling lucky to have a powerful, handsome surgeon. At moments like this, she justified his quick temper and occasional bursts of arrogance to the strong personality required to counterbalance her timidness. In the years of dating Jones, Jewett had become less withdrawn and more willing to speak her mind.

Jones returned her stare with a tight-lipped, provocative smile. "How's your alcohol allotment?"

A light and occasional drinker, Jewett rarely came close to fulfilling her quota. "I haven't become a lush in the past week. Why?"

"Let's grab a few drinks before we go home." Jewett glanced at her watch to discover it was already after 21:00. She knew they needed to go to work in the morning, but she doubted she could find much sleep tonight anyway. "All right. Sure, I guess so."

Jones grabbed her hand, and they whisked past the few remaining diners to the back of the restaurant. Jones pushed open the door to the stairs, and rock music slammed against Jewett's ears. She hesitated at the top of the carpeted stairwell. Compared with the weekend crowd, the bar seemed scarcely half full. Six couples jiggled and leaped on the dance floor amid an array of colored lights. Three of the nine tables supported patrons in groups of two and three. Four lone men sat in front of the canopied bar. The walls were painted in jagged rainbows, interrupted by the stairwell on one side and the outer door on the other. Jewett trotted down the steps, letting the restaurant door snap closed behind her.

"Give me your alcohol card." Jones gestured toward an empty table near the stairs. "I'll get the drinks."

Jewett nodded and complied, not bothering to specify. Jones knew what she liked and had good taste in liquors. She sat, watching him head toward the bar. Alone, thoughts of Stanley Schober returned to her, and tears formed against her will. She dropped her forehead to the tabletop.

Shortly, the sound of a chair leg scraping the floor drew Jewett's attention to the seat across from her. A beer mug clicked against the table, and a masculine voice followed. "Hey, beautiful. What's a nice girl like you doing in a place like this?"

It was, without a doubt, the stalest, most archaic pick-up line Jewett had ever heard. Discomfort forgotten, she raised her head slowly, expecting to discover a man as timeworn as his pitch. Instead, she met a set of keen blue eyes no older than her own. Aside from age, which she estimated at thirty-five, this man seemed in every way the opposite of Kaign Jones. Jewett guessed he would stand half a foot shy of Jones' six-foot-three frame. His features were round, capped with a wild, blond mop of hair tinged slightly red. His nose was crooked, as if broken and healed, his cheeks hollowed and gaunt like a wrestler desperate to make weight before a match, contrasting sharply with well-defined muscles hidden by a loose-fitting shirt. Despite the flaws, the full effect of the stranger's appearance seemed oddly pleasant, if several levels below the status of most of Jewett's friends.

"I'm not interested," Jewett mumbled, flattered despite her annoyance. A long time had passed since anyone but Jones had called her beautiful.

Undaunted, the stranger sat. "Oh, come on. A couple drinks, a little light chatter. You're not over your allotment, are you?"

Why today? Jewett rolled her eyes and spoke in the coarsest, least attractive voice she could muster. "I'm sorry. I'm with someone. Please leave."

The stranger's expression went grimly serious. "You just look like you need someone to talk to."

From over the stranger's shoulder, Jewett could see Jones returning, clutching a glass in each hand, and she wanted to be rid of the smaller man before an argument ensued. "I'm not your type, and I'm sure as heck not going to fall for that cornball pitch. Does my boyfriend have to physically move you, or will you *just go away?*"

The stranger rose, raising his hands as if in surrender. "Sorry I insulted you by calling you beautiful." Forgetting his beer, he spun, a graceful sidestep all that saved him from crashing into Jones.

Knowing Jones' temper too well, Jewett flinched.

Jones slammed the filled glasses to the tabletop. "Look, pal. I don't know who you are, but get the hell away from my girlfriend! We doctors have enough stress without lowlifers like you adding to it."

"Kaign . . ." Jewett started, planning to finish by saying she had control of the situation.

But Jones interrupted, jabbing a finger toward the stranger's face. "I have a mind to report you to the authorities!"

Ignoring Jones' threatening stance, the stranger glanced at Jewett as if to question her choice of date. His manner remained calm as he returned his gaze to Jones, but his voice contained a flat tone indicative of building rage. "You're wrong on both counts. First, I'm a cop. Reporting me won't do you a bit of good since talking to a loud-mouthed jerk's girlfriend isn't illegal. Second . . . I'm not sure you *do* have a mind."

Jones' square jaw clenched so tightly it began to shake.

Jewett gasped in alarm. She glanced to the other patrons, but the volume of the music kept their dispute private. *Let it go, Kaign. Just let it go.* She hoped Jones could maintain the control necessary to stop bandying insults with a policeman; but she also knew his temper could flare beyond rationality, even over such a small slight.

The stranger reached for his beer.

Apparently misunderstanding the sudden movement, Jones took it as a physical threat. He placed himself between the man and Jewett. "All right, you little asshole. Let's take this outside!"

Jewett clasped her hands, knowing from experience that nothing she could say or do would defuse the situation. Jones would see any interference from her as patronizing, and that would only fuel his anger. *He wouldn't really fight a cop.* She tried to reassure herself. *He wouldn't risk his hands in a fistfight . . . would he?* The answer seemed clear, the challenge already made.

The stranger stopped mid-movement, looking directly at Jones with raised brows. "Look, buddy. You're probably what? Forty years old? A little overweight and . . ." The stranger tried to pacify Jones but only succeeded in infuriating him.

"Outside!" Jones screamed. "Right now!"

"Really?" The stranger shifted away from Jones.

Jewett shook her head.

"Right now!"

The shorter man pulled a spiral notebook from his pocket. "That would be in violation of city ordinance X47185: public brawling." He looked up, his mockery obvious despite his level tone. "Off the record, it's also criminal stupidity." He returned the notebook to his pocket, wrapped a hand around his beer, and boldly turned his back on the seething surgeon.

"You . . . you . . . jackass!" Jones sputtered.

Jewett finally dared to touch her boyfriend's hand in silent warning. Since the other man had turned his back, Jones might not see the gesture as belittling.

"Let's get out of here." Jones seized Jewett's arm and drew her toward the exit.

Jewett went happily, glancing over her shoulder once as they exited. Leaning casually against an empty table, the stranger watched them leave with clear amusement, a slight smile playing across his lips.

"Cocky bastard," Jones muttered under his breath.

Under the circumstances, Jewett could only agree with Jones' assessment.

CHAPTER 3

The following morning, after three hours of restless sleep, Patricia Jewett arrived for work. Approaching the plastiglass front doors of the C. Everett Koop Memorial Hospital, she discovered a crowd inside. Cheering men and women filled the reception area, where someone had shoved the padded benches against the walls to make more room in the center. In a far corner, a podium stood on a platform. Atop it, Benjamin Nash was amplified over the crowd, the ceaseless click of cameras, and the constant blare of the overhead speaker as receptionists attempted to process patients who lacked the strength or physical function to tunnel through the crowd.

The double doors opened outward, and it was all Jewett could do to control the urge to trip them open without warning, spilling Moralists onto the sidewalk. Instead, she muttered a few timid "excuse me's," and the crowd miraculously shifted enough to let her inside.

The reception area to Koop felt uncomfortably stuffy after the cool, spring air. The mixture of cosmetic smells—perfumes, colognes, powders, and deodorants—made Jewett queasy. She glanced up at Benjamin Nash, trying to sift his words from the general hubbub. Around him, a half dozen Secret Service agents in suits eyed the crowd suspiciously. No doubt, it would take hours to sort the chaos. Jewett was already late for rounds, and patient care at Koop would grind to a halt. She knew the President wore Kevlar bulletproofing beneath his tailored clothing, and she understood why. Had she possessed a pistol and Kaign Jones' temper, she might have shot the President on the spot. Lacking either, she contented herself with a mental image of Nash tumbling to the ground and tried to slide through the masses.

". . . commend the spectacular job our hospitals are doing to support the cause of life, the cause of all men and women," Nash was saying.

An elbow jabbed painfully into Jewett's ribs, and the irony was not lost. *That's right, Mr. President. Show your support by preventing us from doing our jobs.* Jewett staggered, and the mound of a stranger's foot filled the arch of her shoe. "Sorry," she mumbled, taking an awkward shuffle-step into a paunchy, aging woman.

"Watch where you're going!" The stranger shoved Jewett into a young man aiming a camera. He sidestepped into the person next to him, and the push rippled forward, then violently back through the throng.

Jewett cursed herself for not using an alternate entrance when she first noticed the crowd. *What was I thinking?* Focused on the comments around her, alternating between those helpfully squeezing aside to let her through and those accusing her of trying to sneak a closer position, Jewett lost track of Nash. She ducked and dodged, trying not to hurt anyone as she forced through them. Finally, after nearly ten minutes of maneuvering, she emerged into the artificial light of the corridor beyond the reception area. *Thank God.*

Patricia Jewett glanced at her watch. She had insisted her resident, Curtis Maltorf, have the students ready for attending rounds at 08:30, and it was already 08:50. She broke into a run, dodging the scattered pedestrians in the hallway, arriving, breathless and disheveled, on the chronic care hallway. She slowed as she approached the open bay at the far end, patting wayward strands of hair into place and tucking her shirt back into her pants.

As Jewett entered the bay, she found Maltorf and his five charges by the first bed, discussing anticonvulsant medications. She waited until the red-haired resident paused to take a breath, then interrupted. "Sorry I'm late. I got caught in that mob by the entrance. If they're going to bring in someone as important as the President, you'd think they'd hire some crowd control experts." She examined a tear in her sleeve, annoyance mounting.

The students grunted sympathetically. Apparently, they had all come in early enough to avoid the crowd or used one of the other entrances.

Maltorf turned her a lopsided grin. "Wait till tomorrow, Dr. Jewett. Word is he'll be touring the wards."

Jewett groaned, not daring to contemplate the chaos. "Ready for rounds?"

The students bobbed their heads. Maltorf directed. "Let's start with Mr. Pyrus. Matthew?"

The indicated student plucked a stack of index cards from his pocket and shuffled through them. "Jon Pyrus is a seventy-nine-year-old white male with . . ."

Jewett tuned Matthew out, aware the first rounds with a particular group of students would stretch into an eternity. Over the years, she had become all-too-familiar with Jon Pyrus' history, but it was a necessary part of the students' learning process to demonstrate that they had read and deliberated over their patients' charts, considering treatment options and changes. After rounds, Jewett knew Maltorf would give his charges the "nice job but learn to condense to the pertinent" speech, and the situation would continue to improve until this group of students was replaced by the next and the cycle began again.

Jewett hoped her silence and drifting awareness did not make her seem uninterested. She was as dedicated a doctor as any; usually she enjoyed teaching the rare and the mundane procedures to the students and discussing whatever topics of interest arose from patient affairs during rounds. But today she had to do rounds with new students on the other two open bays as well, and dragging out any topic would assure more people than necessary would have to spend the evening working. Jewett had fallen behind on her research yesterday and knew she would have to stay until 21:00, at least. Focusing her intermittent attention on the "plan" section of the students' droning, seemingly-endless elaborations, Jewett made sure patient care was properly attended without her becoming bored to unconsciousness. Any problem she missed, she felt certain Maltorf would handle.

Not until noon did Jewett and her young retinue finish discussing the last patient on the chronic bay. Maltorf dismissed the students to eat lunch and carry out the plans made on rounds. Nurses wove between the rows of patients, cleaning, replacing lines, and administering medications, clucking half-audible comments about the length of teaching rounds and the irate families barred from the room until their completion.

Patricia Jewett headed for the door to the hallway, hoping to grab some lunch before performing rounds on the subacute bay. After only two steps, Curtis Maltorf drew up beside her. "Dr. Jewett, I need to speak with you about one of the private patients."

Jewett stopped and regarded Maltorf. He wore an expression of grim curiosity, his face unlined beneath his shock of red hair. Maltorf was assigned to three privates, but his concern made it clear which one he wanted to discuss. "It's Stanley Schober, isn't it?"

Maltorf nodded.

Jewett bit her lip, not wanting any more bad news. Before Kaign Jones kept her up complaining about the stranger in the bar until the wee morning hours, she had planned to come to Koop early and assess Schober's condition in detail. A decade ago, she could have accessed his patient data on-line from home, but concerns about privacy had put an end to that practice. She gestured to the hallway. "Come on. We'll talk while we walk."

Jewett and Maltorf wandered along an aisle between patients amid the soft, mechanical hum. A nurse whirled with a full pan of waste material.

Maltorf shuffle-stepped out of her path. "Dr. Schober had a seizure this morning."

Jewett paused at the door, her fingers looped over the frame. Maltorf's assertion sounded ludicrous. "He's paralyzed at the cervical level. How bad a convulsion could he have?"

Maltorf leaned against the opposite side of the door frame. "Fast, furious eye-blinking. The brain wave monitors had an odd pattern I've never seen before, almost like a *petit mal* seizure. There were spikes and waves, but more erratic and less rhythmical than I'd have expected. There was activity on both sides, most on the right, of course, with the vascular accident on the left. Computer read it as a definite seizure, so I loaded him with pikobarbital and told the nurses to repeat the dose if it recurred. Does that sound familiar to you?"

Jewett processed the information, then frowned. The pattern Maltorf described did not sound typical of any convulsive disorder she knew, but she needed to see it herself and compare its relationship to the eye blinking. "Good pick-up, Curt," she said so as not to make him think he had done anything wrong when she changed his plans. "Cancel the order for pikobarb, and tell the nurses to call me if it happens again." She considered, no longer hungry and aware Maltorf would have time to grab lunch while she rounded with the residents overseeing the other bays. "On second thought, let's head down to Schober's room now." Without awaiting Maltorf's reply, she started down the hallway.

Maltorf followed.

Janitors and hospital administrators scurried through the hall, vacuuming stain- and dust-resistant carpets and fruitlessly trying to straighten Impressionist prints bolted to the walls. Strangers with expressions as dour as their plain, gray suits examined the cinder block, presumably Secret Service agents assuring Nash's safety. They had probably come in the night, spending hours searching for bombs and lurkers in the stairwells and bathrooms, as well. As Jewett worked her way past the familiar sequence of bays and rooms, she realized it made sense for the President to visit the chronic care wards; his anti-death campaign was responsible for the patients in this area. On a day already destined to stretch way past normal working hours, she appreciated the fact that, if Maltorf was right, Nash would not tour the wards until tomorrow.

Shortly, Jewett and Maltorf arrived at Stanley Schober's room. Elaine sat in a chair by the bedside, clasping her husband's limp hand. The assigned nurse, Krystal Fantella, readjusted one of the telemeters while a male nurse, whose name Jewett could not recall, demonstrated bed-making techniques to a young nursing student. A romantic comedy flickered across the television screen, its dialogue forming an unusual background to the nurses' conversation.

For the first time since the accident, Jewett got an unobstructed view of her dean's face. Thin, transparent staples bound multiple lacerations. Bruises of red and purple mottled his cheeks, and his jaw appeared swollen. His watery eyes swiveled toward Jewett, though she was unable to tell whether their movement was purposeful or random.

Jewett glanced at the brain monitor. It demonstrated a waking state, its wave amplitudes small and aberrant, unquestionably damaged. There was almost no activity at the site of the stroke. It was impossible to know for certain how much thought he could manage, but Jewett guessed very little, if any, of Schober's higher functions and personality remained. Jewett shuddered at the reality. Without a means to think in abstract terms, understand, or communicate, Schober had become a veritable vegetable.

Jewett felt her face growing warm and managed to bite her lip before she started crying. She turned her gaze to Schober, and he began blinking, the movements quick and asynchronous.

Maltorf leaned over Schober's head. "He's doing it again."

Nurse Fantella shoved between the doctors, fumbling in her skirt pocket. She emerged with a syringe and grabbed for the port of Schober's internal catheter.

"Wait," Jewett said, glancing at the brain monitors. "I want to watch—"

Fantella's reply sounded frantic. "Can't you see he's seizing? I have to give his pikobarb!" She jabbed the needle into the port.

Shocked by Fantella's hostile disobedience, Jewett reached for the nurse's wrist. She knew some nurses bonded dangerously closely with certain patients, especially on chronic or nursery wards. They loved their charges like their own children and leapt on the slightest hint of suffering.

Fantella jerked away, and Jewett's fingers brushed the syringe instead. The port fumbled to the bed covers.

Schober continued to blink. The male nurse backed from the bed in horror at Fantella's display. The student scurried toward the door. Maltorf rightfully said nothing; any attempt to seize control of the situation could only further undermine his attending's authority.

"Look what you've done!" Fantella screamed, snatching up the syringe and entry port in hands shaking with rage. "You've contaminated it!"

Jewett lunged to stop her, but not before Fantella tapped down the plunger angrily, injecting faster than appropriate. By the time the doctor wrestled the syringe from the nurse's grip, Schober's eye activity stopped, and the brain wave monitor registered a sleeping pattern.

Stunned by Fantella's defiance, Jewett threw down the empty syringe on the bed, her mouth opening and closing soundlessly.

Fantella slammed the port closed and jabbed a finger at Jewett's chest. "Chronic care patients are people, too. I'm sick of you doctors mistreating them just because they can't complain! You were going to stand by while . . ."

Jewett finally managed speech, "Krystal, be quiet, right now." Her soft voice trembled with a mixture of embarrassment and rage. "I'll speak with you in the conference room in ten minutes."

Scowling, Fantella rounded the bed toward the door.

Jewett felt dizzy and unstable. Warm tears filled her eyes, and she angrily swiped them away. She knew Fantella was a strong supporter of chronic care and the rights of technologically dependent patients; the nurse had donated many hours to Nash's campaign, and she openly endorsed his policies. Jewett guessed something more than this single incident had made Fantella snap. To oppose a doctor's orders was bad enough; but to challenge the doctor's competence in front of a patient's family could lead to a lawsuit and was grounds for dismissal. Jewett had always encouraged the nurses to speak their minds. They spent more time with the patients and often noticed problems she might miss. Kaign Jones had frequently claimed Jewett's shyness and chumminess allowed too much insubordination; but, until now, she had considered her policies sound. The thought of reprimanding Fantella scared her; she despised messy confrontations. Yet, if she let the outburst go unchallenged, she would lose the respect of all the nurses.

"Elaine, I'm sorry." Jewett's voice continued to quiver and turned hoarse, vividly betraying her need to cry. "I just wanted to see if I could figure out what's going on. The drug masks that. It takes a long time for a seizure to cause further damage to the brain. With the breathing machine going, probably hours."

Elaine Schober squeezed her husband's hand tighter, but her features remained placid. "Whatever you think, dear. I know you'll do what's best for Stan."

Jewett met Elaine's confidence with mixed emotions. Though more relaxed, she also felt the burden of fulfilling Schober's wishes. There was no longer any question that he would never recover. "Thanks, Elaine," Jewett said softly and swept from the room to compose herself before facing Fantella.

Early the following morning, Patricia Jewett startled awake with the same sense of guilt she had experienced as a student when she fell asleep while studying. Disoriented, she opened her eyes and lifted her head from the papers littering her desk. The familiar wall bookshelves of her office filled her vision. She had left the outer door open a crack. Light seeped through from the hallway, banded across the two padded metal chairs she reserved for guests, and ended, as if pointing, on the beeper-phone tucked into its recharger on the far right corner of the desk. Beside it, the fist-sized, plastic desk telephone looked huge and awkward. A digital clock balanced precariously on the left corner of her desk read 01:12.

Jewett sighed. She had only slept half an hour, but long enough to leave an embarrassing spot of drool on the brain wave readout she had been studying and to make her head ache with the need for more rest. The day had gone from bad to worse. Her chastisement of Krystal Fantella had sent the nurse into a fit of hysterical crying, and patient responsibilities did not allow Jewett the time needed to get a full handle on the situation. With a written doctor's order on the chart, Fantella could reasonably argue that she was only doing her job, and the nursing shortage would tend to make the administration lenient. Rounds had stretched until 19:00. Then, after attending to all the problems on the ward, Jewett managed a quick, vending machine supper before rushing to her office and her research. There, she had stared at brain wave patterns until her eyesight blurred and she dozed off. Still, the subtle encephalographic trending differences of a mind capable of awakening and that destined to remain in permanent coma eluded her. And Jewett was in serious danger of losing her grant.

Coffee. Jewett staggered from her chair, feeling as if her head had filled with fog. *I need coffee. The strong stuff.* She stumbled over the cord to the beeper-phone recharger and caught the ledge of the desk for support. She stepped over the cord, walked to the door, tapped it open, and entered the hall. Since she was not on-call, she would not need the pager until she came back on duty. She groaned at the thought. *In all of five and a half hours.*

Movement and the muted lights of the hallway revived Jewett. She trotted through the empty corridor, reassessing her need for coffee. Methyl-theophrine, the active ingredient, had many advantages over traditional caffeine. It worked faster, cleared the mind without the feeling of jitteriness, and was nonaddictive, but it carried side effects of its own. Laymen called it MTP, with the pun intended; its diuretic effects tended to turn the urine clear. When it wore off twelve hours after ingestion, exhaustion would strike so hard few drinkers could accomplish more than sleep.

Deciding she would prefer being wide awake tomorrow afternoon than now, Jewett amended her plans. Circumstance had made it a bad day for everyone. By the time Jewett found a moment to bring her complaint to the administration, they were gone for the day; so Krystal Fantella got stuck with her double nursing shift. Curtis Maltorf was on in-house call for the night. Jewett had heard Kaign Jones' name on the overhead speakers within the hour, which meant he was working tonight as well, probably on an emergency case. Jewett turned, the abrupt motion jogging dizziness through her. Not feeling well enough to drive home, she started back toward the chronic care ward. *Maybe I can use the student cot in the residents' on-call room.*

The click of Jewett's footsteps echoed through the vacant hall. She wandered past a framed line of 1990s movie photo stills on spotless blue walls, passed the right fork leading to the department of sports medicine, and continued. A wide array of prints by western artists lined the next section of hall. Jewett slowed as she neared the left turn that would take her onto the chronic care ward.

Just as Jewett pivoted to turn the corner, a high-pitched, feminine squeal touched her ears, silenced with unnatural suddenness. The sound came from the first private room on the right, the one belonging to Stanley Schober. Before Jewett could think, a man in chronic care greens whipped around the corner and collided with her. The force drove Jewett backward. She caught a glimpse of eyes recessed between a surgeon's cap and mask before her rebound into the wall slammed the air from her lungs. She folded forward, dropping nearly to one knee before catching her balance. By the time she managed to scramble to her feet, the man was gone.

Jewett's thoughts took off in a thousand different directions, then channeled to a single realization. *Someone in Schober's room needs my help!* Dashing around the corner, she swung into the chamber, taking in the situation at a glance. Nurse Fantella sprawled, motionless, on the floor. The wires connecting the cardiac electrostimulators to Schober had been slashed, and he was seizing, his lids snapping open and shut wildly. Jewett could hear the distant buzzing of his alarm at the nurses' station.

Aware Schober's heart functioned relatively normally, and the electrostimulator served only as an adjunct, Jewett ignored Schober and rolled Fantella to her back. A scarlet stream flowed from a gash beneath Fantella's breastbone. *Oh God!* The doctor's hands became slick and sticky. The salt odor of fresh blood grew nearly overpowering. Jewett clamped her fingers to Fantella's throat, smearing a line of blood along the flesh. No pulse met her touch. Jewett shouted, activating the intercom. "I need help! Bring the crash cart!" Hoping to keep blood and oxygen flowing to

Fantella's brain, Jewett slapped Schober's emergency mask over Fantella's nose and mouth, hooked it into the side port of the ventilator, and activated it. It would work at the same rate and rhythm as set for Schober, but it would have to serve until help arrived.

Jewett positioned her clenched hands over Fantella's chest and compressed the heart. With pressure, blood gushed through the hole. *Heart or great vessel slashed.* Jewett swore, now beyond her specialty training. The crash cart rumbled through the hall. Still kneeling, Jewett tried to reposition Fantella. Beneath the limp arm, Jewett's hand touched something cold and metallic. Wrapping her fingers around it, she pulled it free and found herself clutching the hilt of a stiletto. Horrified, she shoved it away, watched it skitter across the floor and beneath Schober's bed. *Murder!* "Call Kaign Jones," she screamed at the intercom. "We need a cardiac surgeon, now!"

Three nurses burst into the room, maneuvering the cart, and followed by several more. Curtis Maltorf slipped in behind them. A collective gasp rumbled through the newcomers before they set to work. Two tended Schober while the others whipped out equipment, trying to anticipate Jewett's orders. IV fluid bags appeared. Armed with the infrared vein locator, Maltorf jolted three peripheral intravenous catheters into Fantella's empty, shrunken vessels. The room became overcrowded with assistants and onlookers.

Jewett tried to find a supervising nurse in the crowd. "Use the artificial blood, isotonic, and wide open. Give me the portable electrostim. Someone check and make sure the mask hasn't slipped."

The nurses prepared the solution while Jewett accepted the electrostimulator and hooked up the wires. The red light blinked rapidly, seeking a heart pattern. Apparently unable to find one, it started a standard beat of its own. Immediately, the error button flared accompanied by an angry buzz. Jewett bit her lower lip, fearing the muscle of Fantella's heart was too damaged to conduct the electrical impulse. She hit reset with the same results. "She needs a surgeon. Where's Kaign?"

As if on cue, Jones' voice bellowed over the crowd. "I want three nurses and my resident! Everyone else, clear out." The group opened to let Jones and his resident into the room. Nurses filed out, leaving only three in addition to the two reconnecting Schober's electrostimulator. Though Jones could have gotten little more sleep than Jewett, he appeared unchanged, his curls still perfectly in place and his operating room scrubs flecked with blood. "What happened?"

"I think someone stabbed her in the heart." Jewett backed away to let Jones take over. "I found her like this, and I can't get the electrostim working."

Jones knelt in Jewett's place. With no time for transportation or sterilization, Jones pulled a clean scalpel from a wrapper and set to work on Fantella's chest.

No longer in charge, Jewett felt her nervous energy vanish. Suddenly, she could scarcely keep her eyes open. Her vision swirled, doubling Jones, and the world seemed crimson-smeared. She stepped back, catching Maltorf's arm. "You got a student tonight?" On a quiet evening, it was customary for a thoughtful resident to send his student home early, though it was technically against the rules.

Maltorf flushed. "No," he admitted without elaborating.

"Good." Jewett hoped her calm acceptance would put Maltorf at ease. "I'm exhausted. I'll wash up and catch some sleep on the student's bed. Call the police. I left my pager in the office, charging, so when they get here, give me a buzz on the phone in the on-call room."

Maltorf's face creased in concern. He led Jewett from the room. "You all right?"

"Fine." Jewett yawned. "I haven't slept much in a long time. If Fantella makes it, she'll be on surgery's service at least overnight. Let me know if you need my help. And don't forget to call me when the police get here."

Maltorf clapped a hand to her arm. "You get some rest. We'll take care of things."

Jewett wobbled down the corridor to the on-call room across from the chronic care hallway. She hated to leave Maltorf, but she also knew the laws controlling residents' hours would assure him tomorrow off while she would have to work. Fantella was in good hands, and it might be hours before the surgery was completed.

Jewett shouldered into the room without bothering to turn on the light. Having done all her training at Koop, she knew the location of every piece of furniture without looking. Parallel resident and student cots lined two walls. At the head of each lay a shelf piled with journals and stapled articles. A bookshelf at the foot of the resident's bed held textbooks while the similar slot on the student's side supported the glowing screen of the computer terminal. Telephones, placed within easy reach of sleepers, occupied the wall at the head of each bed. A wall clock over the entryway glowed the time in red numbers bright enough to read but did not significantly disrupt the darkness. Between the beds, a door led into the bathroom.

Jewett walked directly through. She showered with the orange, hospital soap that effortlessly removed patient secretions and microorganisms. Then, dressed in a fresh pair of chronic care greens, she crawled between the cool sheets of the student's cot and stared at the overhead speaker. With all the excitement—the stabbing of a nurse, the stranger in the hallway, the police on their way, and the botched attempt on Schober's life—Jewett anticipated being unable to sleep. But her years of training had taught her composure even in the gravest of medical emergencies, and too many hours without rest had fully sapped her body of adrenaline. Within six seconds, Patricia Jewett was asleep.

CHAPTER 4

Dr. Patricia Jewett awakened on the student bed in the on-call room with the dull, thick-headed feeling that accompanies several hours of sleep after a long period of deprivation. She opened her eyes. Light from the hallway filtered under the door. Combined with the faint, ruddy glow from the digital clock, it supplied enough illumination for Jewett to see the resident's bedspread lay smooth and undisturbed. *Maltorf didn't sleep.* She rolled, stretching luxuriously, then glanced at the time: 09:15.

Realization buffeted Jewett. *Murder! Was that a dream?* Shocked fully awake, she shook her head and sat up.

The events of the previous day had an ethereal, nightmarish quality; but the image of Krystal Fantella remained too vivid to dismiss, her skin sallow and rubbery in death, blood soaked through her chronic care greens. *I told Maltorf to call me when the police arrived. Why didn't he?*

Jewett sprang from the cot, letting the covers slide into a heap on the floor. Ordinarily, she would have made the bed even though the maid would have to replace the sheets, but now she had more important things to consider. The pinpoint, yellow glow of each telephone revealed they functioned. *Even if the phones weren't working, someone could have knocked.* She shoved open the bathroom door, brushed her teeth with a disposable, hospital toothbrush, ran a hairbrush rapidly through her long, dark hair and changed into fresh greens. *I have to let the police know what I saw.*

Jewett dashed into the main hallway of the chronic care

unit. She stopped first at Schober's private room. He rested, alone. The television on the wall at the foot of his bed lay dark. The brain wave monitors indicated he slept. Janitors had cleaned the floor until it shined, and no evidence of the tragedy remained. *Maybe it really was a dream.* Now at a walk, Jewett continued down the hall, past the private and semiprivate rooms.

As Jewett went by, a nurse poked his head through the doorway to the subacute ward. He backpedaled with the stiff suddenness of a child caught gawking at his parents making love. Uninterpretable mumbling followed. Jewett ignored it, quickening her pace as she ambled around the neurological ward and through the doorway to the chronic care unit.

Noticing the students waiting by Jon Pyrus' bed, Jewett started her apology as she stepped through the opening, "Sorry I'm late I . . ."

The abrupt silence that met Jewett's appearance startled her. She trailed off, glancing around the bay. Scattered between the cots, the half dozen working nurses stared at her. Beyond them, at the station at the far end of the bay, a dozen more pairs of eyes watched her in a tense hush. Near the entryway, Jones stood with a brawny stranger dressed in the gray bulletproofing and uniform hat of the Des Moines police force.

Rising fear turned Jewett's stomach sour. She opened her mouth to explain, but before she could speak, Jones caught her forearm.

"Pat, where have you been?" Jones sounded more angry than concerned, and his voice emerged loud over the hum of ventilators.

Intimidated, Jewett stammered, focusing on Jones as if he was the only other person in the room. "In—in the on-call room."

"What the hell were you doing there?"

The answer seemed obvious, but sarcasm had never been a normal part of Jewett's manner, and her apprehension made a gibe unthinkable. "Sleeping." Seized by the urge to defend her actions, she continued. "You know I hadn't slept much in more than forty hours, and I asked—"

Jones did not let her finish. "Damn it, Pat! Don't you realize the trouble you've gotten yourself into?" Jones was in one of his rages, and Jewett knew from experience her best strategy was to say nothing until his fury dwindled. Any phrase or tone she used would be considered argumentative or patronizing; in either case, it would only fuel his temper to the point of verbal violence.

Not wanting to drive Jones into a frenzy, but needing desperately to understand the seriousness of her predicament, Jewett addressed the policeman. "Trouble?"

To Jewett's relief, Jones allowed the policeman to answer. "Dr. Jewett, I'm Officer Early. Could we talk someplace private?"

Jewett nodded vigorously, though Early's avoidance of her question made her uneasy, and the nurses' unabashed staring drove her to the verge of panic. "This way," she said, leading him from the open bay to the conference room beside the neurological area. She opened the door, assailed by the pleasantly familiar odors of carpet cleaner and wood polish. Two padded bench-chairs lined the walls, long enough to accommodate a patient's family and several members of the health care team. The far wall consisted of a whiteboard for small-scale teaching and illustration of anatomical concepts. Otherwise, the room was empty.

Officer Early sat in the center of one of the benches. Jones filed in behind him and took a seat directly opposite. The policeman frowned but did not ask Jones to leave.

Closing the door, Jewett sat beside Jones, her hands clasped in her lap.

Early cleared his throat. "Dr. Jewett, you must realize the seriousness of leaving the scene of a murder."

Murder. Though she had used the term before, it sounded so much more horrible and final from the officer's mouth. *So Krystal couldn't be saved.* Jewett glanced up, met Early's blue eyes and looked away. Tears blurred the room, and her stomach felt as if it sank into her pelvis. She had not known Fantella all that well and hated their last interaction, but she could scarcely believe the vibrant young woman was dead. "I didn't leave. I told you. I was sleeping in the on-call room right across the hall."

A short silence ensued as Early seemed to deliberate over the best tactic to use.

Feeling obligated to fill the silence, Jewett continued, "My resident was supposed to wake me when you got here." *Damn Maltorf. Where is he anyway?*

Early pursed his lips and tried to meet Jewett's skittish gaze. "Doctor, I need to bring you down to the station for questioning."

Dread seized Jewett, making her feel stretched thin and small. The calm assurance that accompanied medical emergencies disappeared when Jewett found herself facing the alien territory of police headquarters. Despite her efforts to remain composed, her mind conceived images of blinding interrogation lights, questions snapped at her like whips, her every syllable or pause suspect. She had taken part in the early research on brain scan lie detectors, studies that proved at least partial effectiveness. Her later investigations, unfinished and not yet published, uncovered some of the same problems the previous machines displayed: a high percentage of false positive results when used on timid, morally conscious people, especially people with a compulsive streak and the tendency to ruminate over words. *People like me.*

Apparently recognizing Jewett's dismay, Early added quickly, "It's just routine, Doctor."

Jewett knew she was being ridiculously paranoid, but the realization did not make her decision any easier.

Jones responded first. "If it's just routine, why only take Pat? You questioned everyone else right here."

Jewett had planned to make an entirely different point, but Jones' question intrigued her and she awaited a reply. If they had talked to Curtis Maltorf with the others, they should have known exactly where to find her.

Early sighed, balancing his elbows on his knees and lacing his fingers. Though Jones had asked, Early looked directly at Jewett as he spoke. "You were first on the scene, and I expect we'll get a lot more useful information. Besides, it's getting late. I didn't expect to be here this long, and I've got to get back to headquarters."

The excuse seemed flimsy. They had already spent most of the night at Koop. A few more minutes, even hours, seemed unimportant, especially when it came to a murder investigation. Emboldened by Early's talk of work, Jewett met his gaze. "I appreciate your need to get other things done, but I have patients. My resident was on-call last night, which means he had to cover emergencies and admissions for all the medical wards, as well as anything that came in through the E.R. Whether or not he actually handled any patients last night, the law says he gets the next day off, and the swing resident has to take over for him today. He or she won't know the patients and will rely on my help if anything goes wrong." It pleased Jewett to see Early deliberate over her words, though he shook his head.

"Doctor, I'm sorry. You should have considered that before you left the scene."

"Damn it!" Jones slammed his foot against the floor tile. "When Pat left, it wasn't a murder, yet. I was still trying to sew Krystal's aorta and pulmonary artery back onto what was left of her heart." The point hardly mattered. Completed murder or just attempted, it was still a crime scene. Apparently realizing that, Jones took another tack. "The room was packed with gawkers. I ordered all nonessential personnel out so I could work." That, too, seemed unimportant since nearly every other worker had still managed to remain available when the police arrived. "Patricia Jewett is a doctor, *Mister* Early. If she shirks her duty, people die. If you do, a couple reports get filed late."

Early did not appear to change. Only the blanching of his intertwined hands betrayed his advancing annoyance. "Dr. Jones, I don't recall inviting you into this discussion. One more outburst, and I'm going to have to ask you to leave."

Jewett felt Jones spring taut beside her, and she touched his arm in warning.

Early addressed Jewett. "Doctor Jewett, I didn't want to mention this yet, but it is common knowledge you argued with the victim yesterday."

Apparently this was news to Jones. He glanced quickly at Jewett.

Jewett fidgeted, not daring to believe the policeman wanted to make an issue out of such a matter. "Nothing beyond the range of normal doctor/nurse disagreements." It was not strictly true. Fantella would never have acted that way around a bolder attending, and even Jewett usually commanded more respect.

Jones broke in, "If I killed everyone who angered me,

we'd have replaced every nurse, receptionist, and orderly at Koop three times over."

No longer able to rein his irritation, Early snapped back. "I wouldn't brag about that if I were you, Doctor." A knock on the door interrupted Officer Early. "Yes?"

"It's Dr. Cambridge. May I come in?"

Through the door, Jewett recognized the voice of the head administrator. Cambridge had donated most of his fortune to Koop, enough to have the research wing of the hospital named after him.

Early sighed. "Come on in."

The door slid open a crack, and Cambridge's thin, elderly face appeared. Though safe and inexpensive lens surgeries had become routine, Cambridge still wore a pair of wire-rimmed glasses on his pinched nose. It gave him the priceless air of an antique. "What seems to be the problem?" His shifting gaze invited any of the trio to answer.

Officer Early spread his hands diplomatically. "I need to bring Dr. Jewett to headquarters for questioning, but she's worried about leaving her patients."

Pleased Early had made her sound dedicated rather than paranoid, Jewett formed a weak smile.

Cambridge looked appropriately concerned. "Of course, we'll cooperate with the police in any way we can. Dr. Jewett has a competent resident who can take over patient care." His gaze probed Jewett questioningly.

Jewett sat straighter. "Well, you see, sir, that's the problem. Curt Maltorf took in-house call last night. I haven't seen him since I went to bed." As she considered the implications of what she just said, a new concern seized her. Until that moment, she had only considered how his absence had affected her. "He was supposed to call me when the police got here. I hope he's all right."

"Maltorf." Cambridge tapped his nose with a fingertip. "Young man? Redhead?"

"That's him," Jewett confirmed.

Cambridge stopped tapping, ran the finger up the top of his nose and pushed his glasses further onto its bridge. "He's been in the Emergency Room resuscitating a patient for the last eight hours."

The tension in the room dropped tangibly. Patricia Jewett squirmed, suddenly embarrassed. With the mystery of Maltorf's disappearance cleared, she felt as if the situation had been blown out of proportion. Her fear of police headquarters had risen from a momentary lapse. A few years ago, she would have gone with Officer Early, timidly and willingly. By example, Kaign Jones had shown her some things were worth fighting for. Unfortunately, she had not yet taught him other things are not worth the effort.

Cambridge continued, "I could call Dr. Bartram. He knows the chronic patients."

Jewett frowned. Bartram had served as ward attending the previous month, but it seemed unfair to pull him from the one month a year he had to catch up on his research. *Unfair?* Jewett shook her head, wishing she had snagged enough sleep to fully clear it. *Krystal is dead. Dead! How can I compare losing a few hours of research time to that?*

Cambridge addressed Early. "Of course, it would make things easier if you questioned Dr. Jewett here." His tone was friendly, rising slightly at the end as if in question.

Officer Early glanced at his watch. "I'm already late, and I have my orders." He sighed, apparently uncomfortable with compromise. "I'll tell you what I'll do. I think my superior's still here talking with the operating room nurses. Lieutenant Scott's a nice guy. If he's willing to question you here, fine. But he's doing you a favor. And if he says no, you have to promise me you'll come without an argument." He glanced sidelong at Jewett.

Jewett did not know whether the officer spoke the truth or was using a ploy, but she did know she had material information that the police needed. She did not know if anyone else had seen the man in scrubs who had crashed into her in the hallway. She answered quickly, before Jones could intervene. "That's fair."

"Come on." Early clambered to his feet, his stance and movement lighter, as if in relief. Cambridge held the door, and the others filed into the hallway. Ignoring the curious eyes peeking from rooms and bays, Early trotted from the chronic care ward into the main corridor.

Jewett and Jones followed Early through the winding passages on the familiar route. Jones whispered as they walked. "You going to be okay, Pat?"

"Fine." Jewett reassured Jones. "I can handle it."

"You sure?"

Jewett nodded.

"Don't let them corner you into anything. You're not under arrest, you know."

Though stated in the negative, the reference jarred Jewett. Despite Early's vague mention of the argument, it never seriously occurred to her she might be considered a suspect. "I'll be fine."

As they entered the surgical wing, Jones gestured toward the hall to the operating suite. "I have to go." He stopped, kissed Jewett, hard, on the lips, and trotted off.

Jewett quickened her pace to catch up with Early and found him leaning halfway into one of the patient conference rooms. He kept his hips pinched between the frame and the door as he conversed with someone inside the chamber. Unable to see around Early, Jewett tried to decipher the conversation.

The other man was speaking, ". . . no problem. Let her in."

Early back-stepped, swinging the door open. He waved Jewett inside.

This conference room mirrored the one on the chronic care ward, though the padding on the bench-chairs was green instead of orange, and the whiteboard held a crude drawing of an opened abdominal cavity. A man in a gray-drab suit sat at the far end of the right bench, his head bent over a clipboard of scrawled notes. He held a pen. The brim of his police hat hid his face.

Jewett entered, and the door clicked closed behind her.

At the sound, Lieutenant Scott glanced up. Blond hair poked like straw from beneath his cap. Blue-gray eyes regarded her from over a crooked nose. The gaunt features were unmistakable. He rose, extending a hand. "Dr. Jewett, I'm Daniel Scott."

Lieutenant Scott is the jerk Kaign challenged in Webster's Bar. Jewett clasped his hand before she could think. It felt firm, warm, and dry compared with her clammy palm. She inhaled a mouthful of saliva and broke away in a fit of coughing. "You," she managed at last; the hoarseness of her voice robbed it of the aversion she intended to convey.

Scott retook his seat and waved Jewett to sit across from him. "You can call me Scotty. Everyone does."

Jewett remained standing, not daring to believe Scott did not recall the events of the previous night. "You," she said again, this time managing to communicate her dislike of him quite adequately.

Scott tapped his pen against the papers. "Or, you could just call me 'you,' though that pronoun stuff tends to get confusing in a crowd." He met Jewett's gaze, his manner remaining business-like.

Surprised beyond concentration, Jewett reminded, "You tried to pick me up in a bar."

Finally Scott smiled, slightly. "I know. No question. This is fate." He glanced at his notes. "Now, please sit down, Dr. Jewett. I need to ask you some things. Where were you at about one o'clock this morning?"

Jewett simply stared. "Look, I've been having 'one of those days' for three days now. I can't go through with this."

Scott pinned the pen to his clipboard with his right hand and unfolded his left for emphasis. "Go through with what, Doctor?"

"This!" Jewett waved both hands to indicate an exchange between her and Scott. "Being questioned by a cop who tried to pick me up in a bar. With a ridiculous line, no less." It was not that Jewett refused to assist in any way she could; she just wanted to discuss what she knew with someone less biased and grating.

"What's a nice girl like you doing in a place like this?" Scott nodded. "I was rather proud of that line. Made it up myself."

Jewett loosed a garbled sound of irritation and whirled to leave.

"Wait."

Jewett stopped but did not turn back.

Scott's voice went even more serious. "Refusing to answer is not going to look good for you."

Jewett considered, saying nothing. Scott had a point, but the thought of trusting him with her information discomforted her. "I'm not refusing to answer. I just want a different questioner."

"Dr. Jewett, if I got shot in the line of duty and wound up with you as my doctor, would you look in my underwear?"

The assertion was so ludicrous, Jewett spun back to face Scott. "What?"

"If I got shot in the chest, would you peek down my drawers?"

"Lieutenant Scott, I'm a professional."

"Exactly." Scott made his argument in a pragmatic tone devoid of triumph. "So am I. All I want to do is question you. The same way anyone else would."

Jewett hesitated, aware Scott was right; but the memory of the previous night in Webster's Bar still remained strong. The cop had deliberately baited Jones, as if taking some perverse pleasure from the surgeon's discomfort. "Fine." She perched on the far edge of the opposite bench-chair. "I'm sorry. A coworker was brutally murdered last night. I'm upset about Krystal, I've had a very rough few days, and, frankly, Lieutenant, you bug the heck out of me." She clamped a hand over her mouth, scarcely daring to believe she had spoken the words aloud. *God, I AM tired.*

"I do my best." Scott shoveled a fresh piece of paper to the top of the stack. "Now, tell me what happened this morning."

Jewett launched into her story, beginning with awakening on a stack of brain wave scans and ending with Jones cutting open Fantella's body on the floor, careful to mention the running man and the stiletto.

Scott listened in relative silence, adding only an occasional "uh-huh" or a nod to encourage her to continue. When Jewett finished, he met her gaze. "Now, this man who ran into you. Did you get any kind of a look at him at all?"

"I told you." Jewett tried to keep hostility from her tone. "He was wearing a surgical mask and hat and greens. All I saw were his eyes."

"What color?"

"Pardon?"

"His eyes," Scott said. "What color?"

Jewett tried to reconstruct the incident in her mind. "I'm really not sure. I would have remembered if they were unusual. Hazel probably. Maybe light brown or dark blue."

"Well, that narrows it down." Scott kept his voice level and nonjudgmental, but the sarcasm of his statement reached Jewett.

"I'm doing the best I can," she snapped. "The guy knocked me down. I didn't know he'd killed anyone at the time. I was more interested in my balance than his eyes."

"We still don't know if he's the killer." Scott raised his hands in a peace-making gesture. "Age? Build?"

"Our age, I guess. Mid-thirties." Jewett thought some more. "Reasonably fit. Average height, I'd say. Somewhere between you and Kaign."

Scott muttered as he wrote. "Somewhere between a short, burly, obnoxious cop and a tall, paunchy, arrogant surgeon. Got it. Thank you, Dr. Jewett. Don't leave the state."

Annoyed anew by Scott's insulting Jones, Jewett glared. "Are we done?"

"For now." Scott set aside the clipboard. "Except for one more question."

Jewett nodded stiffly.

"Are you free for a date tonight?"

So much for professionalism. Jewett leaped to her feet.

Scott rose more calmly. "Is that a yes or a no?"

"No. Of course not." Jewett smoothed her shirt with her

hands. "I have a boyfriend. A serious boyfriend. We're practically engaged." It was only partially true. She and Jones had never discussed marriage; it was just a common assumption.

"Really? You have a boyfriend?" Scott's forehead crinkled. "Then, why were you out with your brother the other night at the bar?"

"You know Kaign's not my brother."

"He's not?" Scott wore a blank expression that might have passed for innocence if not for the exaggerated incredulousness of his tone. "I just assumed. Why else would a woman of class be out with a clod?"

"You . . . you . . . !" Not wanting to antagonize a police lieutenant, she swept from the room without finishing.

Scott's voice followed her, faint and nearly uninterpretable amid the mingled conversations of the hallway. "She likes me. I can tell."

Kaign Jones glanced at his watch as he headed for his private office in the surgery suite and noted he was twelve minutes late for his 09:30 clinic appointment. *Damn!* He quickened his pace to a jog as he rounded the hall between the operating room and the surgeons' office. He was always a stickler for punctuality; this delay upset him more than usual because the patient he had left waiting, Sharly Chalmers, could supply exactly the comforting his frazzled nerves needed.

Jones maneuvered the familiar corridors from habit, seeing little. The sequence of office doors and the paintings on the wall had become a blur he long ago ceased to notice. He kept his head low, not bothering to identify or acknowledge the few people he passed in the hallway. *Can't spare the time.*

A Time to Die

Shortly, Jones kicked open the door to his private office. The six leather chairs of the waiting area were all empty. A movie flickered across the television screen, the volume off. A curly-haired, middle-aged woman typed at a word processor behind the desk. The surgeons at Koop were known for being difficult to work with, so the administration rotated their nurses and receptionists, seemingly at random, so none of the underlings would feel permanently trapped with a particularly difficult physician. Jones suspected it also kept the surgeons from complaining about unequal treatment. He had worked with this woman before, but her name escaped him.

The woman glanced up as Jones entered. "Sharly Chalmers is in room one. Phone messages in the tray." She gestured vaguely.

Jones unhooked his beeper-phone from his pants pocket and slapped it to the desktop. "I'm running behind. Hold my calls. Anyone else waiting?"

"No one's scheduled till ten-thirty."

Jones skirted the desk and headed back to the patient area eagerly. He always scheduled plenty of time around Chalmers' monthly visits. She was different than any of his other patients, a last carry-over from pre-Moralist politics. Born with a complex congenital cardiac defect, Chalmers had been sickly as a child. Four years ago, at the age of nineteen, her damaged heart had crashed despite multiple corrective surgeries. While she lay in congestive failure, hovering near death despite the best medical efforts, a young athlete had been brought to Koop after a diving accident, brain dead and technologically dependent. His parents had been as violently opposed to ventilators as Stanley Schober. As if by fate, he proved nearly a perfect HLA match for Chalmers. A group of cardiologists decided to covertly circumvent the letter of the law and perform the transplant.

Jones entered the short hallway of his clinic, the closed doors numbered one and two on the right, three and four on the left. He recalled how he had opposed the cardiologists' intentions, but they had chosen to proceed despite his protests. Once the choice was made to discontinue the athlete's life support, Jones did agree to perform the surgery; it gave him an opportunity he would probably never find again. Chalmers got a new life with fewer restrictions than she had ever known. And she was grateful to Dr. Kaign Jones. Very grateful.

The memory of Chalmers' heroic, if secretive, surgery revived the familiar pride that accompanied overcoming hopeless odds to snatch a human being from the brink of death or beyond. Jones paused with his hand on the door to room one, reveling in a sensation of power that tingled through him and seemed to grow with every case and each passing day. Thoughts of his remarkable success with Chalmers allowed Jones to banish the memory of his early morning failure. *Krystal Fantella was dead long before I had a chance to save her, her heart too severely damaged to patch together.* He opened the door, habitually shielding his patient from the view of the empty hallway, slipped inside, and closed the door behind him.

Sharly Chalmers sat on the examining table, wearing only a hospital gown, backwards, so it opened in the front. She had left the ties undone, and the fabric fell casually across her chest, held agape by nipples only half covered. The scar just left of the midline scarcely marred the curves that ended at her crossed legs where the gown lay pinched between her thighs. She tossed back blonde hair that fell in thick waves to her shoulder blades. "Good morning, Candy

Kaign." She laughed softly at her own pun.

Jones paused, torn between the inevitable excitement and the repulsion it incited. It seemed grossly unnatural to find a patient alluring, even one he had known on a sexual basis many times before. Besides, there was always Patricia Jewett to consider.

Noting Jones' hesitation, Chalmers sprang from the table. The gown fanned open, pleasuring Jones with a full view of large, firm breasts and a flat stomach before it fluttered back into place. "I heard you had a difficult morning." She caught his arm sympathetically and pressed up against him. Her thigh touched his groin casually, as if by accident.

Desire shivered through Jones. *It's not as if Pat and I are married.* He felt himself responding to Chalmers' advance; and, suddenly, nothing else mattered. *For all her knowledge and research, Pat's plain-looking and she knows it. Sometimes a man as powerful as me just needs a beautiful woman.* "It was a bad morning, but it's definitely getting better." Reaching beneath Chalmers' gown, he pulled her tightly against him.

Chalmers laughed again, quietly.

That evening, Jewett sat stiffly beneath Jones' encircling arm, watching the channel seven newscaster interview President Nash. She had not known Krystal Fantella well and, gradually, work had dissipated her grief and shock from the murder, leaving only the annoyance inspired by Lieutenant Daniel Scott. The foam cushions of her living room couch seemed to have turned to stone, and she squirmed, seeking a more comfortable position. "Can you believe the nerve of that jerk?"

Reluctantly, Jones looked away from the interview. He lowered one shoe from the coffee table, careful not to kick the telephone. "Are you still thinking about that cop?" He had come to her apartment under the pretext of consoling her, but his tone sounded more disgusted than sympathetic.

Jewett clasped her hands and pressed her knuckles to her face. She did not want to concentrate on Scott, but Schober's accident had left her emotionally wrung out until nothing remained but ire. "He's so damned smug, I just feel like slapping him. I've never known anyone able to rile me like he can. Do you know what he called you?"

"A clod, yes, you told me." Jones' hand tensed on her shoulder. "Forget about him. He's nothing. Just some little weasel who asked you for a date." He removed his arm from Jewett, caught up the remote control, and turned down the television sound. "Let me tell you about this case I did this afternoon."

Jewett nodded, drawing her knees to her chest and balancing her stocking feet on the rim of the couch. It had become routine for Jones to talk about his work. Somehow, he always seemed to get the difficult patients, the weakest hearts, and the most dangerously positioned vascular defects.

The news credits rolled across the screen. Jones turned the television off and twisted to face Jewett directly, sloping toward his left hip. "It was a two-day-old with transposition of the great arteries. She also had a hypoplastic right ventricle which made the procedure particularly formidable. I figured I'd try the new Bariset procedure, the one that saved the little boy out in California, but no one thought it possible . . ."

Jones' voice faded into the distant corners of Jewett's mind. An image of the man who had collided with her in the hallway replaced it, but she still found herself unable to fill in the details of his appearance. She had concentrated on the memory so hard in the last few hours, the simplest consideration frustrated her. Her thoughts wandered to Stanley Schober, but she had no tears left to cry. The mental picture of his room drove her mind to Fantella. She had been one nurse among the hundreds, one who Jewett had never known on a social basis but a hard worker, young, pretty, certainly not deserving of death. *Then again, who is? Death is an enemy to be conquered.* The second idea came unbidden, words repeated from Nash's campaign speech, now inscribed on the outer wall of C. Everett Koop Memorial Hospital. *Why would anyone hate Krystal enough to kill her?*

The introspection brought Jewett's thoughts back to the inquiry in the surgery conference room. She pictured Scott's crooked-nosed face and compact frame, his manner as snide and abrupt as it had been when he had swaggered up to her in the bar. Her arms tensed around her calves, and she found herself mouthing the word "bastard." She bit her lip and glanced up to Jones' sharply-delineated features.

". . . the patient's father asked me to autograph the sutures." Jones paused, as if awaiting praise.

Caught day-dreaming, Jewett simply stared.

"It was a joke. Get it? It was *that* good." Jones closed Jewett's hands between his. "I didn't expect applause, but you could say something. What's your problem?"

Jewett forced a shaky smile. "I had the worst day of my life. I'm upset."

Jones' grip went uncomfortably tight against Jewett's knuckles. His voice developed the sharp edge that warned of coming rage. "You're still thinking about that damned cop!"

Jewett avoided the accusation. "Among other things. Kaign, a nurse got murdered today . . ."

Jones leaped to his feet, releasing Jewett with a throw-away motion. "How come whenever something bad happens at the hospital, you don't want to talk about it, but this cop makes one comment and you can't talk about anything else?"

Jewett considered. "I don't know. I guess because I was depressed before. Now, I'm mad. When I'm sad, I don't like to think about it. When I'm angry, I like to talk it out."

Jones' chest heaved, and his eyes went nearly black. "I'm sick of hearing about the guy. I don't think it's reasonable he's on this case. He obviously has a personal involvement in it. He hates me, and he resents you. I'm calling the police department and making them take him off the case."

Jewett stifled a chuckle. "Kaign, please. They're not going to call a police lieutenant off a case just because some surgeon tells them to. Calm down."

"Who are you telling to calm down?" Jones glared down at Jewett. "What do you mean some surgeon? I happen to be the best TCV man at Koop." He made an abrupt, wild gesture. "I happen to be world renowned. And you're calling me some surgeon? They *will* listen to me."

Usually, Jewett said as little as possible and let Jones' tantrums work themselves out; but, this time, her own anger goaded her to fight back. "I wasn't questioning your abilities as a surgeon, Kaign. I know you're good. I just think you're getting upset over nothing."

Jones scowled. He dropped onto the cushion beside Jewett, arms folded across his chest. "I wouldn't be upset if you didn't keep talking about the son of a bitch."

Jewett unfolded her legs, banging her heels on the coffee table. She bit her lip so hard, her teeth left indentations. She had never felt so angry in her life. "First, I wasn't talking about him, I was talking about Krystal. Second, some nurse hands you the wrong scissors, and she's public enemy number one and the topic of our every discussion for a week. I mention one jerk twice, and you're turning it into World War Three!"

"Twice!" Jones screamed. "Twice? All day long all you've been saying is . . ." He shifted to a high-pitched nasal parody of Jewett's voice. ". . . He really pisses me off this. He really pisses me off that." He returned to his normal shout. "You're obviously infatuated with the stupid, ugly, little cop."

Jewett's mouth fell open, and several seconds passed before she managed speech. "Where did you get that ridiculous idea?"

"You can't stop thinking about him."

Now, Jewett screamed. "I can't stop thinking about him because he's an annoying, obnoxious . . . fucker!"

Jewett rarely cursed. Apparently caught off-guard, Jones did not have an immediate reply.

Though soft, the buzz of the telephone startled Jewett. The caller ID displayed an unfamiliar number and a string of dashes in the name area. She grabbed the receiver, not bothering to quell her hostility before speaking. "Hell-*oh!*"

A moment of silence emerged from the other end. Lieutenant Daniel Scott's voice followed. "That's amazing, Doctor. How'd you know it was me before you answered?"

"Who is it?" Jones demanded.

"I need to ask you another question," Scott said, simultaneously.

Jewett answered Jones first. "It's him. He wants to ask . . ."

"Give me the phone." Jones snatched for the receiver.

Jewett dodged out of the way. "What's your question?" She addressed Scott but watched Jones. The surgeon breathed at twice his normal rate. His eyes went hard, and the grimace of rage on his face frightened her.

"Well, I was thinking." Scott spoke conversationally, ignoring the exchange. "I asked if you'd go out with me this evening, and you said you were busy. I forgot to ask about tomorrow night."

"No," Jewett said.

"Give me the phone!" Jones raged. "Give it to me right now!" He held out his hand, palm up.

"Okay." Scott continued to pretend he could not hear Jones, though Jewett made no attempt to hit the filter button. "Some other day then. When's good for you?"

"When hell freezes over!" Jewett snapped the connection and slammed the phone back into the recharger.

Jones punched the table so hard, Jewett felt the vibrations of the blow. "Why didn't you give me that phone? He asked you out again, didn't he?"

Still seething from Scott, Jewett said nothing.

"Didn't he?"

"Yes."

"That son of a bitch! I'm going to tell him off." Jones reached for the telephone and the recall button that would pulse back the calling party's number.

"Don't." Jewett reined her temper, frightened by the possibility of violence. She caught Jones' wrist. "You're getting upset over nothing. So he asked me out. I'm not going to accept."

"You're damned right you're not going to accept!" Jones shook free of Jewett's grip then seized her hands in each of his own. "Who does he think he is asking you out? I can't believe he dared."

Jewett tried to calm Jones. "You're getting worked up over nothing."

"I insist that you don't see him ever again."

Jones' assertion was ludicrous. Jewett stared. "I can't help but see him. He's the cop in charge of the murder investigation."

"That doesn't matter. You're not allowed to talk to him."

"I'm not allowed to what?" Jewett felt her face growing warm again.

Jones' grip tightened. His fingernails bit into Jewett's flesh. "I absolutely refuse. You can't talk to him. You're not allowed. You don't have my permission."

Jewett tried to pull away, but Jones' grip remained firm as a vice. "This is the twenty-first century, not the eighteenth. I don't need your permission. I'm not your property. I'm not even your *wife*. I can do anything I darn well please. And let go, you're hurting me."

Jones looked down, as if noticing he had a hold of her for the first time. He released his grasp and turned away. "Well, of course you don't need my permission. But you still can't talk to him."

Jewett rubbed her wrists as circulation returned. "I can talk to whoever I want."

Jones whirled back, as if struck. "That's the way you want it? Fine." He jabbed both index fingers at Jewett. "I catch you talking with him, we're through."

Jewett continued to massage her wrists, not wanting to meet Jones' gaze. A choice between a man she hated and one she loved was no choice at all, but the ultimatum hurt. *What next? Will he forbid me calling my mother?* Tears stung her eyes, as much from outrage as sadness.

"And I'll tell you something else." Jones seemed to take no notice of her lapse. "I'm the best thing you ever had, and you'll never get anyone as good. You're thirty-six years old, skinny, plain, and shy. That cop thinks you're unattractive enough to be desperate. He only wants . . ."

The telephone blared through Jones' words. He reached for it, but Jewett caught it first. "Hello!" she said, the word snapped out like an oath.

On the other end of the line, Daniel Scott sounded pensive. "It's Scotty again. But I can see you knew that."

"What do you want?" Jewett glared defiantly at Jones as she talked.

Jones planted both hands on the back of the couch, kneading the fabric in quick, angry strokes.

"I was leafing through one of those newspapers you get at the drugstore, and I found this article that said the earth's core is cooling about one degree a year. So I figure hell ought to freeze over in about . . ." Scott paused as if calculating. ". . . eleven hundred years. I wondered if you'd like to set a date and time?"

Jewett stared at Jones' sturdy, lean hands, followed his arms to his handsome face, and found his eyes narrowed in threat. Driven by a series of horrible coincidences, it was the first time Jewett had found the nerve to fight back; and the feeling of challenge remained strong within her. "Tomorrow night. Seven o'clock. Pick me up here."

Jones stared.

Scott went silent, apparently stunned. "O-okay," he said at length, his voice soft and devoid of its usual jaunty confidence. "I guess I'll see you then."

Jewett severed the connection and tossed the receiver toward its recharger. It landed crookedly across the base. The position offended her obsessive-compulsive tendencies, but she made no move to straighten it.

"What was that all about?" Jones demanded.

Jewett met his gaze. "It was," she said, "exactly what you're thinking it was."

Jones' voice dropped into a flat tone beyond his normal, screaming rage, quieter, yet more dangerous. "Woman, you just made the biggest mistake of your life." He spun with the grace befitting a man of his looks and occupation, ripped open the door, stomped through, and slammed it closed behind him. The gentle purr of his sports car sounded incongruous as it grew more distant and faded into nothingness.

Patricia Jewett flung herself onto the couch. The room seemed unnaturally hushed, as cold and empty as her life had become. She buried her face in her sleeve and wept.

CHAPTER 5

The following morning, Patricia Jewett stood outside the plastiglass entryway to C. Everett Koop Memorial Hospital beneath a curtain of clouds tingeing the world gray. The smell of rain filled the air, a dirty, smog-tainted damp that seemed to permeate everyone and everything it touched. Though Jewett knew it was ridiculous, she could not shake the feeling that the hospital had somehow caused the tragedies of the last few days, since each occurred shortly after she began a day of work. Last year, the same magical thinking had associated the infectious gastroenteritis she developed with the goose paté she had ordered at Webster's Convention hours before, the mental connection springing from a natural defense mechanism the brain uses to prevent repeated poisonings. But, as nonsensical as her rational mind knew it to be, it took an effort of will for Jewett to slide into view of the opener.

The door swung outward, and Jewett stepped onto the tile floor of the reception area. Once amid the milling chaos of patients, staff, and relatives, she paused to check her reflection in the metal rim of the newspaper dispenser along the left wall. Medicated drops and Clairol's new line of post-cry cosmetics adequately hid the redness and swelling around her eyes. From the corner of her vision, Jewett saw the front page headline of every local paper included the words "nurse" and "murder."

Picking up the *Gazette*, Jewett looked more closely. The vague story quoted Kaign Jones twice, first concerning the irreparable condition of Fantella's heart. Later, he apparently attributed the homicide to a professional, someone who knew the only ways to kill were to destroy the heart, sever the head, or hide the body an hour or more until the unoxygenated organs became damaged beyond salvation. *The killer had to understand enough anatomy to know how to approach, find, and mangle a heart still inside the body.* Though accustomed to thinking about blood and death in practical terms, Jewett felt uncomfortable musing about one of her own coworkers in this manner.

Jewett turned away from the newspaper machine and headed toward the chronic care area, her mind on Krystal Fantella. It seemed to Jewett as if God had punched a tiny hole in the cosmos. For most of the world, life continued unchanged. At Koop, the supervisor would rearrange the nursing schedule. Fantella's friends would know a heaviness or perhaps an emptiness. Then, the fabric of the universe, the intangibles and tribulations of the world, would fold in to fill the void Fantella had once occupied; and, for all but her closest friends and relatives, life would go on as if she never existed.

Jewett walked past the sports medicine wing, her thoughts dwelling on death. Its permanence became almost imponderably frightening. The idea that, some day, she would cease to exist, know and understand nothing, while a new generation took their turn at living and loving seemed too vast to comprehend. Each time she came close to coming to grips with its significance, her mind skipped off on tangents: the possibility of an afterlife, reincarnation, the supernatural. She wondered how much of human religion arose from the inability to ponder or accept death, how much of the metaphysical came from a deep-seated need to believe there was something, *anything*, beyond the grave.

The gloom of the day seemed to haunt Jewett through the corridors of the hospital. As she turned the corner onto the main hallway of the chronic care ward, a familiar voice jarred her from the bleak depths of thought. President Benjamin Nash's exuberant speech floated out into the crossway, though distance garbled his words. *I forgot all about him. I thought the murder would keep him away.* Jewett shook her head. *Surely, the President of the United States has better things to do than spend two whole days in Des Moines, Iowa.*

A half dozen people Jewett recognized as family members of patients on the subacute and chronic wards peered through the doorway to Stanley Schober's room. Protective of the solitude of patients in the private rooms, Jewett slipped gently through the onlookers and into Schober's room.

Nash stood near Schober's bedside between a pair of nondescript, young Secret Service men in steel-colored suits. Nearer the door, three female and two male nurses listened raptly, dressed in chronic care greens. A woman wearing a polyester jumpsuit with a patch reading "Channel 7" knelt in the left near corner, the triple lenses of her portable camera recording the scene from multiple angles. In the opposite corner, at her husband's head, Elaine Schober hunched in a chair, looking miserable. Her hand brushed his forehead repeatedly, though her gaze was fixed on the President. On the wall at the foot of the bed, the television screen lay blank.

As Jewett entered, Nash broke off long enough to exchange a pleasant nod before continuing his speech. "For all the strides we have made toward eliminating death, yesterday we took a step backward. The Lord made many people, and he placed goodness in all of them. In the last few years, we have done well avoiding the temptations of the devil: smoking, substance abuses, obesity, the wanton butchering of babies, those things that threaten or take human lives. Yesterday, someone succumbed to the most evil of all vices and took the life of a sweet, young woman with much reason to live. Krystal Fantella . . ." Nash choked on his words, apparently overcome by grief. He bowed his head, white hair cascading around his face, and the others imitated his sorrow.

Jewett sneaked a peek at Schober. His lids were fluttering furiously. *He's convulsing again.* Concerned, Jewett rushed to his bedside, accidentally jogging one of the Secret Service agents. He glared, but Jewett ignored him, taking the opportunity to watch the brain scan monitor while the nurses' attention remained focused on Nash.

". . . I knew Krystal from the volunteer work she contributed to my campaign. She believed in God and the right to life. She treated her patients like family . . ."

Jewett studied the brain waves as they looped across the monitor. The initiating focus lay on the left, just outside the fully damaged area and was electrically conducted to the right. Though nonstandard, it almost certainly indicated seizure activity.

Nash's dark eyes glistened with tears. ". . . and as if her death was not sad enough, Krystal was carrying a child."

Surprised, Jewett ripped her gaze from the monitors. The coroner's report must have become available shortly before Nash's speech. Fantella had shown no evidence of pregnancy and apparently had not even visited an obstetrician by the time of her murder. Jewett saw Elaine's eyes roll toward her husband, saw the look of bewilderment steal over her face as she recognized the seizure. Worried for Schober and his wife, Jewett interrupted the President. "I'm sorry, sir. This patient is having a seizure. You're going to have to leave."

"Of course." Nash let his arms drop to his side. "But first . . ." He glanced surreptitiously at her nametag. ". . . Dr. Jewett, I'd like to try something. May I please?"

Jewett said nothing. It seemed unreasonable to deny the President of the United States anything, but she had an obligation to patient confidentiality as well. Behind Nash, the nurse assigned to Schober darted from the room to get a syringe of his anticonvulsant medication.

Nash approached Schober's bedside. The Secret Service agent Jewett had bumped shifted with the President, giving her a look filled with dangerous warning. He could have reacted violently to her touch, construing it as a potential attack on the President. Given his training, he probably should have, and Jewett doubted he would pardon her twice. His partner moved between Nash and the small crowd near the door. Jewett stepped to Elaine's side and caught her arm reassuringly to indicate she would not let them do anything harmful to Schober. To Jewett's surprise, Elaine felt relaxed beneath her touch, her expression more curious than concerned.

Nash raised his hands and flung his gaze toward the ceiling. Recalling Nash used to be a televangelist, Jewett sighed, prepared for the pretentious stunts of a man accustomed to simulating miracles for his money. Still, Jewett knew Nash had succeeded as a politician because he toned down the theatrics, keeping only those tactics that contributed to his charisma. Suddenly, Nash placed his palms squarely on Schober's chest.

And Stanley Schober stopped blinking. His eyes wrenched wide, gleaming with a look mimicking wonder, and everyone in the room matched his expression.

A Time to Die

Jewett had never believed in quack medicines, chiropractics, and cure-alls, but there could be no doubt that Benjamin Nash had relieved Schober's convulsion. Even the Secret Service man stared into Schober's face in disbelief. The only person who seemed unaffected was Nash. He lowered his head in a gesture of humility and whispered a short prayer, mouthing the name of the Almighty repeatedly. To say anything aloud would have broken the mood, so Nash turned and headed for the door. The crowd parted to let him through, then trailed him into the hallway.

Jewett's hand fell from Elaine's arm, and she turned her attention back to Schober. His eyelids opened and closed faster than before. *Damn! I should have known it wouldn't last.* She drew breath to activate the intercom just as Schober's nurse, Rick, entered with the syringe dangling at his side. Jewett motioned the nurse closer. "Give him 2 mg."

Rick's features wrinkled in question. "Outside they told me . . ." He glanced at Schober, stopped speaking, and administered the drug. Schober's scan fell into a sleeping pattern.

Jewett waited until the nurse left the room and only she and Elaine remained. Elaine dropped back into her seat at the head of her husband's bed. Strength melted from her face, leaving the lax uncertainty of a bewildered child.

Moved, Jewett wanted to remain and comfort her mentor's wife, but she could not afford to delay morning patient rounds again. To do so would inconvenience residents, students, and nurses, as well as patients' families. *When everything goes as it should, this ward runs almost too smoothly. But it only takes one difficult family or admission to throw off the entire day's schedule.* "Will you be around this afternoon? We need to talk."

Elaine Schober nodded. "Whenever you're free, dear."

Jewett headed for the door, appreciating Elaine's forbearance. In times of serious illness, it was often understandably difficult for relatives to remember that other patients and their families required Jewett's attention, too. In the doorway, Jewett stopped and twisted her head to peer over her shoulder at Elaine. "I'll come back after rounds."

Elaine nodded again without looking up.

Jewett exited into the corridor and walked toward the chronic care open bay. She glanced through the doors of the other bays as she passed. In the subacute and neurological areas, the nurses and students worked with their usual exigency; apparently President Nash had left the ward. *Unless he's in the chronic bay.* Jewett winced at the thought. It seemed a vile coincidence for Nash to choose to cover ground in the exact same order as Jewett, causing the maximal amount of disruption to her hospital routine. *The way the last few days have gone, it wouldn't surprise me.*

But when Jewett arrived at the chronic bay, she found the students and Curtis Maltorf waiting at Jon Pyrus' bed. Instead of a crowd around a dynamic, white-haired President, she discovered a disturbance of a different kind. A squeal of delight rose above the machinery hum and the voices of nurses herding patients' families from the room before rounds. Jewett turned toward the sound. The parents of the six-year-old near-drowning victim, Judson Payne, hovered over their child. The mother lay stretched across her boy in a loving hug. The father was talking at one of the nurses and shifting rapidly from foot to foot, as eagerly as a dance step. From over the father's shoulder, the nurse showed a stricken glance to the huddled group of doctors-in-training, requesting help.

Rounds or not, this one can't wait. Jewett hurried down the row of comatose or compromised patients, the students and

Maltorf trailing behind her. She had grown accustomed to the bittersweet joy the Paynes received from their neurologically devastated son. They loved their child as any parent, lavishing toys and attention despite little or no return of their affections, content with the rare grunt or spontaneous smile Judson could manage. Jewett had never seen the Paynes this excited; infected and on antibiotics, Judson was unlikely to perform even up to his normal single-digit I.Q. *They have to be misinterpreting what they're seeing.*

As Jewett pulled up to the bedside, Mr. Payne plucked at her sleeve excitedly. "Doctor, look! Jud's moving! He's getting better, isn't he?" He stared into Jewett's face, anxious for confirmation.

Jewett studied the child. He had rolled to his side, his neck and spine bowed backward. His arms lay rigid at his sides, every muscle extended as if he attempted to stretch out to as tall as possible. His tongue rolled from his mouth and returned. As she watched, he went flaccid, then resumed his stiffened position. *Decerebrate posturing.* Grief fluttered through Jewett, but she kept her expression unreadable as she considered the best way to approach the explanation. She had seen it too many times before: parents, who equated movement with improvement, rejoicing while their normally limp child convulsed or reached the agonal, gasping phase prior to death. Judson's brain scanner revealed a classic seizure pattern. The numbers on the electrostimulator were peaking higher than she had ever seen them; it had taken over the electrical work of his heart. The ventilator, too, now performed every breath for him.

"Doctor?" Doubt entered Mr. Payne's voice, and Jewett knew she had hesitated too long.

This was the part of doctoring Jewett hated most. It seemed so cruel to dash a parent's hopes, no matter how falsely based; so simple, *so necessary* to encourage them to believe. Yet, to allow them to build up expectations would only give them that much further to fall, and to avoid the truth would destroy her credibility as a physician. "Mr. and Mrs. Payne, I'm sorry. I'm afraid the infection must have done some more damage to Jud's brain. He's doing what we call 'posturing.' It tells us he's lost some of the function of his brainstem, the part of the brain that controls breathing. That's why the ventilator . . ."

"No!" Mrs. Payne swung around toward Jewett. Her voice cracked as she spoke, betraying hysteria beneath a surface of rage. "You're wrong! He's my son, and I know him better than anyone. He moved. He did move. He's getting better."

Mr. Payne wrapped his arms around his wife.

Jewett lowered her eyes. Mrs. Payne's reaction was normal and expected. It was impossible to get angry at circumstance, and the doctor made a convenient, if inappropriate, substitute. But grasping the reasons behind the anger did not make the words sting any less. Jewett tried to make peace. "I don't have a son, so I can't possibly understand how you feel. You know I love Jud and care about you, and I want the best for all of you. Doctors do make mistakes. Sometimes we're wrong. Unfortunately, I don't think this is one of those times."

Mrs. Payne burst into tears. "Yes it is! Yes it is! I saw him move."

Mr. Payne pulled her tighter, obviously torn between comforting her and dealing with his own emotions. He spoke apologetically. "She'll be all right. We need to talk for a while."

Jewett patted the beeper on her hip. *Some time alone is exactly what they need right now.* "If you want me, the nurses know how to reach me."

"Thank you, Doctor." Mr. Payne turned, steering his wife toward the door.

Jewett watched the Paynes leave amid an uncomfortable hush. Once beyond hearing, she turned to Judson's nurse, still standing at the bedside. "Arynatine 0.1 mg IV q4 hours, prn." Her heart ached at the sight of a couple usually able to find the best in every situation, now crushed by fate.

The nurse trotted off toward the station.

Jewett arched her arm to indicate the doorway. "Let's start rounds."

Despite the morning's excitement, rounds went without a hitch. By noon, Jewett had finished discussing every patient on the chronic and neurological bays and in two-thirds of the private rooms. Saving the subacute bay for after lunch, she rounded the corner of the neurological area into the hallway and nearly collided with Jones.

"Kaign." Jewett startled backward, smacking her hand painfully on the door frame.

Still dressed in the pink scrubs of the operating room, the tall dark surgeon looked jarringly out of place on the chronic care ward. Since his job was more difficult and demanding, they nearly always met in the surgery wing. And, after the argument last night, Jewett had wondered if she would ever see Jones again. "We need to talk," he said.

Jewett nodded, nursing her aching fingers.

"I saved us a table in the roof cafeteria."

Jewett had planned to speak with Elaine Schober immediately after rounds, but she did not want to miss an opportunity to repair her relationship with Jones. Besides, she enjoyed the rare opportunity to eat on the roof. Originally built as a cafeteria, it had little decor, but the food tasted as good as any restaurant. It admitted only staff, and the prices were prohibitive enough to keep all but the attending physicians from dining there on a regular basis. Usually, Jones was too busy for lunch, and Jewett did not enjoy eating there alone. Occasionally, she would treat her residents or students to a lunch on the roof, but she usually reserved the privilege for the end of their month working together. "Let's go."

To Jewett's surprise, Jones clasped her hand as they wandered through the corridors toward the elevators. His fingers twined between hers in a grip that seemed as protective as romantic. They left the chronic care ward, passed the on-call quarters, and headed deeper into the hospital. As they walked, Jewett looked out the plastiglass windows lining the outer wall. The sun had burned through the clouds. Jewett glimpsed the sky through the translucent, ultraviolet-absorbing lens that covered the patio and allowed the patients, staff, and families to enjoy the sun's less harmful rays. Patients in electronic wheelchairs intermixed with visitors and staff, eating from biodegradable containers at plastic-coated, metal tables. A group of children chased one another around the concrete floor, their mouths open, though no sound emerged through the windows.

The scene ended abruptly at the fire stairs. Across the hall, the display indicated the elevators currently occupied the sixth, ninth, and fourth floors respectively. "Up," Jones said distinctly, choosing the voice-activated mechanism over the button beneath the display. The third elevator responded immediately, its orange digits counting down to one. The doors slid silently open on an empty car. Without exchanging a word, Jewett and Jones stepped inside. The doors whisked shut.

"Roof." Jones spoke into the intercom. The button lit to

indicate the elevator had accepted the command, and the car glided upward so smoothly the only indication of movement was the changing display of numbers.

Discomforted by the quiet, Jewett considered speaking, but every conversational opening she could think of sounded inane. *Kaign came to me. Best to let him talk first.*

Jones did not break the silence until they left the elevators and crossed the corridors to the rooftop cafeteria. He turned toward Jewett amid the mingled din of voices spilling from the room. "I told them to hold us a two-seater along the far wall. See if you can find it while I grab the food." He added as if in afterthought, "Want anything specific?"

Too nervous to eat much, Jewett shook her head. After nine years, Jones knew her food quirks and dislikes nearly as well as she did. The governmental fitness programs had affected even the hospital cafeterias, but they accepted whatever special diets the doctors recommended for patients and tested employees only on a periodic basis. Here, Jones' seventy-five percent rating would allow him free access to food, at least until the next body fat analysis.

Jones headed off toward the food line.

Jewett stood in the doorway of the rooftop cafeteria, gaze sweeping the familiar, tan-painted cinder block walls. Diners occupied nearly two-thirds of the thirty-odd tables, and conversations rumbled together, only the occasional medical word decipherable over the hum. Spotting a suitable table, she headed for it. As she walked between the chaotic patterning of tables, chairs, and attending physicians, she paused to wave at friends and acquaintances. A few people flagged her down to ask about Stanley Schober. She answered in cold, Latin terms, alternately hating and appreciating the professional distance it gave her. Each time, she waited for the inevitable comment of sympathy, then suggested that the well-wisher visit Elaine. Stopped seven times, Jewett reached the table after Jones had already arrived with the meal. She sat across from him.

Jones slid a plateful of food and a bottle of imported soda water across the table. Before Jewett had a chance to look at her meal, Jones caught her hands in each of his own. He leaned forward, his elbows propped on the table on either side of his plate, his dark eyes large and soft. "Pat, about last night . . ."

Jewett held her breath, her food forgotten. Her heart quickened with excitement. Never before had she fought back against Jones' criticism, and she did not know what aftermath to expect.

". . . I did overreact. I said some stupid things I didn't mean."

Jones would rarely admit he was wrong; he found it easier to change the facts than his mind. Jewett recalled the words of a colleague in medical school: "You see more maliciousness among surgeons than any other specialty. It's the nature of the training, I think. They like the power and enjoy watching people cower when they speak. But, you know, Pat, it's the ones who fight back they respect." Jewett recalled that same student, when scorned by a staff surgeon, looking the man squarely in the eye and calling him arrogant. The student had gotten an outstanding commendation from the surgery service and subsequently became an eminent orthopedic surgeon.

Jones met Jewett's gaze, his expression somber as a scolded puppy. The fluorescent lights sparked through his eyes and formed shadows across stately features that had never appeared so handsome. "Pat, I love you."

Jewett smiled, not daring to believe one good thing had

happened in a week that seemed to be falling into shambles. "I love you, too, Kaign. I love you so much."

"Then you forgive me?"

"Of course I forgive you."

Jones released Jewett's hands and dropped his curled fingers to the tabletop. "Good. Let's celebrate tonight at my place. Candlelight, champagne, the works."

Jewett's arms hovered awkwardly. It sounded so inviting, but she had to refuse. "Not tonight."

Jones' features blanked. His soothing, playful tone went strained. "Why not, dear?"

Jewett knew nothing good could come of what she had to say, but she had risked too much already. "You know I have a . . ." The word "date" would not come out. ". . . thing tonight."

"A thing?"

The tips of Jones' ears turned pink, but Jewett saw no other signs of anger, yet. "You know. I promised to see Lieutenant Scott tonight."

"So? When he finds you're not home, he'll get the hint and leave." It all seemed so easy to Jones.

Jewett felt tears building and fought them down. "I can't do that."

"Why not?" Jones snapped. All gentleness disappeared from his manner. "The guy's a jerk."

"True. But the jerk's also a man, and I can't do that to him." Jewett did not want to lose Jones again, and the thought of him making a scene in a cafeteria full of friends horrified her. Still, she desperately wanted him to understand. "Do you remember how you called me plain?"

"I was mad." Jones defended himself. "I didn't mean it."

Jewett would not let Jones bypass the point. "I know I'm no Chelsea Brooks." She picked a popular supermodel-turned-actress. "I know what it feels like to be stood up, and I'm not going to inflict it on anyone else. I told Scotty I'd see him . . ."

"Scotty?" Jones interrupted, his lips a blanched line. "So now you're giving the guy pet names?"

"That's what he calls himself," Jewett explained. "Don't worry. I love you. I promise not to have any fun. I won't let him touch me. We'll go to a restaurant and straight home."

"No." Jones rubbed his hands as if trying to restrain the rage that usually hit him in a wild, unreasoning storm. "You have a choice. An ignorant, low-life jackass or me."

Though pleased by Jones' composure, Jewett resented the ultimatum. "Kaign, I love you, and I don't want to fight with you. I want to spend the rest of my life with you. If you asked me to marry you, I would." She had blurted out the last sentence unintentionally, but, once said, she watched for Jones' reaction.

Jones stared, apparently caught off guard. "I don't think I'm ready for that kind of commitment."

The words sounded ludicrous from a man who had dedicated his life to one of the most demanding fields of medicine, and the line seemed as cliché as Scott's pick-up in Webster's Bar. Deeply embarrassed, Jewett amended quickly. "That wasn't a proposal. I'm just trying to say you don't have to worry about Scott—" She cut off the last syllable. "I love you, and I don't even like him."

"Fine!" Jones' boldness returned swiftly. "Then your decision is made. I'll see you tonight at six-thirty."

"No." Jewett remained firm, the image of her medical school companion encouraging her when it seemed simpler and safer to comply. If she gave in now, he would never learn to respect her. "Like him or not, I promised to go out with him. That's what I'm doing."

Jones glared in warning. "This is your last chance. You go, we're through."

Emotion warred within Jewett. This conversation had started so well, she could not understand how it changed so drastically. *I'm about to lose the man I love for one I hate.* Her lip quivered. She wanted to beg Jones to stay, but she knew the instant she tried to speak, she would burst into tears in front of a room full of staff physicians.

Apparently interpreting Jewett's silence as defiance, Jones slammed his fist to the tabletop. The side of his hand struck the tines of his fork. It flipped, end over end, off the side of the table and clattered to the floor. Jones stared at the blood welling at the puncture holes in his little finger in disbelief. Suddenly, he sprang to his feet, whirled, and blustered from the cafeteria.

A lump filled Jewett's throat, and she felt unable to eat. Wanting to be alone and afraid a friend might try to comfort her, she lowered her head and, looking only at her feet, followed Jones from the cafeteria.

The hallway stood empty to Jewett's relief; the first person to speak to her would surely break the tenuous barriers she had erected to keep in the tears. Instead, she forced her thoughts to Elaine and the promised conference. At first, memories of the incident in the cafeteria intruded. But, gradually, as Jewett rode the elevator down and walked the familiar route to the chronic care area, her professionalism overcame her personal crisis. Her argument with Jones seemed petty compared with Elaine's situation. Still, Jewett found it difficult to dismiss in the same way the personal disappointment of not finding concert tickets so often takes precedence over starvation in a third-world country or the murder of a stranger.

Jewett had mastered her tears by the time she entered

Schober's private room. She found Elaine sitting in a chair at the head of Schober's bed, watching a soap opera on the television. At the sight of Jewett, she snapped off the set and pulled another chair from the opposite side of Schober's bed. She patted the seat. "How are you, dear?"

"Fine." Jewett lied as she sat. "Are you all right?"

Elaine looked up. A gray-streaked curl fell across her forehead, but she did not bother to brush it aside. "Stan's chances for recovery are what? One in a thousand? One in a million?"

Jones was forgotten as Jewett turned her attention to Elaine's question. Her answer was necessarily evasive. "About that, probably, but there's no way to know for sure. When it comes to the brain, we still don't have enough knowledge to be much more than vague."

Elaine's lower lip quivered. "Please, dear, don't sugar-coat. You can be straight with me."

Jewett took Elaine's hand. "I'm being as direct as I can. His cervical spine . . ." She broke off, remembering that, although Elaine had spent much of her time around physicians and medical students, she was still a layman. "His neck was broken. With our current technology, we can't restore muscle function below mid-chest level. There's just no way to know how much thinking he can still do."

"The seizures?" Elaine pressed.

Jewett had not wanted to talk about that particular prognostic indicator. "Their persistence is a bad sign. I'm seeing activity on the monitor, so he's not 'brain dead' in the classic sense; but the frequency of the seizures suggests the electronic impulses are more abnormal than purposeful." Jewett translated from habit, "In other words, his brain works, but it's unlikely he's actually able to think like you and me."

"That's what I thought." Elaine knotted her hands in her lap. "I took Stan's will to a lawyer today and showed him the part where Stan wrote if he ever became technology dependent, he wanted any machines discontinued."

"And?" Jewett encouraged. She was too young to directly recall the "Living Will" agreements of the 1970s and 1980s. Durable Power of Attorneys had become popular during the 90s and into the twenty-first century, but the Moralist Party had seen them outlawed. She doubted any mention of such a desire in a will would hold any sway, either.

"He called it invalid." Elaine hiccupped, as if on the verge of tears, and Jewett was gripped with the sudden sensation that she might lose her own control. "He said legally a will can't be followed until after the death of its subject."

Jewett hesitated just long enough to make certain she could maintain composure. "I'm sorry, Elaine." She tried to comfort. "Maybe it's for the best. Stan's not suffering, and as fast as technology is developing, it's possible we might be able to help him in a few years."

Elaine pulled free of Jewett's grip. Her expression changed instantly. She looked hurt, as if betrayed by her own child. "Do you really believe that?"

Abruptly uncomfortable, Jewett shrugged. "It's possible." Her reply sounded as defensive as it was.

"Possible?" Elaine snorted. "Possible in the same way as taking a two-hundred-piece model airplane, tossing it into the air, and having it land fully assembled. Why should Stan suffer for that kind of possibility?"

Jewett suppressed the urge to answer with anger, reminding herself it was a normal part of the grieving process for patients' families to become antagonistic. "Please, Elaine. I don't write the laws; I just obey them."

Elaine sagged in her chair.

Seizing the moment, Jewett continued. "Stan doesn't know what's happening. He's not suffering. If it helps, think of all the patients who went through an ordeal to make Stan the outstanding doctor he was." Jewett did not have details, but they were easy enough to guess from her own experiences. "The veteran who sat through Stan's first grueling two-and-a-half-hour history and physical exam. The athlete who said nothing while Stan fumbled the IV catheter placing device three times, jabbing her with needles until he got it right. The first woman with an abnormal baby who needed comforting but got a stammering first-year resident named Stanley Schober." Jewett took Elaine's hand again, and this time she did not pull away. "Someday, the procedures we perform and the information we gather from Stan will save the lives of other people's husbands."

Elaine met Jewett's glance. "Pat, dear. How many of your colleagues really, deeply believe the length of life is more important than its quality?"

Jewett considered. *I owe Elaine the truth.* "About a third, I guess. Those are the ones who believe we can't draw lines or pick and choose who lives or dies. That's playing God. We have to use all the technology and medical knowledge at our disposal to help every patient as much as possible and let God decide where our expertise will fail. Probably an equal number think, like Stan, that we have to draw lines somewhere. Unfortunately, each one has his own personal opinion on where to draw those lines. The rest of us see both sides and follow the law."

Elaine stared toward her husband, but her eyes seemed focused somewhere distant. She rocked back in her chair. "Stan always hated that phrase, 'playing God.' "

Aware of that fact, Jewett nodded.

"He always approached the issue from the opposite

side." Elaine clarified, "The abortion of abnormal fetuses."

Jewett said nothing, aware reminiscing would help Elaine handle the situation.

"The anti-abortionists would inevitably use the argument, 'Who speaks for the baby?' As if both sides weren't trying to do exactly that." Elaine smiled. "Stan would always bring up the remarkably high suicide rate among the severely handicapped. He knew the exact numbers, of course. He'd say . . ." She imitated his strong bass. ". . . 'So obviously, if the fetuses could speak, some *would* choose to be aborted. Since they can't speak, we have to make our best guess based on family emotions and resources.' " Elaine stroked her husband's forehead with her free hand, as if to apologize for the satire. "Then, he'd remind the speaker that the expression, 'Who speaks for the baby?' implies that the baby ought to have a choice. But, since we outlaw abortion, then outlaw decisions made by minors, they can't choose whether to live or die until age eighteen. Then, we outlaw suicide!"

Jewett nodded sympathetically, wondering when or if Elaine would come to the point.

Elaine rose, disengaging her hand naturally and without malice. She gripped the headboard of her husband's bed. "Pat, I can't help thinking of Stan as having made that kind of choice. He's past the age of consent. It's cut and dried. The line is drawn. On what basis could anyone deny his last request?"

Jewett sighed, finding it difficult, if not impossible, to argue. "I want to make one thing clear. Whatever your convictions, I'm on your side. I can only use my knowledge to steer you." She looked up to Elaine who watched intently, waiting for her to finish. "Unfortunately, my loyalty has to go to the law first and the patient second. I don't like it that way, but I'm no good to my patients in jail. The law states that to discontinue life support on a living person is murder. Plain, glass-clear, certain."

The muscles of Elaine's forearms bunched as she tightened her grip on the wood. "Who comes up with this nonsense?"

The answer was obvious. "Politicians. Voters." Jewett rose to speak with Elaine on her own level. "Mostly well-intentioned people who see life in absolutes. If it isn't good, it's bad. If it's not white, it's black. If it isn't death, it's life. The only way to oppose that is with knowledge. But you can't send everyone to medical school, and most people will only seek out enough information, whether facts, half-truths, or outright lies, to prove their point." Jewett broke off, stunned by her own argument. For the sake of her patients and their opposing views, she had always made an effort to remain neutral. *How can you tell people like the Paynes who love their devastated son as much or more than their normal daughter that Judson has no right to live?* Jewett had often wondered what direct opponents of the Moralist party would call themselves. *The Immoralist Party? Pro-death? Anti-life?*

Elaine studied her husband's face, her eyes glazed with tears. "It just doesn't make any sense."

Jewett felt obligated to present the other side. "The problem is we know patients like Stan can't think like we can, but that doesn't mean they can't think at all. Sure, he believed he would want to die rather than become technology dependent; but, now that he's here, he might fear death more. There's no way to know for sure, and that's where the Moralists hold the advantage." Jewett quoted Sir William Blackstone: " 'It is better that ten guilty persons escape than one innocent suffer.' Since death is permanent, it makes a certain amount of sense to keep everyone alive in case one would want to live. That reasoning works for fetuses, too."

Elaine clenched her lips into thin, white lines, her expression shifting from pensive to an emotion Jewett could not yet decipher.

Jewett finished her contention. "Think of the ALS patients." She clarified, "The ones with Lou Gehrig's disease. Their bodies stop working, but their minds remain sharp. Used to be we let them all die. Now, some have adjusted to living on machines. They've gone home. I've had many use their communications boards to thank me."

Elaine's hands slid from the headboard and balled into fists on its ledge. Her wrinkled cheeks flushed, and her dark eyes narrowed. There could be no doubt anymore she was angry. "I'm not buying it, Pat. There's only one reason for this kind of cruelty." She uncurled her fingers just long enough to gesture over her husband. "The younger generation wants eternal life, so they're using us as lab rats."

Jewett had never seen Elaine lose her composure before. She tried to protest, but Elaine continued, undaunted.

"This is wrong, and you know it. Stan was a vital, active man. If he has any ability to think at all, he *is* suffering. I love him, and I'm going to fight this stupidity every way I can." Elaine wore the same distant, righteous glare as Nash's followers when they talked about abortion. "Are you with me or against me?" Her gaze probed Jewett questioningly.

Jewett glanced from Elaine to Schober, not daring to believe she had just been cornered into another ultimatum. She recalled the lectures given by doctors from Schober's era and before, when health care decisions were made by a team consisting of the doctor, the patient's relatives, the patient, if possible, and perhaps the family clergyman. According to Schober, the changes had begun in the late 1970s with the Baby Doe laws and diagnosis-related group payments, which took treatment decisions from doctors and families and gave them to politicians, insurance companies, and lobbyists. Then had come a long stretch of conservative politics, followed by the Moralist party. Jewett had read the old classics, back in the days when doctors visited patients at home and knew there was a time, before technology outstripped ethics, when death was a foregone conclusion rather than a decision. "Elaine," she said softly. "I understand. You know I'm with you."

"Good." Elaine's features relaxed into a mass of peaceful creases. "Then you'll understand this. I'll do everything I can within the law. But, if I have to . . ." Her eyes rolled down to Schober. ". . . I will break it."

Shocked speechless, Jewett made no reply, but she followed Elaine's stare.

Stanley Schober was seizing again.

CHAPTER 6

A battered, gray Dodge pulled into Jewett's driveway at 19:10, dashing her hope that Lieutenant Daniel Scott had forgotten their date. Peering through the crack between the kitchen curtains, she watched him clamber from the driver's seat. Like her, he wore a dress shirt tucked into crisp, clean pants, a safe compromise between casual and formal. The car door remained open as he leaned over to retrieve some object from the passenger seat. She caught a full view of his behind, more tight and compact than his burly build led her to expect.

Jewett flushed at her assessment. *Nice butt or not, the guy's a patronizing jerk who picks up women in bars.* The thought rekindled her annoyance. She picked nervously at the switch that opened and closed the curtains, careful not to activate it and reveal her spying. *I can't believe I lost Kaign for a single date with an idiot. What was I thinking?*

Scott backed away from his car, now clutching a bouquet of the short-stemmed, uniform hybrid roses carried by most of the flower shops. Slamming the car door, he headed toward the house. He waddled as he walked, and Jewett assessed his peculiar gait from habit. Unable to pin it on a medical diagnosis, she guessed it had something to do with his build and short, thick legs.

Oh, why did I agree to do this? Jewett stepped away from the window as Scott covered the last few feet of walkway before the recessed porch. *Dinner and that's it.* Her mind kept focusing on Jones' assessment the previous night:

"That cop thinks you're unattractive enough to be desperate. He only wants . . ." Jones had never gotten the opportunity to complete his sentence, but the implication was clear. Jewett crossed into her living room and closed the door next to the kitchen entryway that led into her bedroom. *If that jerk so much as tries to kiss me, I'll scream.*

The doorbell chimed. Revolted by images of Scott trying to pin her to the couch or car seat with roving hands and lips, Jewett considered pretending she was out. The thought of him pressed against her, her nostrils full of a rank mixture of sweat and unfamiliar cologne, made her ill. More than nine years had passed since she had dated any man other than Jones; remorse and uncertainty tainted her thoughts. *What if he tries to rape me?*

The doorbell rang again, as if in answer, and Jewett realized how ridiculous her imagination had become. *The guy's a cop, for Christ's sake.* She caught the knob and wrenched open the door before her mind could fly off in some other nonsensical direction.

On the porch, Scott smiled and extended the bouquet. His pale eyes met hers, and she looked away uncomfortably. "Hi, Doctor," he said. "I was afraid you weren't home."

"So was I," Jewett mumbled beneath her breath. Then louder, "Hi. Thanks." She accepted the roses, suddenly realizing she would have to let Scott inside while she rummaged for a vase. She twisted her head, seeking a suitable substitute. An oversized, half-filled mug of standard, caffeinated coffee sat on the table between the couch and the television. Quickly, she shuffled the few steps between the door and the table, jabbed the flowers into the mug, and turned back to Scott who had not moved from the porch. "Let's go."

The corners of Scott's mouth twitched as he wrestled a

smile. "Well, we don't have to worry about those flowers getting any sleep tonight. You haven't eaten yet, have you?"

"No." Jewett checked her pocket for her wallet. It would not be the first time she had forgotten her key card. Reassured by the bulge in her hip pocket, she tapped the button to lock the door.

Scott reached for Jewett's arm. Surprised by the movement, she dodged aside, tripped over the edge of the porch, and staggered onto the grass.

Scott watched her antics, his hand frozen casually in mid-air. "You know, Doctor, you really shouldn't drink coffee on an empty stomach."

Upset about Jones and flustered by her clumsiness, Jewett felt jumpy as a hunted deer. "Just don't touch me, okay, Lieutenant Scott?"

Scott raised his hands in a gesture of surrender. "Call me Scotty, please." He back-stepped to give Jewett plenty of space on the porch. "I come in peace, but you're welcome to frisk me."

Jewett returned to the concrete of the walkway. She realized she was acting like a graceless idiot, and that only made her angry. "Don't patronize me."

Scott dropped his hands to his sides. "I know you've had a bad time, and I'm not trying to patronize you. I want to help. If I'm making you feel that uncomfortable, you don't have to go out with me. Really. I've always held this strange belief that dates should be fun." He met Jewett's gaze as he spoke, his stance relaxed, his blue eyes friendly beneath tousled, blond hair.

"Maybe canceling this would be best." A spot of scarlet caught the corner of Jewett's vision. She turned her head toward it and saw a familiar car parked around the corner, a red Mazda C-999. *Kaign's car! He's checking up on me.* Rage boiled up in Jewett. If she broke the date now, she would have to admit she needed Jones. *He'll throw it at me every argument.* She whirled back to Scott. "On second thought, let's have some fun." She seized his hand so abruptly, this time, he jumped. "How about Webster's Convention?"

Scott followed Jewett's gaze; but, if he saw Jones' car, he made no mention of it. "Sounds good." He clasped her hand in his and headed for his car.

Immediately, Jewett knew regret. *It's one thing to date the guy because I'm mad at Kaign, but I can't make him pay inordinate sums of money on me.* "Wait, Scotty. Let's go somewhere else."

"Why? I like Webster's."

"Webster's is too . . ." Jewett caught herself, not wanting to insult Scott.

"Expensive?" Scott finished. "I can handle it." Jewett stopped at the passenger side of the car. Stripes and dents furrowed the body. Spots of rust showed through, protected and permanent beneath a transparent sealant. Ten years had passed since she had seen a metal car on the highways. "Why don't we go somewhere else?" She spoke politely but in a tone intended to end the discussion.

Disengaging his hand, Scott passed around to the driver's door. "I'm a cop, not a seamstress. You think I face off with rich lunatics carrying assault weapons for a pat on the back? Combat pay keeps us honest. What decade are you in?"

Jewett wandered toward the back of the car, gaze locked on the paint job. "Forget what decade I'm in. What *century* is this car from?"

Scott paused with his hand on the door handle. "What are you looking for?"

"A gas tank."

Scott laughed. "I had it converted over." He pulled open his door and leaned across the frame. "Get in. Unless you can come up with a better argument than money, we're going to Webster's."

Jewett climbed into the passenger's seat while Scott tapped in the destination on the dash keypad. The map viewer snapped to life, showing the nearby streets and the best route to Webster's Convention. A lever jutted from the floor, looking conspicuously out of place. Uncertain, Jewett stared. Realization struck her. "This is a . . ." She could not dredge the term from memory.

"Stickshift." Scott cranked the car into reverse, a smile playing over his lips.

"How? Why would you want to . . . ?" Jewett trailed off as the car glided smoothly from the driveway.

Scott slammed the stick into gear. "I bought the car, used, when I was fifteen. My first, of course. I love the way it handles. Anyway, I got so used to it, nothing else feels quite right. I'm sure there're better cars out there, and I've probably spent enough updating this one to buy a few. I've just kind of fallen into a rut." He glanced at Jewett. "You know how that is."

In the sideview mirror, Jewett watched the red Mazda pull away from the curb and wondered if Scott was baiting her.

In the entryway to Webster's Convention, Patricia Jewett stared into the darkened, ruddy interior. Electric candles, one per table, gave the room the appearance of an ancient cult ceremony, its worshipers in neat rows. Careful not to accidentally brush Jewett, Scott followed her toward the hostess. From the way his gaze skipped about the furnishings, Jewett guessed if he had ever visited the upper floor of

Webster's, it had not been in the recent past.

Dressed in Webster's customary black and red, the hostess cradled the portable body fat measuring device in the crook of her elbow. Jewett recognized the blonde ringlets dangling across her forehead above an artificial smile and identified her as the same hostess who had weathered the argument with Kaign Jones.

"Arm, please." The hostess apparently recognized Jewett as well, because her smile vanished. She froze with the probe extended and glanced quickly at Scott. The welcoming grin reappeared, now genuine.

Jewett rolled up her shirt sleeve, revealing a slender arm, and felt the cool touch of the probe against her skin.

"Menu A," the hostess said. "Sir?"

The waiter plucked the appropriate menu from the burnished rack, but Jewett turned to watch Scott work his cuff over the smooth, vein-riddled bulges of his forearm and tried to guess his menu letter. His short, stocky build had originally leaned her toward the later letters; but, seeing his loose clothing hid brawn rather than fat, she became less certain.

The hostess poked the probe into Scott's arm. From over her shoulder, Scott met Jewett's gaze and mouthed the words, "May I try that again, please?"

Shielding the digital display with a cupped hand, the hostess stared. She looked up. "Excuse me, sir. May I try that again, please?"

Jewett pursed her lips, trying not to laugh. Behind her, the waiter at the menu stand chuckled. Sparked by the waiter, Jewett clamped her mouth tighter, but a snort of mirth escaped through her nose before she regained full control.

Scott simply smiled indulgently. "Certainly."

A Time to Die

The hostess shook the body fat measuring device several times, then again pressed the probe against Scott's skin. "Menu A," she said with a shrug of resignation. Scott claimed the appropriate menu from the waiter, and the hostess led them to a table along one of the inner walls. Its red tablecloth supported the candle, two settings of silverware, and two glasses of ice water beside napkins folded into swans.

Jewett sat, running her hands along the plush, red fabric that lined the walls. It felt thick and soft, a welcome change from the usual wallpaper or painted-over cinder block sealed with plastic. She waited until Scott took the seat across from her before speaking. "That happens to you a lot, doesn't it?"

"That probe stuff? Yeah." Scott spread his menu over the linen tablecloth and silverware. "The fitness push has all been geared to aerobic exercises. People used to think muscles make you clumsy, give you high blood pressure, or magically turn into fat as you age. That's all been dispelled, of course, but kids mostly do whatever exercises their parents did. Environment and all that." He slid the cloth napkin from beneath his menu and spread it across his lap. "Anyway, people equate big with fat."

"Yeah." Jewett studied the entryway where the hostess conversed with the menu waiter. Dropping her gaze back to the table, she opened her own menu. It was formality. She and Jones came to Webster's Convention frequently enough to know the choices by heart.

Scott glanced through the columns in silence for several seconds. Jewett sipped her ice water, watching a tall figure enter the door to the restaurant, backlit by the sun streaming through the gap behind him.

Scott looked up. "Ever had the trout here?"

As the newcomer approached the hostess, Jewett recognized his long, square-cut features. *Kaign!* Her eyes widened. Ice water dribbled down her chin. Hastily, Jewett righted her glass, seized her napkin, and dabbed at her neck. Scott half-rose to help, but Jewett waved him back to his seat. "I'm all right."

Scott glanced at the doorway before retaking his chair. "If I knew you felt so strongly about it, I would never have suggested trout."

Trying to recover her dignity, Jewett replied to Scott's comment, though her eyes trailed Jones to a distant table. "I've never had any great urge to eat a food when the best thing anyone can say about it is it doesn't taste like what it is." She dropped the napkin to her lap.

Accurately guessing Jewett's point, Scott closed his menu. "You really are living in the wrong decade, Doc. Fish hasn't tasted 'fishy' since they came up with that spice everyone uses to cook it. What do they call it? Marvel fish?"

"Parahydroxyallithone." Jewett used the generic title. "I think the brand name is Miracle Fish."

"Miracle Fish. Marvel Fish." Scott threw up his hands. "Either way, it sounds like something with gills that ought to fly out to the table and rescue damsels in distress."

Jones leafed through his menu. With exaggerated nonchalance, he edged his head toward Jewett and Scott. Jewett looked away quickly and grabbed Scott's hand.

"Doctor?" Scott said, closing his fingers around hers.

Jewett winced. Embarrassed by her transparent play, she hoped Scott had not noticed or, if he did, he would not mention it. "Yes?"

"I know you don't like me much, but this would feel more like a date if you let me call you by your name. Would you mind?"

Flustered, Jewett returned his stare. "Of course not. Pat's fine."

The flickering light of the electric candle sent highlights skipping through Scott's eyes. His smile was cryptic, suggesting he understood more than he was letting on. "Tell you what, Pat. We'll see if I can't get you past this childhood prejudice."

Having lost the thread of the conversation, Jewett was uncertain of the reference. "What?"

"I'll get the trout and let you try some."

"Oh." Jewett sneaked a peek at Jones, discovered him glaring in her direction, and rapidly returned her attention to Scott. "Sounds good."

"You ready to order?"

Jewett nodded.

Scott groped beneath the table with his free hand, pressing the button that would summon the waiter.

Hoping Jones had not seen her notice his entrance, Jewett resolved to keep her gaze from him for the rest of the meal. *Best to make him believe I'm enjoying my date with Scotty. Once Kaign thinks I can have fun with another man, he'll stop treating me like I'm so desperately unattractive I need him to make me presentable.*

Shortly, a tall, lean waiter arrived, his black pants crisp and his shirt unwrinkled beneath his red vest. "My name is Cody. What can I get you tonight?"

Scott inclined his head toward Jewett to indicate that she should speak first.

"I'll have the braised turkey with wild rice. Lemon and spices on the salad," she said.

The waiter pivoted toward Scott.

"Stuffed trout," the lieutenant said. "With that paraydroxyWonderFish stuff. And I'll have the L. & S., too."

The waiter hesitated. "L. & S., sir?"

"Lemon and spices." Scott smiled. "Come on, Cody. Get with the lingo."

Cody stared, the corners of his mouth twitching.

For one horrified moment, Jewett thought the waiter was going to cry. Then, Cody's face split into a broad grin, and his stiff, Webster's façade crumbled. "Two L. & S. salads coming up. Anything to drink?" He collected the menus.

"Sure." Scott released Jewett's hand and leaned back in his chair. "Pick out a good, white wine. Something classy that'll impress the lady by showing that you, at least, have taste."

"I'll think of something." Cody turned and trotted toward the kitchen.

Jewett wanted to confront Scott about his treatment of the waiter; but, before she could find the words, he spoke first. "Hope you don't mind about the wine. If you want, I'll talk them into putting the whole bottle on my allotment."

Customarily, the waiter split table drinks equally between its patrons; government alcohol allotments proved more than generous enough for a casual drinker. "I can handle it." Jewett watched Cody disappear into the dark interior of the kitchen. "But I can't believe you embarrassed the waiter."

"Embarrassed him?" Scott hitched his chair closer to the table. "He's probably sick of the usual stuffy codgers. He was enjoying it as much as me."

"Lingo? Codgers? Where do you come up with this ancient slang?" Jewett shook her head in disbelief. "A lot of high-class waiters would have gotten angry or insulted by what you just did. How did you know this one wouldn't?"

Scott addressed Jewett's questions in order. "First, I like

old movies. Real old movies from before action-adventure and violence became swear words. And, for some reason I can't explain, I've always been a good judge of character. Ever see those old cop shows where some white-haired veteran Irishman works on hunches?"

Jewett nodded, hating to admit she frequently combed the early morning stations for a restored black and white oldie.

Scott continued, "I just got this feeling Cody needed to laugh, so I went with it."

"I see." Jewett thought back to their initial meeting. "And I just look like the type who would fall for a ninety-year-old pick-up line?"

"No," Scott explained. "You looked like the type who needed cheering up. I was just getting started when . . ." He fumbled with the pronunciation, apparently having obtained it from the written report of another officer. ". . . *Kay*-gen pulled the scalpel from up his ass and tried to give me a close shave."

All the anger from the incident in Webster's Bar returned. "Kaign." Jewett restored the name to its single syllable. "The 'g' is silent. And you were asking for it."

"What did I do?"

"You antagonized him."

"Ah, come on, Pat." Scott cupped his hand over hers. "I was walking away, and he came after me. And what kind of a name is Kaign, anyway?"

"It's a family name."

Scott mumbled something unintelligible.

"What?"

Scott waved Jewett off. "Never mind. It wasn't nice."

"Tell me," Jewett pressed.

Scott considered, then apparently decided she could

handle the insult. "I said, 'A family name, huh? Probably dates back to when he killed his brother, Abel.' "

Familiar with the bible story of Cain and Abel, Jewett grimaced at the pun.

Scott grinned as another thought occurred to him. "Only Abel would be spelled A-b-e-*g*-l."

Caught off guard, Jewett smiled, then clapped her free hand to her mouth to hide it. Torn between laughter and rage, she forced down the smile before speaking. "I love Kaign very much. Could we talk about something else, please?"

"Of course." Scott turned appropriately serious. "I'm sorry. I warned you it wasn't nice."

Before Jewett could think of a reply, the waiter whisked from the kitchen and set bowls of salad in front of Scott and Jewett. Apparently noticing they were engaged in conversation, Cody did not speak; he returned the way he had come.

Scott used the interruption to change the subject. "Anything interesting happen at the hospital today?"

Jewett selected a fork and dipped it into her salad. "A thing or two." The task of trying to explain Stanley Schober's case to a layman seemed overwhelming. "But I spend enough time working. I really don't like to discuss cases outside the hospital." She scooped up a forkful of lettuce and placed it in her mouth. *That's one of the things I really like about Kaign. He always has something to say and never expects me to talk about my day at work.* Jewett's gaze roved over the other patrons.

Scott took several mouthfuls of salad, chewed, and swallowed before speaking. "What do you like to do or talk about in your free time?"

Jewett did not want to admit she had given up painting, piano, and basketball for the grueling hours of medical school and never restarted any of them. Now, she spent her time at home with Jones or hunting down old movies on the television. She caught her stare sliding toward Jones and quickly redirected her attention to Scott. Forgetting his question, she returned one of her own. "How's the investigation on Krystal Fantella going?"

Scott winced, full fork halfway to his lips. "We're fated to tread on broken glass tonight, aren't we?"

"What do you mean?"

Scott lowered the fork. "Well, I do have a couple questions I have to ask you, but I was hoping to wait until you figured out I'm really a great guy."

That's not likely to happen. Jewett kept the thought to herself. Instead, she took another mouthful of salad. Scott's reluctance raised her guard. "Go on."

Scott finished his salad quickly and pushed the bowl aside. Jewett continued eating while he spoke. "Have you come up with a better description of the man who bumped into you in the hall?"

Mouth full, Jewett answered by shaking her head.

"Well." Scott shifted in his chair as if uncomfortable with his next statement. "Turns out no one else in the hospital saw him that night."

Jewett swallowed, suddenly defensive. "That doesn't surprise me. It was after one o'clock in the morning."

"Agreed," Scott said. "But that means you're the only one with any information on him at all. We've got a mechanical hypnosis environment at the station, and we thought you might be able to recall more details in it."

Jewett sighed, now on common ground. As one of the top brain wave experts in the field, she had participated in most of the studies on mind-related equipment. "I won't refuse, but I can tell you it won't work."

"How do you know?"

Jewett pushed away her own nearly empty bowl. "If you look at the studies done on the mechanical hypnosis environment, you'll find my name listed." Recalling she had only been a resident at the time, she added, "Last of nine, but listed anyway. Curiosity is an asset to a scientist, and I've yet to meet a researcher who doesn't use himself as a white rat, at least for harmless experiments." She got to the point. "I'm one of the one-third of the population who can't be machine hypnotized. For the record, traditional hypnosis doesn't work on me either." Not wanting Scott to think she was inventing excuses, Jewett specified. "It's all documented on the computer, if you need to verify."

"That won't be necessary."

Cody reappeared from the kitchen with a serving tray. Shielding the contents with his body, he placed it on a portable stand and removed two steaming plates of food. He placed the turkey in front of Jewett and the fish in front of Scott. Collecting the salad bowls, he exchanged them for a pair of chiseled, plastiglass wine glasses. He spoke in a dignified monotone, "Sir, knowing your tastes would differ from those of the lady, I brought a vintage for each of you." He turned, his back still blocking Jewett's view of the serving tray. "This is yours." Cody pivoted to face Scott, clutching a bottle of Joe's Orchard Apple Wine. He twisted off the top and held it out. "Would you like to smell the aluminum cap?"

Scott smiled, playing along with the charade. He sniffed at the cap. "October, a very good month. Would you have a paper bag I could drink it from?"

Without pouring, Cody set the wine on the table. "That one's on us. This is for the lady." Without looking, he reached behind him and emerged with another bottle.

He showed the label to Jewett.

Jewett rarely drank alcohol; and, when she did, Jones always chose the vintage. The name on the bottle was unpronounceably French. Uncertain what to do, she nodded approval.

Peeling away the foil, Cody coiled a corkscrew into the cork and pulled it free. He poured a small amount of the amber wine into her glass and waited expectantly.

Jewett tasted it, not quite sure what to expect. It had a pleasant, mildly sour flavor. "Good," she said.

Cody filled both glasses and left the bottle in the center of the table, beside the other. "If you need anything else, call. The hostess will need your alcohol allotment and credit cards on the way out." His tone remained level. "I took the liberty of adding a twenty-five percent gratuity." He collected the tray and portable serving stand.

It was standard for restaurants to add a fifteen percent tip to all orders, and Jewett knew Cody was joking. She took another sip of wine.

"Make it thirty percent," Scott said. "I've paid more than that for a good laugh. And I'll pay for that guy at the corner table dining alone, too."

Jewett choked on the wine.

"All right. But between you and me . . ." Cody glanced surreptitiously in Jones' direction. "That guy's a well-known surgeon. He can handle his own tab."

"That's okay." Scott raised a clean fork. "I owe him."

"It's your money." Cody tucked the portable table beneath his arm and headed back to the kitchen.

Scott cut a corner from the trout with his fork and shifted it to Jewett's plate. "Taste."

Jewett took her fork, speared the meat, and ate it. It tasted light, more like lobster than fish. "Why did you do that?"

"I promised you a taste. You can have more if you like."

"No." Jewett tipped her head toward Jones. "I meant paying for his dinner."

"I don't know. It seemed funny." Scott used the edge of his fork to carve off another piece of trout. "Actually, I was feeling a bit guilty about insulting him. I shouldn't have made that 'Abel' crack. Anyway, what were we talking about?"

Jewett turned her attention to the rice. "Krystal Fantella. What have you found out?"

"Mmmm." Scott swallowed before speaking. "Did you know she was pregnant?"

Jewett spoke between bites. "Not until the President of the United States announced it this morning."

"Oh, yeah. Wasn't that kind of weird, the President deciding to come to Koop at the last minute, then staying for two days?"

"I wouldn't say 'weird.' Koop is a renowned chronic care facility, and Nash was in the area to visit hospitals." Jewett recalled the crowd in the lobby. "I'd just say inconvenient. With a little more warning, we might have been able to reroute patient traffic. My guess is they make these sudden changes in plan on purpose, to foul up would-be assassins or terrorists."

Scott continued eating, wrinkling his nose with obvious skepticism. "That sounds a bit paranoid to me. Anyway, about the nurse. Isn't it common for women to discuss things like pregnancy with their friends? The coroner said she wasn't far along, but she should have known."

Jewett shrugged. "She might have talked to friends. My social life outside the hospital is pretty limited. I like the nurses, but I only see them three times a year when I'm on the teaching service. I'm not the one Krystal would have told. What else did the autopsy show?"

"Not much. Are you sure you want to talk about it over dinner?"

"Oh, please." The idea that Scott would think her squeamish aggravated Jewett. "As a student, I used to grab lunch between a bowel resection and an appendectomy. What do you think Kaign and I discuss while we eat?" Only then it occurred to Jewett that Scott might feel uncomfortable with the topic.

If so, Scott did not show it. "The killer knew exactly where to stab. Her heart was badly damaged by the long knife we found under the bed. The blood matched hers perfectly. Only one set of prints on the handle."

Jewett knew her fingerprints were on file since they were routinely taken before anyone could seek employment. Since most parents had their children's fingerprints cataloged in case of emergency, only a rare United States citizen did not have his fingerprints mapped on the government computers. "Mine?"

"Yeah," Scott confirmed. "The only hair and skin we could uncover belonged to hospital personnel accounted for by the emergency treatment."

Jewett did not like the direction the investigation was taking. "Making it probable one of us killed her."

"Or a trained, professional hitman." Scott chewed thoughtfully. "Two things still don't fit, and I hoped you could shed some light on them."

Jewett looked away from her meal. "I'll try."

"Several of you said the lines of the heart stimulator of the comatose patient Fantella was treating were cut. It sounds to me as if the killer attempted a double murder."

"Not if it was one of the chronic care personnel."

"Oh?"

"Anyone who can read an electrostimulator would know that particular patient's heart worked without it. It's just standard backup technology to keep the heart operating to its maximum ability. It protects the heart and the other organs from becoming damaged or throwing clots." She returned to her turkey. "If a person in the know really wanted to murder the patient, and I can't imagine why anyone would need to kill a virtually braindead . . ." Struck by the memory of Elaine's threat, Jewett trailed off. *Even if Elaine would sever her husband's lines, she could never have killed Krystal.* Jewett recovered quickly. ". . . patient, they'd know enough to cut the ventilator tube."

"Interesting."

Jewett had to admit it was. "You said two things didn't fit. What's the other?"

Scott hesitated. "Actually, I probably shouldn't be discussing this part with you since it's not released yet." He shrugged. "Maybe you'll have an answer. How much do your nurses get paid?"

"I don't know exactly. Not enough."

"So it would seem strange if one of them had a fat credit account?"

Jewett finished the turkey, assuming Scott had already considered the obvious explanations, such as an inheritance or a miserly attitude. "Maybe. I suppose. Krystal did?" She raised her second glass of wine.

Scott emptied the bottle into his glass and nodded. "Possibly a gift. A rich boyfriend or parents. There're plenty of legitimate explanations, but I'm a cop and we're paid to be suspicious." He drained the glass.

Jewett sipped more slowly. "About ready to take me home?" She tried to close all other options. *If he thinks I'm going to bed with him just because he spent a lot of money, he's crazy.*

"Let's go."

Jewett fished her alcohol allotment card from her wallet and handed it to Scott. He rose and headed for the counter deeper inside the restaurant to settle up credits.

Jewett sneaked a glance at Kaign Jones. His meal only half eaten, the surgeon had swiveled to watch Scott. She used the moment to study his profile. The familiar straight forehead, sharp aristocratic nose, and strong jaw evoked memories of joy and laughter: picnics along the Des Moines River, cuddling safe and warm in front of the television set. *Sure, Kaign's got a temper; and sometimes it makes him say things he doesn't mean. But he wouldn't be here if he didn't love me.* Guilt settled over her, and the urge seized her to throw herself into his arms and ask for forgiveness. To do that, however, would mean to confess she had pretended to enjoy Scott's company, and it would be cruel to abandon Scott. *If I don't go through with this, Kaign's never going to change, and I'll have to live with his demands and rages forever.*

Scott started back to the table, seemingly oblivious to Jones' stare. Jewett tore her gaze from Jones and rose to meet Scott. He returned her allotment card, gave a final wave to Cody near the kitchen door, and they exited Webster's Convention into the coalescent radiance of the street lamps.

On the sidewalk, Scott headed away from the parking garage. Thinking he had made a mistake, Jewett trotted after him. "Wait, Scotty. You're going the wrong way." She stayed close. Even well-lit, the city streets were not safe for a person alone at night.

Scott continued walking. "No I'm not."

"Yes. You are." Jewett pointed behind them. "Don't you remember? I can see the lights of the mall we passed from here. The garage is that way."

Like a dog or a young child who has not yet learned the meaning of the gesture, Scott regarded Jewett's finger rather than the direction it indicated. "Who said I was headed for the car?"

The question caught Jewett by surprise. "I just assumed . . . I mean, I thought . . ." Realizing she was babbling, Jewett drew her intentions together as Jones had taught. "I told you. It's time to take me home."

Scott did not slow his pace. "Why?"

"Because . . ." Jewett hesitated. *What am I supposed to say? Because I don't like you? I don't trust you?* ". . . I have to go to work in the morning."

Scott glanced at his watch. "Pat, it's 20:45. I seem to recall a couple of doctors just arriving in Webster's Bar significantly later than this the other day." Scott turned a corner, passing a high rise.

A few arguments came to Jewett's mind, but none of them seemed worth turning into a discussion. "Taking a woman somewhere against her will is kidnapping." She trailed Scott, keeping close to the streets and away from alleys and storefronts.

"Don't be absurd."

A crowd of youngsters passed, dressed in the dull black and gray synthetics of city camouflage, exchanging street slang so rapidly it sounded like a foreign language. Unconsciously, Jewett swerved closer to Scott. "At least tell me where we're going."

At the next intersection, Scott stood on the pedestrian plate, and the light turned green. "It's a surprise." He started across the road.

Defiantly, Jewett stopped at the corner. "I'm not going until you tell me."

In the center of the street, Scott turned. "That's your choice. I'm not holding a gun to your head."

"So, you'd let me walk back alone?"

A trio of elderly women crossing the opposite direction watched the exchange with unabashed curiosity.

Scott shrugged. "If that's what you want."

Jewett watched the women swerve around Scott, feeling trapped. The idea of walking the city streets alone, even just the few blocks back to Webster's Convention, frightened her, but Scott did not seem likely to call her bluff. *Unless I use his own tactics against him.* Jewett fought a smile. "All right. But I can picture the headlines." She adopted the loud, sensationalistic tones of a newspaper vendor from an old movie. "Cop's Date Murdered in Streets Because Cop Too Lazy to Walk Her to Car. Cop's defense:" Jewett imitated a stereotypical villain's stupid sidekick voice, "Well, garsh. I thought that was what she wanted."

The women stared, making a wide detour around Jewett.

Scott howled with laughter. "Sarcasm! That was sarcasm! I didn't know you were capable." He set his clasped hands beneath his tilted chin. "I'm in love."

A silver sports car glided toward Scott. Ordinarily, the light would have changed for the only vehicle on the street, but Scott's presence kept the light green for pedestrians. Jewett watched in horror as the driver slammed on the brakes, skidding into the crosswalk. A man's head shot out the window. "Out of the road, asshole!"

Bathed in the headlights, Scott looked unperturbed. "That's *Officer* Asshole, sir."

The driver went quiet, clearly uncertain whether to believe him.

Scott continued, "It's people like you overriding the computers that set traffic technology back decades. And I'll be out of your way as soon as this young woman agrees to accompany me *to a public place where there'll be lots of other people.*"

Embarrassed by the scene, Jewett flushed. "You're insane." She darted into the street, glancing at the driver as she passed. "I'm sorry. I really am." Grabbing Scott's arm, she hauled him across the road to the opposite curb.

The light changed, and the car continued on its way, the driver shaking his head in helpless frustration.

Once revealed as a public place, their destination became obvious to Jewett. She and Scott headed toward Des Moines Park half a block up the street. "Is there some law that says men have to publicly humiliate themselves at every opportunity?"

"I'm sorry." Scott's apology sounded honest. "I really didn't mean to block traffic, and I had to give the guy a warning. It goes with the increased pay. I'm a mandatory reporter. Even off-duty, if I see someone disobeying traffic laws, I'm legally obligated to mention it." The border of the park became visible, an abrupt meeting of gray sidewalk and green grass. Beyond, trees waved in the spring breezes, a last remnant of country looking out-of-place amid the high rises. "Besides, letting him know I was a cop probably kept him from jumping out of the car and trying to punch my nose through the other side of my head."

Jewett nodded, all too acquainted with the dilemmas raised by the status of mandatory reporter. As a doctor, she was legally obligated to report suspected child, elderly, or spouse abuse, possible mercy killings, and abuses of law or power by colleagues. In theory, a parent who did not strap his child's shoulder harness in a car could sue Jewett for seeing and not reporting the negligence should an accident occur and the child become injured. "Fine. Now explain why you risked your life to get me to go to the park."

Scott stepped from the wide sidewalk onto the narrower park pathways. "I just got this urge to show you my favorite place in the world."

"Your favorite place in the world is Des Moines Park?" Knowing Scott, Jewett would have expected he preferred pool halls, bowling alleys, and barrooms. She walked alternately behind and beside him to give the sparse clusters of other pedestrians room to pass.

"Actually, it's in Des Moines Park." Scott led Jewett to where the pathway ended in a central square. In the middle, a rectangular basin held flowing water originating from the trunk of a statue of an elephant and draining through slits in the sides. The blue-tiled bottom made the water look clear despite dirt left by children playing in it during the warmer months. A concrete ledge encircled the basin, damp from wind-blown droplets, and multiple walkways radiated from it like the spokes of a wheel. A few people perched, in groups, on the ledge. Scott sat and patted a place beside him.

Reluctantly, Jewett took a seat. Since all the paths converged at the fountain, the traffic here was thickest. Overhead lamps bathed the water, lending an even sheen that made it seem to glow. Wind chopped eddies across the surface, and the less uniform light of the moon struck the wavelets like jewels. A couple walked by, and Jewett noticed a subtle bulge in the woman's neck. She assessed it with the carelessness of long routine. "Goiter. Probably congenital, possibly thyroiditis."

Scott's gaze never strayed from the couple. "What?"

Realizing she had spoken aloud, Jewett winced. "Sorry. Force of habit. When I was a medical student, my friends and I would come here as a study break and play Sidewalk Diagnosis."

The couple continued down one of the pathways, and Scott turned his attention to Jewett. "What's that?"

"We'd watch people. By the way they walked or talked, the equipment they used, or external abnormalities, we'd guess their medical diagnoses." Jewett dismissed the game with a snort. "Stupid, huh?"

"Not at all." Scott watched a portly, middle-aged gentleman stride past. "In fact, you just gave me a great name for the game I like to play here: Secret Diagnosis."

"Secret Diagnosis?" Jewett humored Scott, knowing she had to give him at least a few minutes at the fountain before talking him into driving her home or risk another public spectacle.

"I believe everyone has a deep, dark secret he hides from the rest of the world."

Jewett studied Scott, waiting for him to laugh. It seemed like the sort of distraction he would have found silly.

"I told you I have a good feel for people. I've never been wrong yet." Scott returned her look, his pale eyes white in the lamplight.

"Never?" Jewett found the assertion difficult to believe.

"For example. That guy who just passed." Scott beetled his features in concentration. "He's cheating on his wife with his best friend's secretary."

"Uh huh." Jewett's tone betrayed skepticism. "Now how do you confirm it? Call his wife and ask?"

"Of course not. I don't even know his name." Scott twisted away, but not far enough to hide his tight-lipped grin. "Besides, if I'm wrong, it would break my perfect record."

"Perfect, I assume, because you never check any of them out."

Scott shrugged, not bothering to deny the assertion.

"Did you used to stop people and ask if they did, in fact, have V.D. or . . . Hunga-Bunga Syndrome?"

"Hunga-Bunga Syndrome?" Jewett rolled her eyes in resignation. "Anyway, at least we had some factual basis for our diagnoses. What makes you think that guy's an adulterer?"

Scott dabbled his fingers in the water, watching the rings widen until they struck the larger disturbance of the waterfall. "He's in the park alone at night and going somewhere. He's paunchy and not particularly attractive. The way he's dressed, he's got money to waste; but the way he walks suggests he's insecure. Those are the jerks who question their virility and cheat."

"And the best friend's secretary?" Jewett reminded.

"The guy kept looking around, like he figured he'd get caught, so it's more likely than usual someone he knows could turn him in." Scott flicked water from his fingers. "I made up the details to be funny."

"It didn't work."

"I noticed." Scott looked up as a pair of men passed, one as skinny as Jewett, the other obese, his joints recessed in folds of fat. Scott waited until they disappeared from sight before speaking again. "The scrawny fellow lost everything in the stock market."

"Sure." Jewett tried to sound interested, but her tone revealed impatience. "And the other one?"

"Lost everything in the *super*market."

Jewett snickered but caught herself before it became an outright laugh. "That's not funny. It's mean. I'll bet the guy's got a genetic syndrome or a pituitary lesion."

Scott tapped his hand against the concrete. "I can't do anything right for you, can I? I was just trying to make you smile. I didn't say it loud enough for him to hear me, and I have heavy friends and coworkers who would have been rolling on the floor with laughter." He cringed. "No pun intended."

Jewett scowled. "I just can't believe you're cruel enough to make a game out of insulting people."

"I don't do it to insult people." Scott rested a foot on the ledge and glanced around the fountain. "Usually, I'm serious. For example, I'll do myself." He screwed up his features as if in heavy consideration. "My deep, dark secret is that I have a terrible habit of interfering when I see a beautiful woman in a no-win situation."

Anger flared anew. "Is that another crack at Kaign?"

Scott made no reply.

Jewett leaped to the ground. "Take me home."

Scott did not move. "Not until you try a Secret Diagnosis. Just one. On . . ." He waited until a trio of middle-aged men trooped past. ". . . that fellow." He pointed out the one on the end, a willowy brunet in blue jeans and a T-shirt.

Jewett was in no mood for games. "I'm leaving now."

"If you try this one guy, I'll walk you to the garage and drive you straight home."

Jewett folded her arms across her chest without turning. "I want to go now."

"If you try this one guy, I'll take you back."

"Cop's Date Murdered in Streets Because Cop Too Jerky to Walk Her to Car," Jewett revived her facetious headline.

"Fifteen-yard penalty for repeating jokes. Besides, I'd just be embarrassed by that headline. Think where it would leave you." Scott pulled up his other leg. "Come on, Pat. All I'm asking you to do is try to guess some guy's secret."

Jewett sighed and snapped out the first thing that came to her head. "He wears women's clothes. Now, let's go."

"Hold it." Scott caught her sleeve. "What kind of women's clothes?"

Jewett turned back. "The deal was I just had to guess his secret."

Scott kept a straight face. "But you have to be specific. It's the rules."

"What rules?"

"My game. My rules."

It seemed faster and simpler to agree than fight. "Dresses."

Scott looked pensive. "What color?"

"Floral patterns."

"Nylon or silk stockings?"

"Ah, come on," Jewett protested. "This could go on all night."

"Nylon or silk stockings?" Scott pressed.

"One of each," Jewett blurted in exasperation. Then, the ridiculousness of the answer struck her, and she broke into laughter. Realizing she laughed alone, she gasped out, "What am I laughing at?"

"Introspection?" Scott suggested on cue; and, suddenly, they were both laughing.

I've been a jerk. Jewett knew she ought to share the thought with Scott. "Look, Scotty. What's your angle?"

"My angle?"

"I haven't exactly been fun to be around. Why did you want to take me out? And why are you trying so darn hard to make this work?"

Scott patted the seat Jewett had vacated. "I told you. I have a terrible habit of interfering when I see a beautiful woman in a bad situation."

Jewett remained in place. "No. I'm not buying that. I've lived with me a long time, and I know I'm not beautiful."

Scott started to protest, but she cut him off.

"At first, I thought you were just trying to be obnoxious. Then, I figured you were trying to get some cheap sex." Jewett ran her fingers along the damp concrete. "But instead of trying to get me to your bedroom, you took me to a public fountain and made me laugh. You spent a lot more money than necessary. What's your angle?"

Scott was silent several seconds. "May I speak now?"

"Of course."

"First, beauty is a personal thing. I happen to think you're beautiful, so you're beautiful." Scott indicated the ledge again, but Jewett shook her head suspiciously. "Second, even if you're not beautiful, and you are, if men only dated beauty queens, how come ugly women get happily married, too? I told you I'm a good judge of character. You looked like a woman I'd get along well with. The only way to know for certain was to spend some time with you."

Jewett clambered back to the ledge, torn between guilt and doubt. *If he's serious, I used him.* "How did I do?"

Scott looked at his shoes, obviously self-conscious. "Actually, not as bad as you probably think. A few times, I could tell you were having a good time because you got mad at me for it. You came with me hoping to have a terrible time, and whenever you started to enjoy yourself, you sabotaged the date."

Guilty. Now Jewett stared at her feet. "I have to be honest. I never wanted to date you. I was trying to make Kaign jealous."

"What, you think I didn't know that?"

Jewett looked up sharply. "You knew that?"

"I would have to be deaf, blind, and stupid to miss it."

I guess I haven't exactly acted subtle. "So why did you go along with it?"

"I was enjoying your company." Scott's gaze roved around the fountain. "Besides, it was hilarious. I've never seen a world-famous surgeon act like a jealous six-year-old before." His jovial manner returned, and he smiled. "Back to Secret Diagnosis. There's a guy on the other side who just wet himself and sat by the fountain to camouflage it."

Jewett followed Scott's stare to Kaign Jones perched on the ledge, face buried in the evening newspaper. "That's Kaign. What's he doing here?"

"For one thing, sitting in a pile of pigeon shit." Scott slid to his feet. "This has gotten ridiculous. I'm going over to talk to him."

Scott's tone was friendly, but the idea stabbed dread through Jewett. "No!" She softened her tone. "No, please. He's my boyfriend. Let me talk to him."

Scott shook his head. "No, if you go, he'll try to intimidate you and create a scene."

The logic was lost on Jewett. "But if you go, he'll try to intimidate you and create a scene, too." She remembered the muscles she had glimpsed beneath his sleeve. "I don't want you to hurt him."

Scott rested a reassuring hand on Jewett's leg. "I'm not going to hurt him. I'm a cop. We're taught restraint. Could you imagine if every time a cop pulled over some idiot for speeding and got called an asshole, the cop shot him?" Scott considered his own words. "Granted, it would cut down on traffic problems, but it wouldn't go over real well with those headlines you've been creating. I can handle him." He turned and headed around the fountain.

Jewett shrank back onto the ledge, afraid for what she might have caused. *I wanted to make Kaign jealous, not get him killed.* She wrung her hands in her lap, rubbing them repeatedly as if washing them. *I shouldn't have let Scotty go. I should have stopped him.* She tensed to jump down and catch him, but she had delayed too long.

Scott's voice floated to her beneath the burble of the fountain, his tone level and firm. Though soft, it carried. "Dr. Jones, I don't know why you're following us, but you're upsetting Pat. She's staying out longer with me than she would have if you had just waited at home. Why don't you leave quietly? Call her in the morning, and ask her out. I'm sure she'll forgive you."

Jewett slumped, aware Jones would answer with anger.

Jones screamed, "Who do you think you are coming over here and yelling at me? I'm a private citizen. You may be a cop, but you're not on duty. You don't have any right to give me shit!"

Relatively, Scott's reply sounded low as a whisper. "I'm a cop. I'm not on duty. I can give you whatever shit I please so long as it's not illegal. So far, I've given you completely legal shit."

Jewett's jaw went slack. She could imagine Jones' face growing scarlet.

"This is harassment! I don't know what you think you're doing, but you can't get away with it."

Scott had the upper hand. "Look, if I wanted to harass you, I'm a hell of a lot better at it than this."

Jewett spun around, just in time to see Jones spring to his feet, towering a solid half foot over Scott. "Listen, you little peon. I don't know who you think you are . . ."

"Sit down!" Scott's playful wit evaporated. "I don't give a damn how tall you are. When you're lying on the ground, you're not any taller than I am. If you make this degenerate into a fist fight, we're both going to be sorry. You, because you're going to hurt for a few days. Me, because I'm going to have to fill out paperwork to explain why I beat the snot out of a surgeon in the middle of City Park. But rest assured. After I pound you, I will throw you in jail."

"For what?" Jones demanded.

"Being a public nuisance."

"In what way am I being a public nuisance?"

Scott seemed at a loss for words. He glanced around. "You're . . . swimming in the fountain."

"That's a lie! I'm not swimming in the fountain."

"If you don't sit down and shut up, you will be."

Jewett suddenly realized she had stopped breathing. She took a great, shuddering gasp, awaiting Jones' retort that never came. Stiffly, he sat.

Scott's voice dropped so soft, Jewett had to strain to hear him. "Look, Kaign. You're doing this all wrong. Pat loves you. She's only seeing me because you're taking her for granted. Acting like this is hurting you more than me. Personally, I want you to be an asshole. Go ahead. Hit me right in the face, and I'll go home with a black eye. I'll punch you in the stomach, and you won't walk straight for a week. Mine will show up more than yours does. I'll get sympathy, and you'll be in the Emergency Room. Which one of us will come out worse in that deal?"

Jones' reply had the nasal tone that accompanies speaking through gritted teeth. "Get away from me. And stay away from my girlfriend. Can your simple mind grasp that?"

"Fine, I'm leaving." Scott backed away diplomatically. "But if you have any respect for Pat or yourself, you'll count to a thousand before following us home."

"I'm not following you . . ."

Scott turned his back on Jones' denial and headed back toward Jewett.

And Patricia Jewett wished she was anywhere else.

Chapter 7

The buzz of Jewett's bedside telephone roused her to semiconsciousness. She rolled with a groan and caught the receiver without opening her eyes, a maneuver learned during residency when every minute of sleep counted. Then, night phone calls could demand anything from simple acknowledgement to an emergency, and it had proven prudent to determine the importance of each call before committing herself to coming fully awake. "Hello?"

A hesitant male voice responded. "Dr. Jewett?"

"Yes."

"This is Dr. Hanley. I'm the trauma resident, on-call. I'm sorry to bother you."

Jewett wished Hanley would skip the amenities; the longer she talked, the less likely she would be able to fall back to sleep. She guessed by Hanley's discomfort he was in his first year of residency; and, despite her impatience, she tried to put him at ease. "You're not bothering me. What can I do for you?" She let one lid slide open a crack and glanced over the bedcovers to the mirrored dresser supporting a figurine of a unicorn, a chronic care textbook, and her clock radio. The digital display read: 00:19.

Hanley continued, "We have this brain wave scan, and there's a dip on it. The staff thinks it's probably normal; but, given who it's from, we don't want to take any chances."

Despite her efforts, Jewett's eyes fell open, and the familiar furniture of her bedroom filled her vision. When

Hanley did not finish, she asked the obvious question, "Who is the patient?"

A moment of stunned silence followed. "I . . . figured you knew. It's Dr. Jones. The surgeon."

Kaign, my God. Jewett jolted fully awake. "I'll be right there." Torn between the need for information and speed, Jewett slammed the receiver to its cradle. *What if he fought with Scotty? What if he's badly hurt?* Pulling off her nightgown, she rifled through the dresser drawer, jerked out a set of chronic care greens, and slipped into them. *It's all my fault.* Grabbing a pair of shoes and her wallet, she tapped the garage button and raced from the house onto the porch.

The concrete felt cold against Jewett's naked soles. Hopping on alternate feet, she yanked on her shoes. She removed the car key and shoved the wallet into her back pocket as she ran for the opened garage door and her blue and gray Ford Pegasus. Unlocking the door, she climbed into the driver's seat, activated the ignition, flipped the toggle from charge to drive, hit the map pre-set for her customary ride to the C. Everett Koop Memorial Hospital, and pulled away, forgetting to lock the front door or close the garage in her haste.

The five-minute drive to Koop gave Jewett more than enough time to concoct a thousand explanations for Jones' injury, from a fist fight with Scott to a car accident or a suicide attempt. *They got a brain wave scan, so Kaign hit his head, at least. God, why didn't I ask if he's conscious?*

Jewett swung the Ford into her reserved parking spot in Koop's garage. From habit, she wrenched the hand brake. The lever met no resistance. The car rolled forward, the tires bounced from the concrete barrier, and the car ground to a halt before Jewett could think. Too late, she kicked the foot brake, recalling the many times her father, then Kaign

Jones, had remanded her for using the emergency instead of the regular brakes. *Well, this ought to teach me. Lucky it didn't happen in traffic.* She punched the park button, exited the car, and ran through the connecting tunnels directly to the Emergency Room.

Breathless and frenzied, Jewett avoided the patient waiting area by cutting through the film reading room. The back-lit screen held a brain wave series. Seated in a chair in front of the scans, a young resident in Emergency Room scrubs looked up as she entered. Even from a distance, she could discern a relatively normal waking pattern on the printout. Squinting to read the name printed in the corner, she moved closer until she could make out "Kaign Jones." *Thank God, he's all right.*

The resident rose and offered his chair. "Dr. Jewett, I'm sorry. I didn't mean to upset you."

Panting, Jewett dismissed him with a wave and leaned closer without bothering to sit. She spotted the irregularity in the pattern just before Hanley indicated it with a fingertip. She nodded, routinely glancing over the entire series. "One of the more unusual . . ." She took a breath. ". . . normal variants."

"Normal. I thought so. Sorry to drag you all the way in."

Jewett clapped a hand to Hanley's shoulder, "No problem." She caught her breath. "Don't hesitate to call me anytime you have a question." She whisked out the opposite door toward the main emergency area.

Jewett emerged near the emergency station desk. Residents, staff physicians, and nurses clustered around the central table, discussing a case. Multiple computer screens displayed laboratory results or half-finished dictations. The unit clerk was talking on the telephone. Above the station, the digital display revealed nine of the sixteen rooms held patients. Jewett skimmed the roster rapidly, discovered Jones listed in the minor trauma room, and hurried to the door. She knocked but did not wait for a reply before entering.

Jones sat in one of three plastic chairs near the sink, disdaining the central examination table. As Jewett entered and let the door click shut behind her, Jones clapped a hand to his face. "What are you doing here?"

Jewett hopped up on the examination table facing Jones. "They called me in to read the scan. Are you all right?"

"Do you care?"

The implication stung. "Of course I care. Kaign, I love you."

Jones said nothing.

Jewett climbed off the table and took the seat beside Jones. "What happened?" She reached for his hand, but he avoided her touch.

Jones spoke through his fingers. "If the cops were out doing their jobs instead of trying to steal honest citizens' girlfriends, this sort of thing wouldn't happen."

"Kaign, please." Jewett wished she had discussed the case with the resident before seeing Jones, but she had not wanted to waste any time. "What happened?"

Jones let his hand slide to his lap. "One minute I'm walking home from the park, the next I'm lying face down on the sidewalk with the worst headache I've ever had."

"You got mugged?" Jewett's chest felt squeezed. "Oh, Kaign." She reached for him again.

Jones sprang to his feet. "That's what you wanted, isn't it?"

"What?"

"Isn't it?"

The question was so absurd, Jewett resorted to humor.

"That's right, Kaign. I hired them. Paid them extra to take your watch so I'd have something to get you for your birthday."

Jones stared, apparently uncertain how to react to Jewett's atypical sarcasm. "You told your pudgy, midget, cop boyfriend to talk me into walking home late and too far behind to call for help."

Recalling Jones had just gone through a traumatic experience, Jewett reined her annoyance. "I've got about as much control over Scotty as over you. I didn't ask him to talk to you, and I don't remember asking you to follow us. Anyway, he's not my boyfriend. You are."

Jones retook his seat, his head sagging and his shoulders slumped.

Jewett had never seen him look so meek. Sympathy twitched through her, and the urge to comfort him became overpowering. She wrapped her arms around him, pressing her cheek into the warm hollow between the muscles of his chest. "I love you."

Gradually, Jones' arms looped around Jewett's back. "I love you, too. I'm sorry."

They sat in one another's arms without speaking. Jewett felt better than she had in days, listening to the steady, muffled beat of Jones' heart. He said, "What did the wave scans show?" The words vibrated against Jewett's ear.

"It said you're bullheaded and stubborn." Jewett smiled. "Completely normal."

"Normal." Jones disengaged from Jewett without bitterness. "I knew it. The E.R.'s staffed by a bunch of incompetents."

Not wanting Jones to run off on an angry tangent, Jewett spoke soothingly. "Now, Kaign. They're not specialists, and you can't hardly blame them for being thorough."

"I suppose not," Jones conceded. He took Jewett's hand.

"Now, gorgeous. Tell me what happened on this date."

Jewett cringed, not liking the direction of the conversation. Now that their relationship seemed back to normal, she longed to avoid touchy subjects, for a while at least. "I don't want to talk about him. I want to talk about you. Do you have any pain?"

"Nothing ibuprofen won't cure." Jones rubbed the back of his head. "And I do want to know what happened. What did you talk about?"

Unable to dodge the topic, Jewett considered. "Not much . . ." She could not recall discussing many important things with Scott, though there had not been any long, uncomfortable silences either. ". . . except the murder. They wanted to get me into one of those machine hypnosis environments."

Jones crinkled his forehead. "Why's that?"

"To see if I could remember any details of that guy."

"What guy?"

"The one I saw leaving the scene." Jewett examined Jones' eyes for gross evidence of injury. "Are you sure you're all right?"

"I'm fine. Why didn't you tell me about this guy before?"

"I did." Jewett distinctly remembered telling someone. Doubt descended upon her. "Or maybe I told Scotty." Jewett realized her mistake instantly.

Jones stiffened. "Oh, so now you can't tell us apart."

Jewett walked a diplomatic tightrope, trying to keep Jones on the side of logic and reason. "He's investigating the case. I had to tell him. Then, in all the excitement, I forgot to mention it to you. I always tell you everything, so I just assumed. I've known him a day. What we have is special." She held Jones tighter. "Thirty years from now, you and I will be sitting on the porch swing watching our grandchildren play, and we won't even remember Scotty's name."

Jones scowled. "Are you back on that commitment thing again?"

Jewett was seized with the sudden urge to scream. Instead, she released Jones, rose, and placed her hands on her hips in helpless frustration. "First you're mad because you think I'm not committing. Then, you're mad because you think I am. It's like talking to a seesaw." Jewett could not fathom the source of her boldness; but, inspired, she went with it. "I understand you're upset. I just can't take this any more. You know I love you. I would never purposely do anything to hurt you. But next time you need comforting, I'll send you a telegram."

Jones leaped to his feet. He lurched toward Jewett. Afraid he might hurt her, Jewett took a back-step, but Jones curled her into an embrace, his arms trembling slightly. "I'm sorry," he said softly. And they clung.

It was nearly 03:00 before the Emergency Room cleared Kaign Jones, and the two grabbed what sleep they could in surgery on-call. Life seemed to settle back into a normal pattern for Dr. Patricia Jewett. Her reconciliation with Jones restored her flagging spirits, despite the circumstances surrounding it. Ward duties usurped talk of the murder, and Krystal Fantella slipped quietly into the dark recesses of memory. The questions and discussions on rounds proceeded in a logical, educational fashion, and all the patients were doing relatively well. Judson Payne's monitoring unit sported a fresh wreath of black-eyed Susans and his sister's picture taped beside the one of the stub-tailed mongrel that had been the boy's pet before his accident. Though higher than before the infection, his electrostimulator and ventilator settings seemed to have stabilized.

After rounds, Jewett took Curtis Maltorf aside to discuss his private and semiprivate patients. Leaning against the chronic care bay wall, the red-haired resident dismissed the students to their duties and become instantly solemn.

Jewett sensed the change at once. "What's wrong?"

Maltorf minced his words. "I can't quite put my finger on it, but I think Dr. Schober's condition is deteriorating."

Jewett frowned in consideration. In chronic care areas, intuition rarely proved reliable. Parents, students, and less experienced nurses tended to assess a patient's condition by tiny movements or perceived focusing of the eyes, all notoriously unreliable indicators in brain-damaged patients. Often, a young nurse would rush to the resident with nonspecific findings and demand "something" be done for the patient immediately. Most of the time, no treatment was possible or necessary, and the resident would delay and suffer until the new shift brought a seasoned nurse to the post. Jewett expected a more professional assessment from Maltorf. "Deteriorating how?" she pressed. "More seizures?"

"Fewer seizures," Maltorf admitted. "I looked over his convulsion pattern and the amount of pikobarbital needed per day and started him on an appropriate dosage of barobid. I haven't seen a seizure since."

So far, he sounds better. Jewett waited patiently for Maltorf to continue.

"There's the usual stuff. He used to move around, and now he just lies there. Doesn't even bother to open his eyes." Maltorf rocked from foot to foot. "Then there's more objective stuff. His brain wave patterns have flattened out, and his vent settings have climbed."

The latter signs concerned Jewett. Several possible explanations sprang to mind; but, for the purpose of teaching, she turned the question back to Maltorf. "What do you think is going on?"

Maltorf shook his head doubtfully. "I'm not sure. Possibly an infection, but he's got no fever and his blood studies are all normal. I thought about pneumonia, shock lung or ventilator damage. The magnetic images go against those. The only new drug I've got him on is the barobid." Pleased by Maltorf's thoroughness, Jewett smiled. An image of last year's Koop physicians' picnic came to her mind, unbidden. She pictured Stanley Schober playing volleyball with as much energy and enthusiasm as any of the new residents, and sadness settled over her again. Trying to maintain professional distance, she forced away an image of Schober diving for a ball driven desperately out of bounds by a teammate. "Sounds like you thought this out well."

Maltorf added frivolously, "If he was a regular, thinking patient, I'd say he just gave up."

Psychiatric vagaries rarely fit well into medical diagnoses, but theories about the power of the mind to combat or surrender to illness had waxed and waned over the years. "Survival is an instinct, not a conscious thought. Even animals can lose their will to live." Jewett supported Maltorf's consideration of all the possibilities but directed him from his current abstraction. "Of course, there's not much we can do about that, so I'd concentrate on the other ideas you raised. What do you think we should do for Dr. Schober?"

"Well." Maltorf counted off a finger for each contingency. "Infection's most likely, so I'll get regular blood studies, check his urine, and start antibiotics if needed. The lung problems could still be too small for the imagers to detect, so I'll check again in a couple days." He ticked off a third finger. "Fourth generation synthetic barbiturates shouldn't cause suppression, but just in case he's having a paradoxical reaction, I'll stop the barobid and go back to treating individual seizures with pikobarb."

Jewett would have started the antibiotics now and continued the barobid, but Maltorf's plan seemed equally competent and justifiable, so she sanctioned it. "Sounds good. Let me know what happens." She started to leave, then noticed Maltorf seemed ready to say something else. She waited.

Maltorf went right to the point. "I hear you may try out one of those machine hypnosis deals. Must seem weird using one of the devices you researched."

Jewett laughed. "Not half as weird as reading my boyfriend's brain wave scan last night." Curiosity followed. *How did Curt know about the hypnosis environment?* She never intended to keep the information about the fleeing man a secret, but she had only told Lieutenant Scott. *And Kaign, of course. Makes sense he might have told a few colleagues at the hospital, and rumors spread fast among the residents.* "See you this afternoon." She slipped into the hallway, glad Maltorf had made his plans for Stanley Schober from gathered facts rather than vague premonitions. Despite that, she could not shake the "given up the will to live" theory from her mind.

After the excitement of the last several days, the familiar mundaneness of a normal day seemed boring. Rounds on the neurological and subacute bays went as smoothly as the chronic care area, and no new admissions arrived that day. Between patient responsibilities, Patricia Jewett managed to slip in a few hours of research, but even the frustration of her brain wave study seemed routine. She managed to finish her work by 18:30, and, leaving the beeper in her office recharger, headed for the parking garage.

The front doors of C. Everett Koop Memorial Hospital opened onto a comfortable mixture of concrete walkways spidered over well-tended grasses, young oaks, and flower beds. In the nicer seasons, Jewett routinely took the outside route to the garage; the underground tunnels sported an array of ugly pipes, smelt musty, and led past such unimpressive scenery as the laundry room, the storage facility, the morgue, and the crematorium. And, from the chronic care areas, the outside walk proved shorter.

As Jewett left the hospital and stepped into the spring sunshine, the mingled perfume of warmth, damp, and greenery greeted her. The sun hovered, slanted toward the western horizon, and a gray glaze of clouds lay over a sky not dark enough to kick on the dusk to dawn lights lining the pathways. Few other people passed Jewett as she made her way toward the garage. The nursing shift had started hours ago. Most of the residents, students, and physicians had left their duties in the hands of the on-call team; and the visitors would be enjoying dinner at home or with the patients they came to see.

Jewett followed the walkway into the well-lit interior of Koop's parking garage and wandered up the center of the ramp. Bars of steady fluorescence lined the ceiling and the walls at several levels and intervals; the antiglare wavelengths lit the concrete without blinding. Jewett retrieved her wallet and rummaged through its contents for her key card.

Instinct alone caused Jewett to glance up just as a sleek, red sedan whipped around the corner and barreled straight for her. She hesitated, certain the headlight detectors would buzz her presence to the driver. Then, realizing it was not going to slow, she stepped aside to give it more room.

A Time to Die

The sedan veered toward her. The bumper loomed. The tinted windshield filled her vision.

Panic seized Jewett. She dodged between parked cars, smacking her wrist on a side view mirror. Her wallet jarred from her hand, skidding beneath a Volkswagen. The sedan swiped the bumper of the car Jewett dodged behind, then roared past, tires screeching as it took the next corner too fast.

Jewett grabbed at a car for support, her heart pounding. *He nearly killed me. He tried to kill me. Why would someone want to kill me?* She pried her fingers from the door trim and groped beneath the car for her wallet. Finding it, she removed the car key card and stuffed the wallet back into her pocket. Her wrist throbbed from the impact of the mirror, but the pain seemed unimportant. Her gaze darted nervously between the rows of cars, and she skirted every shadow until she opened the door of her own vehicle, slid inside, and locked all the doors. Her heart settled back into its normal rhythm, but her mind remained riveted on the incident.

Hitting the pre-set for the drive home, Jewett snapped on her seat belt, kept her grip light, and allowed the Ford Pegasus to all but maneuver itself. *Maybe it's the murderer. He knows I saw him, and he saw me.* A chill crawled down Jewett's spine. *That makes no sense. Why didn't he go after me right away? Before I could describe him to the police?*

The evening turned leaden beneath layers of clouds, and the dusk-to-dawn lights kicked on, intensifying the shadows of houses, cars, and roadways, providing cover for the evil inventions of Jewett's anxiety. *Of course, until today, no one else knew about the machine hypnosis. Darn it, why didn't I tell Kaign to keep it secret?* She answered her own question, the self-argument making her feel like an idiot. *Because I'm just being paranoid. No one tried to kill me. It was just a stupid accident.*

The car slowed, rumbling up her driveway and into the garage. The dash light flashed to remind her to stop. Mechanically, Jewett reached for the hand brake, then remembered it was broken in time to hit the foot pedal instead. *My God, the brake! Maybe someone did try to kill me before.* Opening the door, she exited the car, the spring breeze cold against flesh speckled with goose bumps. *I can't be alone tonight. Thank goodness I made up with Kaign.*

Jewett pressed the garage closer and slipped out before the panel rolled shut. The concrete of her walkway never seemed so sterile and forbidding, and she listened for sounds of movement beneath the steady click of her shoes on the pavement. Freeing her card key as she walked, she stepped onto the porch and remembered, with sudden terror, she had never locked the door. *What if someone's in there waiting for me?*

Jewett's grip went tight on the key. She froze, incapable of movement, while her thoughts scattered in multiple directions. *I shouldn't go in there.* She edged forward, common sense warring with caution. *Lots of people don't map-set their cars until they leave the garage, including Kaign. It's not as if the driver followed me home. He probably just didn't see me.* Jewett used the moment of reason to gather her self-composure. Now, her house looked reassuringly familiar, a safe haven she could seal against strangers. *I've got too many things to do to just stand here waiting for some nut to grab me off the porch. And if I don't move soon, the neighbors are going to think I've gone crazy.* Jewett pushed open the door and glanced inside.

The customary dark array of television, coffee table, telephone, and couch met her scrutiny. *If someone wanted to rob me, he would have taken the T.V.D., at least.* She edged inside, hyperalert despite rationalization. Using the buttons by the door, she snapped on every bulb in the house. Light bathed the interior, showing nothing out of place. Jewett glanced through the doorways into the kitchen and bedroom. Everything seemed exactly as she had left it: tidy, clean, each item in its proper position. *I'm being ridiculous. Have to calm down.*

Jewett closed the outer door, meticulously activating the lock. She dropped onto the living room couch, took a long, deep breath, and loosed it in a sigh. She intended the gesture to calm, but her nerves still felt on fire. A movement to her left startled her. She sprang to her feet, loosing a short scream and whirled to face the motion. A bar of light whipped across the wall, a headlight from a passing car, then disappeared as the vehicle continued.

Jewett sank back into the couch cushions. She clamped a hand to her chest, feeling the brisk tap of her heart. *At this rate, I'm going to scare myself into a coma. I'm calling Kaign.* Jewett picked up the telephone and hit the first pre-dial. The connection clicked alive. She glanced at the television clock and discovered it was 18:53. The receiver signaled the first buzz, and Jewett remembered Jones would probably not have returned from the hospital yet. *Thursday night. Surgical conference.*

Severing the connection before the second ring, Jewett punched in the code for the surgical wing of C. Everett Koop Memorial Hospital instead. As the first buzz trilled across the line, Jewett suddenly realized she had failed to check the bathroom and closets on entering the house. *What if I've locked myself in with some lunatic?* She swung her legs to the cushions and pressed her back against the arm of the couch, facing the entrances from the kitchen and bedroom.

A click sounded over the phone line. A woman's voice followed. "Surgery. Can I help you?"

Jewett's tongue felt as if it had dried to the bottom of her mouth. "This is Dr. Jewett. Could you page Kaign Jones to my number, please?"

"Certainly." She broke the contact.

Jewett drew her knees to her chest, the receiver cradled in her hand and her gaze still locked on the doorways. A gap of silence followed. It seemed like a quarter hour wait or longer until the telephone buzzed; but, when Jewett glanced at the clock, she realized only four minutes had passed. She switched on the connection. "Hello? Kaign?"

"Yeah, what's up?" Though filled with impatience and annoyance at the interruption, Jones' voice soothed Jewett.

"I think someone tried to kill me," she blurted, her voice tremulous.

Jones' tone changed instantly to one of concern. "What happened?"

"In the parking garage. Someone tried to run over me." A pause followed as Jones assessed the information. "Are you hurt?"

"No. I got out of the way."

Another pause. "What makes you think he tried to kill you?"

Jewett gripped the receiver more tightly. "He came straight at me."

"Were you between him and the exit?"

"Well, yeah." Jewett knew Jones was trying to calm her, but she could not help feeling defensive. "But when I tried to get out of his way, he swerved after me."

"Maybe he misjudged the direction you'd take. Or he sneezed or his gum fell into his lap or something."

Jewett did not like the turn of the conversation, but the

thought of the deep silence and emptiness that would follow breaking the telephone connection frightened her. "Kaign, whose side are you on?"

"I'm not on anybody's side." Jones said gently. "You've had a rough week. First Schober's accident, then Krystal's murder, and me getting mugged. I just think you're being irrational. You're blowing a minor incident out of proportion."

Jewett clung to the receiver. "Maybe I am, but I'm still scared to death. I want you to stay with me. I *need* you."

"Pat, I'm in the middle of a conference." Jones sounded compassionate, but irritation tinged his tone. "We've got a guest speaker from Harvard, and I can always use the continuing medical education credits. As soon as he's finished, I'll come over."

Goaded by fear, Jewett forced the issue. "There're ninety billion ways to get CME credits. One conference isn't going to make a difference. I need you now."

"What if I have a patient who needs this procedure?" Aggravation broke through Jones' attempts to comfort. "Let him die because my girlfriend wants me?"

The logic escaped Jewett. "You'd do a different procedure, the same one you would have done if that same patient came in yesterday." She added quickly, "You were acting irrational last night, and *I* was there for *you*."

"I didn't call you in."

"But I came anyway!" Jewett clamped her free hand between her knees to steady it, knowing she had to find some words, any words, to convince Jones to come. *I just can't be alone tonight.* "I want you here. I shouldn't have to beg you."

Jones spoke slowly, as if to a child. "I'll be there as soon as the conference is finished. I have a commitment to my patients."

"You have a commitment to me, too."

Jones' control broke. "I'll be there in an hour! What the hell do you want from me?"

Warm tears brimmed on Jewett's lashes. "I just want the same commitment you give your work."

"People's lives depend on my work!"

Jewett's vision blurred, and she did not trust herself to talk.

Jones waited for her reply. When he got none, he continued shouting. "Fine! You want commitment? How's this for commitment? Marry me!"

"What?" The word slipped from Jewett's mouth before she could think.

"Damn it, Pat! I said, 'Marry me!' That's what you want, isn't it?"

Jewett managed speech. "That's not a commitment, it's a threat! A proposal isn't something you make in anger, and it certainly isn't something you preface with a swear word."

"Damn it, Pat," Jones repeated. "I don't want to play games. If I didn't mean it, I wouldn't have said it. I'll be over after the conference. You've got an hour to think about your answer. See you then." He disconnected.

Jewett switched to standby from habit and let the receiver slide into her lap. Tears rolled down her cheeks. For years, she had believed Jones would eventually propose, but she always pictured a candle-lit dinner or a picnic by the river and a diamond ring. Suddenly, what she imagined as one of the happiest moments of her life seemed more like a cruel trap. *I can't say yes to that. Can I?* The answer seemed obvious; yet, if she refused Jones' proposal, pride might keep him from giving her another. *He'd take it as an insult.*

Jewett's tears quickened as she realized the full effect of what had become a no-win situation. *But if I accept, I can't be certain how he really feels. Why did I have to corner him?* Uncertainty turned to self-doubt and anger. *I dearly love Kaign, and I don't want to lose him. But what happens five years from now when he resents me for trapping him?*

The chime of the doorbell shattered Jewett's train of thought. She jumped in fright, then hesitated, unsure.

The bell sounded again, followed by a knock.

Jewett approached cautiously and looked through the peephole. Lieutenant Daniel Scott stood on the porch, dressed in his Des Moines police uniform, his expression somber.

Oh, God. The last person in the world I want to see right now. If he's here when Kaign arrives, it's all over. Jewett considered pretending she was not home, but even Scott's company seemed preferable to being alone. Wiping the tears from her eyes, she inched open the door. "What do you want?"

Scott avoided her stare, gaze fixed on his feet. His manner seemed completely out of character, tense and deadly serious. "I'm sorry, Pat."

Jewett's every muscle tightened, and she did not dare believe another tragedy could possibly have happened. "Sorry? Sorry for what."

Scott looked up, his blue-gray eyes cold in the shadow of his hat brim. "Dr. Patricia Jewett, you are under arrest for the murder of Krystal Fantella. You have the right to remain silent . . ."

CHAPTER 8

The following morning, Dr. Patricia Jewett walked from the parking garage to the front entrance of the C. Everett Koop Memorial Hospital beneath a sky glazed gray-blue with calm. No spring breeze stirred, and the trees stood in silence, black and skeletal beneath glassy streaks of white that broke through the clouds. She tried to lose herself in the familiarity of the route, but the events of the previous night haunted her until even the plastiglass doors seemed strange. She seized the handle, choosing to pull it open manually rather than tripping the viewers, a last remnant of power in a life that seemed to have slipped into a wild chaos beyond her control.

One day a respected physician, the next a criminal. Jewett wandered through the hallways with her head low, certain every person she passed stared in judgment. *Innocent until proven guilty. Since I've done nothing wrong, how could any jury convict me?* Jewett continued toward the chronic care ward, aware, blameless or not, the evidence against her might hold up in court. *I had motive in the argument, I guess, though I wasn't even planning to get her fired. Everyone has a right to one really bad day. OK, I had opportunity, but so did everyone else at Koop. Fingerprints on the knife—that one's going to hurt. Knowledge of anatomy, sure, and I practically handed that one to Scotty. A flimsy story no one can corroborate: I was alone in my office when Krystal was killed, and no one else saw the fleeing man.* The phrase she had so blithely quoted to Elaine Schober returned to her now: "It is better that ten guilty persons escape than one innocent suffer." She thought of all the thieves and murderers free on technicalities of the law designed to protect the innocent while she faced a strong chance of serving time, perhaps her entire life, for a crime she could not imagine committing.

Jewett turned the corner onto the ward and headed straight for the chronic care bay without glancing left or right. Tense whispers followed her through the corridor. She could imagine colleagues' stares, felt them mentally pronouncing her guilt and questioning the head administrator's decision to let a suspected felon, who may have murdered one of their own, continue working until her trial. Jewett could not help but respect Dr. Cambridge's willingness to stand behind her despite vocal opposition from the board and the certainty of a lawsuit should anything untoward happen to Jewett's patients, no matter how unrelated. He had personally posted her bail, brushing aside Jones' offer to do the same, and given her the option of taking a paid vacation or finishing her month on the ward. She had chosen work, hoping the routine would allow her to elude ceaseless musing over what she could not change. *And my patients need me. I can't let my own problems interfere with their care.*

Jewett whisked through the entryway to the chronic care bay, and the nurses and technicians became inordinately involved in their responsibilities. The patients, machinery, and monitors had never seemed so well tended. The five students waited for rounds by Jon Pyrus' bed, fidgeting more restlessly than on their first day on the ward. Jewett glanced around the room, but only one gaze met hers. Maltorf looked up from amid the cluster of students, his brown eyes quizzical, his lips bent into a half smile that mixed welcome with sadness.

"Morning," Jewett said, unable to preface the word with the customary "good."

No one moved. The background noises fell beneath the hum of the ventilators, and the routine rattle of a bedpan seemed abruptly out of place.

"Good morning, Dr. Jewett," Maltorf returned, sounding genuinely pleased to see her. "I heard you had a rotten evening. Is there anything I can do to help?"

A collective gasp rumbled through the room. The students' eyes rolled, focusing everywhere except on Jewett.

Jewett appreciated Maltorf's forthrightness and hoped it would pave the way to normal relationships with the remainder of the staff. "Thanks, Curt. The best thing any of us can do is make sure patient care doesn't suffer."

Maltorf grinned fully. "I'm sure we can do more than that. If you think of anything, you know how to reach me." He flicked the beeper at his hip with a finger, his nail making a ticking sound against the plastic. "Matthew, why don't you start with Mr. Pyrus?"

Rounds began with an uncharacteristic, stiff formality. The students stuck tightly to the facts, impeding the usual flow of conversation that raised issues of discussion. Desperate for topics, Jewett seized on a minor abnormality in a routine blood count. She addressed the student caring for the affected patient. "Why do you think Mr. Sorenson has a mild degree of polycythemia?"

The student fiddled nervously with a penlight in the breast pocket of her white coat, its light an orange spot through the fabric. "Lab error?"

"Probably." Unable to stimulate a discussion with this answer, Jewett prompted another student. "Rina? What other things might cause polycythemia in this patient?"

Rina feathered blonde bangs from her forehead. "The

ventilator might be set a bit low." She considered. "The other night, I read an article in a hematology journal, I think it was *Blood*, about chronic care and . . ."

Maltorf snorted, interrupting the student.

All eyes turned to the red-headed resident.

"I'm sorry," Maltorf continued. "That title just kills me. *Blood*." He used the sharp, tongue-dominant pronunciation from an ancient vampire movie, "Bl-ooood."

Jewett let Maltorf finish, appreciating his attempt at humor. No doubt, he wanted to break the tension.

"You know," Maltorf went on. "I always thought the heme guys ought to get together with the GI guys and call their journal *Blood & Guts*."

Several of the students snickered, turning away; others clamped hands to their mouths, horrified by Maltorf's disrespect to an attending physician. Jewett laughed for the first time in days. Then, like the initiating grain dropped into a supersaturated solution, the ward erupted into laughter. The nurses chuckled. The students howled, and the strain that had hung over the room shattered as completely as fine crystal on concrete.

Teaching rounds resumed on a more normal keel, a complementary mixture of education, care plans, and banter; and Patricia Jewett felt a driving urge to hug Maltorf. *Thanks to him, we may still make this work.*

As the doctors-in-training approached the final row of patients, something seemed misplaced to Jewett. She glanced around the familiar, glazed visages, but it still took her a moment to realize what was missing. *Judson Payne.* The boy's bed lay empty, neatly made. Stripped of the flowers and photos, the monitors looked dull and ugly. Discomfort prickled the edges of Jewett's consciousness. *Maybe they took him for some sort of surgical procedure.* The conclusion seemed impossible. *The on-call resident would have contacted me if Jud's condition had deteriorated.*

There seemed only one other possibility. *My God, maybe his parents were right. Jud's been moved to the subacute bay.* Guarded hope spiraled through Jewett. *Always we wish for the one in a million who responds despite hopeless odds, the single tiny miracle that justifies everything we do.* Jewett could picture the Paynes' faces lit with joy and love and belief in the will of God, chattering like new parents. *It couldn't happen to a nicer, more dedicated family.* "Where's Jud?" She looked at the responsible student.

The student became suddenly fully engrossed in her penlight.

Only then did the truth strike Jewett. Horror drained the blood from her face, immediately replaced by a flush of outrage. "He's dead, isn't he?"

Maltorf nodded. "He went suddenly last night."

Why Judson? It seemed grossly unfair to Jewett. So many of the patients lay without friends or visitors, invisible so far as the world outside Koop was concerned. Yet they kept on, day after day, waiting for a godsend to return them to a semblance of life or drive them to the grave. But Judson Payne had people who loved him, caring parents who took joy from the son others dismissed as dead. "Why wasn't I called?" The answer was obvious, yet Jewett could not banish the Paynes' need. *The reasons don't matter. They depended on me last night, and I wasn't there for them.* She did not wait for a reply to her question before asking the next. "Who talked to his parents?"

"I did," Maltorf said. "When the on-call resident couldn't get you, he called me, and I came in. They asked for you. I told them you'd have been here if you could."

Jewett made a mental note to call the Paynes after

checking on Judson's pathology results. Not wanting to lose the lighter mood Maltorf's joke had set, she dropped the topic. "Let's finish rounds."

Teaching rounds on the neurological and subacute bays went as stiffly as the chronic bay's had begun. More relaxed, Jewett kept the answers and discussions as routine as possible; and, by the end of the session, the students and ward staff seemed as comfortable as she dared to expect. The normalcy of her actions allowed them to think of her as the attending physician they knew rather than a potential killer.

Rounds finished, Jewett left the chronic care ward and headed for the basement tunnels. Personally checking the pathology of her treatment failures had become ingrained since residency. It gave her an opportunity to review anatomy and see the effects of technology, medications, and disease on the human body. It supplied her with a chance to understand the deep impact of every doctor's order, clues about how life support equipment might be enhanced to decrease organ damage, and a rare occasion to see where her medical knowledge had failed.

Jewett took the fire stairs down the single flight to the basement. She emerged onto the finished area of the underground hallways that supported the Department of Radiology. A brown carpet with a speckled pattern of white and black lined the floor between painted rainbows that covered the cinderblock walls with color, looking more misplaced than cheerful. Jewett continued past the staff lounge. Soon, the carpeting and murals ended, replaced by dreary blue-gray concrete and copper pipes. She passed the closed doors of janitorial offices, clean but drab-appearing restrooms, and hospital stores. The musical whine of the box folder trailed her through the corridor to a set of stairs leading up to the outside, positioned as if as an escape from the less traveled area of the corridor housing the morgue. Jewett proceeded.

Soon, the sickly-sweet odor of tissue preservatives tainted the hallway. A sandy-haired janitor wandered by, dressed in the dark green jumpsuit of Koop's cleaning staff. He appeared vaguely familiar, which did not surprise Jewett. She traveled the hospital hallways frequently enough to recognize the faces of many staff members with whom she did not directly work. Without exchanging amenities, she turned onto the cul-de-sac leading to the morgue.

Jewett skirted the crematorium, its hall door recessed several yards from the main hallway. The blind stretch of wall in front of it contained a sign: "Danger: Do Not Enter. Authorized Personnel Only." The metal and plastic door looked oddly sleek amidst the ancient, musty concrete of the remainder of the basement. Jewett remembered when the crematorium was built amid a rush of other measures designed to keep rapidly-mutating bacteria and viruses confined. Greedy pharmaceutical companies had goaded doctors to keep switching to the newest, most expensive, broad-spectrum antibiotics and antivirals. Only the hardiest and fastest evolving microorganisms survived; but, no longer needing to compete for nutrition and space, those flourished, creating a wild rash of infections resistant to even the most potent drugs. Soon, it became safer to keep patients at home amid less sensitized bacteria then take a chance with the killer hospital bugs. Something had had to be done. The crematorium was one of the solutions the department of pathology had contributed to the cause.

A short distance further down the main corridor, Jewett opened the door to the decontamination booth and stepped inside. A door on the opposite side led into the morgue, and she knew she was not supposed to open it until she closed the outer door and activated the electromagnetic radiation field that would kill microbes on the surface of her exposed skin and clothing.

Jewett never understood why it was necessary to decontaminate before entering the morgue, especially since staff could move freely between wards and even outdoors without a similar cleansing. *Are they afraid we might sicken the dead?* The best explanation she had heard was that someone entering could contaminate a specimen and cause confusion or error when it came to determining cause of death. The cleansing procedure needed to be repeated to leave the morgue, which made more sense to Jewett. Already, construction workers were building similar booths in the operating suite and the intensive care nursery. Given the high number of immunosuppressed patients, Jewett suspected the chronic care ward would be high on the list of installation sites. *The morgue is a good starting place: low traffic means fewer exposures to the radiation and a chance to absolutely ascertain its safety before exposing the entire staff.*

Facing the morgue entry, Jewett activated the decontamination switch and watched for the confirmatory light to go on. Instead, the display flashed an error message: "Door Open." She turned, seeing the blue beam from the edge of the door shining onto the wall. *Forgot to close the door.*

Turning, Jewett pushed the outer door shut. The beam connected with its receptor plate on the door frame, completing the circuit. The display formed the words: "Working," then "Complete." Jewett opened the door to the morgue and stepped inside.

The entrance opened onto the main room where a pair of plastic tables supported half-dissected corpses. One held a mangled adult. *Accident victim,* Jewett guessed. The other was an infant or abortus. She saw no sign of Judson Payne.

Jewett glanced over the assortment of refrigerators and incubators. A door in the right wall beyond the tables led to the far side of the crematorium. To her left, an entryway opened onto the documentation room. A young man with curly hair and a beard dictated into a word processor. He paused to retype a word misinterpreted by the voice scanners, then looked up to Jewett. She recognized him as Aaron Higitin, the senior pathology resident. He rose and came to greet her. "Pat, hi. What brings you to the depths of hell?"

Compared with the night I had, this is heaven. Jewett smiled. "You have a patient of mine."

"Oh, that's right. The Payne kid from last night."

Jewett nodded confirmation. "What did you find?"

"The usual mechanical trauma. That kid was on the ventilator a long time."

Jewett nodded vigorously.

"I haven't seen the microscopics yet, but I'd bet the house on an overwhelming infection. Hemorrhages, necrosis, and lots of abscesses. I should have the slides done tomorrow, and I can go over them with you in detail."

Jewett wanted a chance to look over the organs herself. "Can I see the body?"

"Sure, why not?" Higitin hesitated, as if trying to recall where he had left it. "He's in the crematorium."

Of course. Jewett knew the law specified the remains of anyone who died of a hospital-acquired infection must be cremated as part of the effort to contain the virulent microorganisms. She also realized the Paynes would have wanted a religious burial and cringed at the added discomfort this situation must have caused them. "Could you go over it with me? Show me the major pathology?"

Higitin glanced at his watch. "Not right now. I've got a lunch date." He hissed in disapproval. "And I'm late as usual. Feel free to root around. I'll save the body until we can go over it together this afternoon." He fished a pair of rubber gloves from his pocket and handed them to Jewett. "If you want a cover gown, there's a box by the exit."

The decontamination booth had made gloves and gowns optional, but Jewett suspected most people still felt more comfortable using them. *Sterile gore is still gore.* "Thanks." She headed for the box as Higitin slipped into the decontamination booth and closed the door behind him.

Jewett took a packet from the top of the stack, unfolded it into a disposal paper gown, and tied it over her chronic care greens. It did not surprise her that Higitin seemed busy. President Nash's promises to eliminate death must have steered many residents away from pathology, though logic dictated accidents, murder, and suicide would make it impossible to completely abolish death.

Jewett opened the back doorway and entered the short operations hallway between the morgue and the crematorium. A row of levers on the wall activated the system and locked the doors. The morgue-side entry to the crematorium stood ajar, and Jewett could see the central table and the box containing the remains of Judson Payne. Beyond it, the door to the main hallway was closed, certainly locked to keep visitors from wandering inside, and Jewett could see the "Authorized Personnel Only" sign through the window.

Jewett entered the crematorium, leaving the back door open. Like the decontamination booth, the system could not be activated without the door securely fastened, a safety feature designed to keep even the most bumbling employee from frying himself. Gas jets lined the inner walls, interspersed with electrical detonators that sparked temperatures high enough to burn bone to ash.

Jewett swung open the lid of the coffin. Judson Payne lay still and silent, his face and limbs looking bloodless in death, more like rubber than skin. She had seen it many times, yet the reality struck her again, the fine trickle of being between life and death. She considered the moment before it, when the staff rushed and fought to keep the blood pressure palpable and stabilize the final, erratic beats of the heart. Then, in the tick of a moment, the invisible evanescent *thing* that is life disappeared, leaving an empty shell looking nearly the same but no longer truly human.

Gaze locked on Judson Payne, Jewett pulled on her rubber gloves and reached for the flaps of skin folded neatly over his internal organs. A hissing sound touched her ears, soft as a whisper. A second later, a cloying odor filled her nostrils. *Gas?*

Jewett whirled. The door behind her had closed, its window overlooking an empty hallway. Panic slammed her thoughts. Once activated, the detonators would spark the gas in seconds, before it had a chance to mix with oxygen. *Oh my God. I'm going to die.* Jewett hurled herself against the door. The force jolted pain through her shoulder, all but knocking her to the ground. "Help!" she screamed in terror, the gas burning her throat.

Think. Got to think. Jewett pounded at the panel, crashing blows that spasmed agony through her fingers. *Got to get the door open.* She clawed at the plastic, her nails sliding from the edge. An image of the decontamination booth flashed into her mind, the blue connecting beam of the door crawling across the wall as she closed it. *The beam. Got to break the beam.* Desperately, she rummaged through her pocket, trying not to think of the explosion that would incinerate her in the blink of an eye. Her frenzied movements knocked the beeper/phone from her waistband, and it crashed to the floor. She ignored it. By the time anyone she managed to call arrived, they would find a pile of ashes where she stood. Catching her wallet, she fumbled out her car key and jammed it between the door and its frame. The key jarred to a stop, wedged not quite far enough.

"Get in there!" Tears of hysteria filled Jewett's eyes, and she pounded at the card with the edge of her fist. "Fucking, god-damned son of a bitch, get in there!" The plastic cut through glove, then flesh. Sharp pain flared through her hand and it went sticky, but she continued to bash at it, shrieking curses in wild, savage frustration. The card crumpled beneath the blows. Jewett howled. Then, the key slid a little further, and the hissing disappeared.

The connection broken, the door opened easily. Jewett staggered into the empty hallway, sobbing in panic. She clamped her hands to her face, smearing blood the length of her cheek. *Got to get out of here.* She broke into a run, crashing through the morgue and into the hall without activating the decontamination booth, unable to shake the fear someone was chasing her.

In the basement corridor, Jewett bolted without direction, her only thought to put as much distance as possible between herself and the crematorium. Blue-gray walls whisked by. She careened around the corner into the main hallway, straight up the stairs to the first floor. She emerged just beyond the main waiting area near the entrance. Among the milling strangers, she paused to catch her breath, and reason broke through the terror that had scattered her wits. *I've got to get help, but I can't let my patients' families see me like this.* Whirling, she ran the opposite direction, toward the surgical wing.

Fear lent Jewett speed. She lowered her head, sprinting through the hallways from habit and trusting people to scuttle from her path. Disembodied voices muttered or snapped at her, their words swirled up and lost in the whirlwind of Jewett's frenzy. Soon, she whipped onto the surgery clinics and skidded into Jones' private waiting room.

Seated in the padded chairs that lined the walls, an elderly man glared at Jewett, and a middle-aged woman glanced up from a fashion magazine. Jewett ignored them, collapsing, breathless, across the nurse-receptionist's desk. "Buzz Kaign. Please. It's an emergency."

The curly-haired nurse stared at the blood beading scarlet across the white, simulated marble countertop. She punched the intercom button to room four. "Dr. Jones?"

"Yes?" Despite the glib confirmation, the voice was not Jones'.

Student, probably. Jewett buried her face in her arms.

"Sam, Dr. Jewett needs to see Dr. Jones right away." The receptionist placed a supportive hand on Jewett's arm, her tone reinforcing Jewett's urgency. "It *is* an emergency."

This time, Jones answered, sounding preoccupied. "Put her in room one. I'll be there in a minute."

The nurse-receptionist snapped the connection, walked around her desk and took Jewett's arm. "Are you going to make it?"

Jewett nodded, unable to stop the warm cascade of tears. Her hands trembled. Docilely, she accompanied Jones' receptionist into the examination room and to the sink. The nurse plucked off the left rubber glove then gently removed the right one. Reaching over Jewett, she punched on the cold water, placed Jewett's cut hand beneath the stream, and retrieved a gauze pad from a pile over the sink. Wetting the gauze, she scrubbed at the blood smeared across

Jewett's face. "Everything's going to be all right," the nurse reassured, her words as routine as the care and equally appreciated by Jewett.

The examination door swung open, and Jones entered, flanked by a young, male student. Both wore white coats over pink surgical scrubs.

Without shutting off the water, the nurse slipped from the room and closed the door behind her.

Jewett flung herself into Jones' arms, sobbing hysterically. She felt his hands tighten around her, his face warm against her scalp. She clung, pressing against him as close and completely as she could, still incapable of controlling her quivering. Jones freed one hand to brush strands of hair behind Jewett's ear. "What happened now?" he whispered.

The student tapped off the spigot, seemingly oblivious to the private display.

Jewett spoke into the folds of Jones' scrub shirt; her gasping pauses and the fabric's muffling rendered her words nearly incomprehensible. "Someone . . . locked me . . . in the crematorium." A fresh wash of tears slid from her eyes. "And started it."

"Oh my God." Jones' grip hardened. "Are you sure?"

Jewett went on the defensive. "I'm not crazy, Kaign. I know what happened. I smelled the gas, and the door was locked. I mangled my car key . . ."

"All right, all right." Jones disengaged, catching her injured hand. The bleeding had started again. "We need to get you home. Then, I'm going to talk to Dr. Cambridge. There's a careless janitor down there who's going to lose his job."

"Careless?" Jewett watched her blood trickle over Jones' fingers. "You think it was an accident?"

"Was there a body ready to cremate?"

Jewett thought about Judson Payne in his little coffin. The pathologists had finished their examination. "Well, yes. The one I was looking at. But Aaron said he'd save—"

His point proven, Jones did not need her to finish. "Of course it was an accident. It was bound to happen sometime. The idiot didn't look inside, just slammed the door and started the thing."

Jewett was unconvinced. "Kaign, I think someone tried to kill me."

Jones turned his student an apologetic look. He walked Jewett to the examination table, and she sat. "That's paranoid, Pat. Why would someone want to kill you?" He addressed the student. "Sam, get me a wet and a dry."

Obediently, the student pulled two gauze pads from the stack and ran one under the tap.

The answer seemed obvious to Jewett. "The murderer. He knows I saw him and about the machine hypnosis."

"That's ridiculous." Jones accepted the wet gauze from the student, using it to wash Jewett's hand. He took a closer look at the wound. "You're the perfect scapegoat. If you're convicted, he goes free. If he kills you, he'll prove your innocence, and the police will go after him." He patted the gash dry with the clean gauze. "This is going to need stapling. Mind if Sam works on it? My 13:00 case canceled, so I can drive you home after I finish up my last two privates."

"That's fine," Jewett said, finally regaining command of her hands. Jones' logic made sense. *Just one more stroke of bad luck.* She clasped the gauze against the injury to staunch the bleeding.

Jones left, closing the door behind him. Sam wandered over eagerly, pulling a spray bottle of topical anesthetic and an unopened staple kit from his pocket. Jewett scarcely felt the cold wash of the anesthetic or the tugs and positionings while Sam approximated the skin and clipped on the sterile, absorbable staples, but it gave her something to concentrate on until Jones dispatched his patients.

Sam was still cleaning the last flakes of dried blood from the wound when Jones returned. "Ready to go?"

Jewett reclaimed her hand from Sam and examined the stapling with satisfaction. The medical students' inexperience tended to make them slow and awkward; but, once past the additional time and pain, they usually did fanatically precise work. "Nice job, Sam."

The student beamed.

Jones caught Jewett's arm and steered her for the door. "Sam, hold down the ward while I'm gone." He tapped his beeper with a finger and glanced at his watch. "I'll be back in time for the 14:00 case."

Sam grinned more broadly, understandably thrilled by Jones' trust and the prospect of taking charge of an attending physician's patients.

Reminded by Jones' gesture, Jewett added, "Could you have someone go down to the crematorium and fetch my beeper? Also, call chronic and let them know what happened and where to reach me."

"No problem, Dr. Jewett."

Jones and Jewett walked to the main entry of the hospital, out into the spring air, and to the parking garage. Once inside Jones' Mazda and headed for home, Jewett's adrenaline dispersed, and she fell into a wrung-out, sleepy lull. Jones kept a protective grip on her hand. It comforted Jewett, even after the warmth of their bodies turned the handclasp slippery with sweat. *I love Kaign so much. I'm so lucky to have him.*

The drive proceeded in silence. Soon, the red sports car purred into Jewett's driveway, and Jones cut the engine.

Loosing her hand just long enough to let them both climb out of the car, Jones walked Jewett to the door, waited while she unlocked it, then entered with her. Jewett snapped the locks into place and sighed in relief. She pitched her wallet to the coffee table. "I've got a spare car key, but I'll need a ride into work tomorrow to . . ." She turned.

Jones snaked an arm around Jewett's waist, and the sentence dropped, forgotten. He drew her tightly against him, her breasts pressed to his chest, his fingers dangling provocatively across her hip. Through the fabric of their scrubs, she felt him, hard, against her thigh. "I was thinking. I have until 14:00, and if you're feeling up to it . . ." He trailed off.

Warmth flooded Jewett. Jones' arousal seemed the most comfortably natural occurrence in days. She wanted him to stay as long and as close as possible, and she knew she could respond to him. Her hands slid to his behind. "I'd like nothing better."

CHAPTER 9

Afterward, alone behind the locked door of her one-story house, Jewett closed the living room's single storm window over the screen and kept the curtains closed. She missed the friendly stripe of sunlight that usually fell across the couch and the sweet-smelling cross breeze that circulated whenever she left the door ajar and the window opposite it open, but she felt safer swaddled between laserlocks and clamps.

Jewett occupied herself with lunch and mindless cleaning and straightening for the first hour after Jones left her. Then, certain she had given him enough time to discuss the crematorium incident with the head administrator, she picked up the receiver and punched out Dr. Cambridge's number. A secretary answered, and Jewett waited while he called Cambridge to the line.

Soon, Cambridge's diplomatic baritone rumbled across the earpiece. "Pat, how are you?"

"Fine." Jewett sat on the couch. "Better. I assume Kaign told you what happened."

"Yes, I'm terribly sorry." Cambridge's tone matched his words. "I know it's not much consolation, but I've already got the wheels in motion to find the responsible person and make sure nothing like that happens again. I can't believe it happened to you of all people. As if things haven't been hard enough."

Jewett tried to look at the situation philosophically. "I got out. Someone else might not have known how."

"Well, yes." Cambridge sounded slightly ruffled, as if

the conversation had taken an unexpected turn. "Of course, the hospital assumes full responsibility. Dr. Bartram's taken over your ward, and you're on paid vacation for as long as you need."

Jewett prepared to protest; but, feeling certain more reasons and pressure than she knew lay behind Cambridge's suggestion, she hesitated. *Cambridge is a good man. I should make things easy for him and bow out.* She pictured Kaign Jones, the confidence he tried so hard to instill in her, and she knew this was one cause worth fighting for. *Right now, doctoring is all I have. I can't let them push me out without a struggle.* "Thank you, sir. But I'm feeling just fine, and I'll be ready to take over tomorrow."

For the first time since Jewett met him, Cambridge seemed at a loss for words. "Do you think that's . . . don't you think maybe . . . ?"

Pleased by her assertiveness, Jewett tightened the noose. "If you're ordering me to leave, I will. But, if I have the choice, I'm staying. My patients need me. I'm not egocentric enough to believe no one else can handle my work, but I know my patients' families believe in me."

Cambridge regained his powers of speech. "And I believe in you, too. I just want what's best for you *and* patient care."

He's cornered. Jewett bore in. "Dr. Cambridge, I was a quiet child, not particularly good at sports or art, rather plain-looking and afraid to take a chance. But I was good at one thing: my schoolwork. And I decided to be a doctor." Jewett flung her arms across the backrest of the couch. "My parents are wonderful people, and they wanted what's best for me. But, while everyone else's folks tried to talk them into becoming doctors, mine discouraged me. Do you know why?"

"Why?" Cambridge sounded genuinely interested.

"Because they thought I couldn't handle it. That I'd faint at the sight of blood or I'd crumple the first time one of my patients died." Jewett stretched out her legs on the coffee table. "But I didn't. I dissected dogs and cadavers and survived failure just like everyone else. The day I can't handle stress, I'll quit; you won't have to put me on vacation. If I wasn't absolutely positive I could manage ward responsibilities, I wouldn't come in. I'd never put my patients at risk. But I *can* handle things. And, unless you fire me, I'm coming in tomorrow."

Jewett knew she had trapped Cambridge between his acclaimed dedication to his doctors and his necessary commitment to his peers and more vocal hirelings. Guilt weighed heavily upon her. *I shouldn't have put a good man in a bad position any more than Kaign should have forced me to choose between an insincere proposal and losing him. But I had to make a stand.*

Cambridge drew breath to speak, and Jewett awaited a tactfully worded dismissal. "You believe you can handle your responsibilities."

Jewett paused; but, when she spoke, it was with unwavering certainty. "Yes. Without question."

"That's good enough for me. See you in the morning." Cambridge disconnected, leaving Jewett gripping the receiver in wide-mouthed surprise.

Gradually, joy replaced Jewett's emptiness. She slapped down the receiver with a whoop of elation. *Finally, my luck's turning around. And it's about time.* She swung her legs around so she lay on the couch, using the armrest for a pillow. Idea and memory swirled through her mind. Aware any chore not requiring thought would leave her free to brood, yet still unable to devote full concentration to a task, she grabbed the remote and switched on the all-news station.

A handsome, young weather forecaster appeared on the screen, then disappeared as the cameras cut to an equally attractive anchorwoman behind the news desk. "Now in the last week of his Midwestern hospital tour, President Benjamin Nash has vowed to continue advocating the rights of the technologically dependent."

A cut of Benjamin Nash appeared in the upper right corner of the screen. He grinned and waved with one hand, the other wrapped around a pretty, blonde child with the bulges of leg braces visible beneath her jeans. The newscaster continued, "One young admirer, Loralie Darenski, came out to show her support."

An image of a nervous brunette materialized on the opposite side of the screen speaking into an extended microphone. A caption beneath the picture identified her as Morgan Darenski, Loralie's mother. "After Loralie fell off her father's motorcycle, we thought we'd lost our little girl forever. She hit her head and was in a coma for forty-eight days. The doctors thought she'd never wake up. A decade ago, they would have turned her off or donated her organs to some other kid. But she woke up, and now it looks like our Loralie's going to be normal again."

Jewett shook her head, as always amused by the misinterpretation. As a physician, she had learned to present the worst case scenario to relatives; false hope was more dangerous than none and bad situations worked out better for everyone when the patient surpassed his physicians' predictions, as he nearly always did. But, it never ceased to amaze Jewett how a poor result was always the fault of the doctors, a good one the will of God or luck. *Miracle or not, what I want to know is what that girl was doing on a motor-*

cycle. Especially without a helmet. That's clear-cut, open-and-shut child abuse.

The anchorwoman went on to another story. "The President's next project is a mainstreaming campaign to encourage the technologically dependent to get involved in national and community affairs, including voting." The background scenes faded, replaced by another view of Nash speaking. "It is our obligation to see all of our citizens lead as normal a life as possible . . ."

The doorbell chimed over Nash's next word. Jewett stiffened. *Who could that be?* She snapped off the remote control and slipped off the couch. *Kaign won't be back for hours.* Jewett's heart quickened as she approached the door, flicked the peephole, and glanced outside.

Lieutenant Daniel Scott stood on the porch, dressed in jeans and a gray sweatshirt. Beyond him, Jewett caught a glimpse of his battered Dodge.

Anger flared, and the memory of her arrest turned Jewett's thoughts bitter. *The bastard! How dare he come back here after what he did.*

Scott touched the bell again. "Pat? I know you're there."

"Go away!" Jewett backed away from the peephole.

"Come on, Pat. I just want to talk."

"That's Dr. Jewett to you, Lieutenant Scott. And I don't want to talk to you. Go away."

"Please?"

"No!" Jewett walked back toward the couch, hoping the distance of her voice would convince Scott the conversation had ended. "If you don't leave, I'm calling the police." Then, realizing how stupid that sounded, she amended. "The real police." *Even dumber.* "Different police."

A long pause followed. "Fine," Scott said at length.

Jewett followed his course in her mind: the single step

from the porch onto the walkway, a minute to reach his car, climb inside, and close the door. She listened for the sound of the motor starting.

The image of Scott's leaving appeared so clear to Jewett that the clatter of the door lock startled a scream from her. She clamped a hand over her mouth as the door swung open, and she groped behind her across the coffee table for a weapon. She discovered only the telephone receiver, but she brandished it as Scott stepped into her living room. "Get out of here!" She shook the plastic threateningly. "You can't come in. Where did you get that key?"

Calmly, Scott turned and closed the door. "I showed your landlord my badge, and he gave it to me."

Enraged at Scott's blatant misuse of power, Jewett hurled the receiver without aiming.

The light plastic flew wild, but Scott dodged aside, throwing a protective arm in front of his face. His gaze followed the receiver as it bounced from the wall and crashed to the floor. He turned Jewett a wide-eyed look. "Does this mean you're not glad to see me?"

Jewett winced, remorseful for having acted in anger. *Just what I need to do, convince the police I'm violent.* "Look, I'm sorry. I shouldn't have done that, but I'm really on edge. I told you to go away. Unless you have a warrant, you're breaking and entering. I have the right to protect myself."

"Agreed." Scott picked up the receiver and handed it back to Jewett. "You missed. Try again."

Jewett snatched away the receiver and slammed it back to its cradle.

"I have a warrant."

Jewett doubted it. Scott's informal dress and use of his private car made it unlikely he was on duty. "To search, maybe. But you don't have a warrant to harass me."

"You're right." Scott lowered his head in an exaggerated display of shame. "I remand myself to my own custody. I have the right to remain silent. If I give up that right . . ."

"Cut it out!" Jewett screamed. "Why are you doing this?"

Scott indicated the couch. "I just want to talk."

Jewett remained between Scott and the bowl-shaped arrangement of chairs and couch, arms folded across her chest. "Fine. I give up. Say your piece, then leave."

Scott sighed. "I'm sorry I had to arrest you."

"Are you?"

"Of course. Do you think it was my idea?"

"Yes," Jewett admitted. "Yes, I do. You're in charge of the case. You take me out and ask questions, pretending it's because you like me. Hoping to catch the murderer, I cooperate. And what do I get for it?"

Scott tucked his hands in his pocket, tossing his blond head in exasperation. "First, I didn't *pretend* to like you. I'm not that good an actor. Second, I think you're innocent. I don't date killers; it's frowned on in my line of work. Third, I'm here because of first and second." He hesitated, as if trying to recall what number he was on. "Fourth, haven't you ever had to do something you didn't want to do because of your job?"

Jewett back-stepped against the chair and sat on the armrest. "No, Lieutenant Scott. My job is to save lives, not arrest innocent people."

Scott met Jewett's gaze, his eyes almost silver in the artificial light. "What about Stanley Schober? You'd like to let him die, wouldn't you?"

Jewett's lawyer had warned her not to discuss the case with anyone, and she cursed herself for letting emotion goad her into it. "Isn't there some law against arresting officers annoying murder suspects?"

"No, luckily for you. Dating them isn't kosher though, which is why we have to get cracking before they pull me off the case."

"One date," Jewett reminded Scott. "And there will never, ever be another." Another thought came to her, and she asked suspiciously. "What do you mean 'get cracking?' And what about Dr. Schober? You can't possibly believe I killed a nurse to get to him. If I was going to try to kill him . . ." She added hastily, ". . . and I wouldn't, of course. I'd have plenty of chances to catch him alone. And I'd know which lines to cut."

"I thought about that." Scott stepped around Jewett to the couch. "I talked to some of your colleagues and confirmed that anyone who works on the chronic care ward would have known Schober didn't need his electrostimulator." He sat. "That leaves three theories."

Jewett was curious; despite her hostility, she could not help feeling Scott honestly wanted to help. He had risked arrest and his job by illegally entering her house to supply her with information he could have kept to himself. "Three theories?"

"First." Scott extended his index finger. "The murderer actually wanted to kill Schober but stabbed Fantella either as a diversion or because she got in his way." Scott tapped at his pointing digit with the index finger of his opposite hand. "The only possible motives for wanting to kill a comatose patient are money and mercy. Since Schober left everything to his wife, and she already has joint control of the bank accounts, money is no longer an option. There's still life insurance, of course; but she has more than enough to live very comfortably without it. Most mercy killers sincerely believe in their cause and aren't the sort to commit other murders, premeditated or spur of the moment."

Jewett added her own ideas. "Oh, it had to be premeditated."

"Why's that?"

"Why else would someone bring a knife into the hospital when the rooms are full of scissors, clamps, scalpels, and a million other assorted weapons? How hard would it have been to snap off the monitor alarms and simply pull the ventilator hose apart? That wouldn't require any weapon at all." Now on a roll, Jewett continued. "Heck, it might even have looked like an accident."

"Okay," Scott said. "So we can assume the murderer wanted Fantella. Which brings me to the second theory." He uncurled his middle finger beside the index one. "That someone, probably a health care worker or professional assassin, killed Fantella. Not knowing Schober's state of consciousness and unfamiliar with electrostimulators, he slashed the lines to ace what he thought was his only witness."

"Until I bumped into him in the hallway." Jewett appreciated Scott's use of the pronoun "he" to describe the murderer. "I assume the third theory covers me."

"Afraid so," Scott confirmed. "It's sort of a catch-all." He added his ring finger to the lineup. "The murderer used Schober as a diversion, a red herring to confuse the police. In that case, he wouldn't actually have to kill Schober, merely give the impression that he tried."

Jewett slid off the arm of the chair and onto the cushion. "I still don't understand why you're telling me this."

Scott rested an elbow on the backrest of the couch and leaned toward Jewett. "Because I like you, and I know you're innocent. Laws are made to protect the common good, and individuals fall through the cracks. I don't want to see that happen to you." He dropped his chin to his knuckles. "What are you doing home today, anyway? The hospital wouldn't give me specifics."

"I was involved in an accident, and I needed some time alone." Jewett detailed the incident in the crematorium.

Scott listened attentively, adding nothing until she finished. "Why didn't you report this to us?"

Jewett shrugged. "I wasn't aware the police took an interest in accidents when no one gets seriously hurt."

"Not usually," Scott said. "But we do when someone tries to kill a murder witness."

"Tries to kill . . . ?" Jewett looked up sharply. "You think it was an attempt on my life?"

Scott's face went smooth with incredulity. "Don't you?"

"No," Jewett admitted. "I mean, I did, but Kaign convinced me it was an accident. And I believe him." She parroted Jones' argument. "Why would the murderer want to kill me now that I'm taking the rap for him?"

"Maybe he didn't plan to, at first." Scott lowered his hands to his lap. "He's probably watching you, saw a chance too good to pass up, and took it. If you were killed, we'd look for another murderer. If you disappeared, burned beyond identification, we would naturally assume you skipped town. When we finally gave up the search, the ash pile in the crematorium would be forgotten, if anyone even noticed it in the first place. No one would doubt your guilt. Case closed."

Jewett shivered at the imagery. "So, someone might have followed me to the crematorium?"

Scott shrugged. "Maybe. Or, if he had reason to know you'd come down, he might have waited in the basement. You said you always check the pathology on your patients. Is that common?"

"Most doctors do it."

"There you go." Scott spread his hands to make his point. "Did you happen to see anyone in the basement?"

"No," Jewett said. She tried to relive the walk to the morgue in her head. "Well, there was the pathology resident, but he's an old friend." She considered. "And a janitor. I remember him looking familiar, which probably means he's exactly what he seemed."

"Or not," Scott added cryptically. He pulled a crushed and battered pad from his pants pocket. "Describe him. It's one more possible lead."

Jewett shook her head in helpless frustration. "You'd think taking a murder rap would improve my powers of observation. I honestly didn't pay much attention."

Scott fished a pen from his other pocket. "Try. Do the best you can."

Jewett sighed and closed her eyes, trying to revive the picture on the back of her lids. "He was wearing a green maintenance jumpsuit."

"Clothes change. Stick with the man."

"Probably a few inches to either side of six foot. Straight, sandy-colored hair." She amended. "Or maybe light brown. I got the impression he was heavy-set, but thinking about it, he might have been more muscular than fat. Like you." She opened her eyes to Scott's amused half-smile.

"Face shape? Nose? Eye color?"

Jewett shook her head. "That's the best I can do."

Scott snapped the pad closed. "Would you know him if you saw him again?"

"I think so."

"That's a start." Scott stuffed the paper back into his pocket. "You know, Pat, I've had lots of suspects try to hide incriminating evidence; but you're the first one who concealed information pointing to your innocence. Anything else I should know, or would you like to just convict yourself at the trial?"

Jewett flushed. "Actually, there was another incident. The other day, before you arrested me, a car almost ran me down in the parking garage. Do you think that had any significance?"

Scott's tone went deeply sarcastic. "No, Pat. There're two hundred seventy-three hit-and-runs a day in this country, and I think it was just your turn."

Jewett started to make a reply, but Scott cut in.

"Don't tell me. Kaign said you were just under stress and drawing connections between coincidences. Right?"

Uncertain where Scott was leading, Jewett replied carefully. "Something like that. Why bring Kaign into this?"

"Because I'm mad." Scott's fist crashed into his open palm. "Because I can't believe a jerk so jealous, so afraid of his girlfriend talking to me, so concerned I might try to steal you, that he passes off attempts on your life and puts you in danger." He jabbed a finger at the air. "You know what makes me even madder?"

The memory of Jones' gentle caresses hours ago remained strong within Jewett, and Scott's accusations made her angry as well. "What!"

"The bastard's right! I'd steal you in a second if I could."

"What?" Jewett's anger dispersed instantly, and nothing immediately replaced it.

Scott buried his face in his palms, obviously embarrassed. "Nothing. I said something I shouldn't have. Let it lie." He shook his head, fingers still clamped to his cheeks. "I can just see this trial. What a team. You'll be in the front convicting yourself while I sit in the back humiliating myself."

Scott's vulnerability raised Jewett's empathetic instincts. She tried to think of something to say, but knew a line like "that's so cute" would only fluster him more. She returned to the original subject. "There was one other possible attempt."

Scott peeked between his fingers. "Oh?"

"The emergency brake gave out on my car."

Scott lowered his hands. "The regular brakes?"

"Work fine," Jewett finished. "Probably coincidence. Kaign's been chiding me for years for using the emergency as my first brakes."

The look that stole over Scott's features mixed thoughtfulness and horror. "Does anyone else know about this odd habit of yours?"

Jewett considered. "My dad always warned me I'd break the emergency. I don't know. I never kept it secret, but it's not the sort of thing that comes up in casual conversation." She tried to follow the track of Scott's questioning. *Kaign knows about the brake, and he underemphasized the attempts on my life.* Scott's implication became frighteningly clear. Rage flared anew, "You're thinking Kaign might be involved."

Scott chose silence.

Jewett sprang to her feet. "Now wait a second! Kaign believes in the sanctity of life more than anyone I know. He wouldn't kill anyone. Certainly not me. He loves me."

"Whoa! Whoa!" Scott defended himself. "Don't jump to any wild conclusions. I didn't say he killed anyone. I was thinking more that he might be supplying information to the killer." He added quickly, "Inadvertently, of course."

Jewett gathered breath to argue, then realized she had nothing to say. *The first attempt did happen right after I told Kaign about the hypnosis machine. And how could anyone know I use the emergency brake?*

Scott shot down his own argument. "Actually, I'm willing to bet the emergency brake thing really is a coincidence. A professional would have taken out both sets of brakes, regardless of what he heard. Anyone else would have had to have access to your car." He rose. "Much as I hate to admit it, Kaign doesn't strike me as a murderer, either. On the other hand, I'd suggest you don't see him for a few days, or at least guard your tongue."

Jewett did not like the turn of the conversation. Scott's advice sounded dangerously close to Jones' ultimatum several days past. "He's coming over after work."

Scott shrugged. "It was just a suggestion. You're more than capable of making your own decisions." He headed for the door. "Ready to go?"

Jewett blinked in confusion. "Go? Go where?"

"To City Park. We could both stand to unwind, play a little Secret Diagnosis, get some fresh air."

"A date?"

"Horrors, no." Scott clutched his chest as if fighting chills. "Just a chance to get out and talk some more. Police stuff."

The idea of leaving the house discomforted Jewett. "I'm staying. Every time I go out, something terrible happens. I'm just going to lock myself inside, go to work in the morning, and lock myself inside when I get back."

Scott placed his fingers on Jewett's arm. "If you're convicted, you'll spend more than enough time locked up. How many chances will you get to go outside with a personal bodyguard?" He patted beneath his armpit to indicate he carried a gun.

Jewett hesitated, feeling desperately cooped up but not wanting to risk her relationship with Jones again. A chill spiraled through her at the memory of their tender love-making just a few hours earlier. *This is police business. Kaign has to understand.* She glanced at Scott, knowing he would not accept "no" as an answer any more than Jones would accept the rationalization. She did not know if she could survive the next several hours alone. Every sound sent her heart skittering into a wild rhythm; and she needed something, anything, to drive her mind from the stress of the last few days. *I could go to jail for a crime I couldn't conceive of committing, for a crime I didn't commit, for the rest of my life. I can't give up the chance to have a police lieutenant on my side.* "Oh, to heck with it. Let's go."

Chapter 10

The sun beamed down on City Park, blurring the grass to a broad carpet of greenery. Where trees towered, their shadows striped long, dark sections in which every blade became discernible: tall, jade, and spear-like. Dr. Patricia Jewett perched on the cement rim that surrounded the pool of the elephant fountain, enjoying the cold spray of water the breeze tossed against her back. Beside her, Scott watched the strolling passersby with more than casual interest.

Jewett pulled one foot onto the ledge and left the other dangling. "What got you started with this Secret Diagnosis game, anyway?"

Scott kept his gaze on the walkway. Gradually, his lips curved into a smile. "Remarkable coincidence. It was a woman doctor."

"A girlfriend?"

Scott loosed a short laugh. "Not hardly." He met Jewett's stare. "I was fifteen and seeing my pediatrician for a sports physical. He had a new, young doctor working with him. A student or something." He gave a low whistle. "Beautiful."

Jewett could not help noticing how the sun lit Scott's eyes, pale and piercing, softened by a central ring of darker blue. "I don't understand."

Scott nodded. "That's because you were never an adolescent male who had to strip for a gorgeous female doctor. I was afraid I was going to . . . well, you know, get . . ."

"An erection?" Jewett supplied.

Scott flushed, the color appearing awkward on his hollowed cheeks. "I was going to say 'excited,' but you got the idea. I thought I might embarrass myself. So I tried to remember some of the tricks people use to keep from getting flustered."

Jewett considered. "Like imagining the audience or, in this case, the doctor in her underwear."

"Exactly."

Jewett winced. "I see the problem."

"So, instead, I pictured that under her skirt and blouse was really a cross-dresser."

"A man?"

"With a hairy back."

Jewett snickered. "I guess it worked."

"Well enough." Scott shifted his attention back to the milling strangers. "I didn't actually believe it, but it did relax me. That's when I realized it's impossible for a person to be embarrassed, angry, or sad when he's laughing."

Jewett recalled an argument with Jones several years ago while taking a drive. She could no longer remember the issues, only that while Jones was screaming, the radio started playing the song they considered their own. The coincidence had dispelled the tension, and they both broke into wild laughter, their disagreement forgotten. "I know what you mean. So, when we first met, what secret did you attribute to me?"

"What makes you think I picked a secret for you?" Scott responded carefully, but a bit too fast.

Jewett called upon the smidgen of psychiatric training she retained from medical school. "Because Secret Diagnosis is your way of dealing with uncomfortable situations. And no matter how self-assured you try to look, dating another guy's girlfriend has to feel awkward."

"All right. You caught me." Scott pressed his hands to the concrete, still watching the crowd. "I did come up with something, but it's not funny and we'll both be happier if I don't share it."

Curiosity piqued, Jewett pressed. "Why?"

"If I tell you, you'll get mad."

"I won't get mad."

"Yes, you will."

"I will not."

Scott made no reply.

Jewett twisted toward him. "Come on. Tell me. I won't get mad."

Scott shook his head.

Jewett tried another tactic. "If you don't tell me, I'll imagine something worse. And I will get mad."

Scott accepted the challenge. "Oh yeah? Like what?"

Jewett considered. She had always preferred watching or listening to humor over creating it, but Scott's secret intrigued her. "Like . . . I have a pet toad. Because, over time, people tend to look like their pets."

Scott chuckled. "I like that one. I'll have to remember it."

"You're avoiding the subject."

"I know." Scott met Jewett's gaze, his smile casual, as though he could think of nothing more pleasant than sitting in front of a fountain chatting with her.

Frustration turned Jewett's tone from gentle interest to insistence. "Come on. Just tell me the darn secret."

"All right." Scott still sounded reluctant. "When I saw you in the bar, I knew you were upset and someone was not doing an adequate job of comforting. As I've said, I find you quite attractive . . ." He raised a hand to keep her from disputing his assertion. ". . . but I could tell by the way you carried yourself that you weren't comfortable with your beauty. So, I imagined you had a boyfriend who didn't appreciate what he had and spent his time whittling away your self-esteem."

Whittling away my self-esteem? Jewett had heard the exact words from her father several years ago, after Jones had made a disparaging remark at a family gathering.

Scott dropped his hand to his thigh. "And you were just waiting for a short, waddling cop to come along and rescue you from the beast."

Still stunned by Scott's choice of words, Jewett ignored the jest. Then another thought occurred to her. *Scotty's making this up to insult Kaign.* She fought down rising anger, aware she had promised not to get mad. "I don't believe a word. Your secret diagnoses are short put-downs to make you laugh. You're just saying this stuff to make it look like you had a grip on my relationship with Kaign before you met us."

Scott looked away in defeat. "I already told you I'm not that good a liar, and I'm great at reading people. Would it help if I came up with some facts about your life I couldn't possibly know? Like how you and Kaign got together?"

Jewett rocked, intrigued. "Yeah. Do your best."

"You won't get mad?"

"I won't get mad." Jewett agreed.

"And you'll let me finish before you say anything?"

Jewett hesitated. "Sure, all right. I'll let you finish."

"And you won't insist on going home at the first implication I think Kaign is anything but perfect?"

"No, no, no." Growing impatient, Jewett signaled Scott to continue.

"Okay." Scott settled into a comfortable position, half-turned toward Jewett, his hands behind him on the ledge supporting most of his weight. "You two ended up matched together in classes because you were both at the top of your class." He tilted back his head, and the blond mop of hair fell into one of his eyes. "Or maybe it was alphabetical."

As promised, Jewett remained silent. Scott's description showed a lack of knowledge about medical school, where every student attended all their classes in a huge lecture hall without assigned seats. The associated laboratory courses were divided into alphabetical sections, not by academic standing. Coincidently, Jones and Jewett scored in the top ten percent of their class. *Lucky guess.*

Scott continued, "You and three-quarters of the other women in your class thought Kaign was gorgeous. He probably dated most of them, but only once or twice. Your friends said he was arrogant, self-absorbed . . ." He studied Jewett's face as if to read her reactions. ". . . full of himself. But, damn it, the guy was good. Tall, dark and handsome. Smart."

Confident, Jewett filled in, recalling how the male medical students gave one another nicknames. Jones' certainty he would ace every test earned him the title "Cocksure Kaign."

"How am I doing?"

"You told me not to talk until you finished," Jewett reminded.

"Right." Scott rolled his eyes upward in thought, then returned his gaze to Jewett's face. "You wanted Kaign to notice you, so you gave him every hint in the world. You probably called him for assignments you already had. Asked his opinion on things you knew. Maybe even had some friend tell him you liked him."

I wasn't that juvenile. "Now wait a second," Jewett interrupted. Catching herself, she went quiet and waved Scott to go on. *I did dress up and blush a lot in Kaign's presence. Scotty's not doing badly. He has the general idea.*

"You finally got up enough nerve to ask him out . . ."

I arranged to "accidentally" bump into him at a party, but close enough.

"At the end, he got you into bed, and you were too scared of losing him to refuse."

Finding Scotty's hunch too close for comfort, Jewett bit her lip.

"Afterward, he treated you exactly the same, distantly, as if the date never occurred, until . . ." He paused to consider. "Now I'm guessing, and I need your confirmation." Scott leaned forward. "Surgeons make lots of money, so would I be correct in saying surgery residencies are more competitive than chronic care?"

Jewett nodded. "In general, the better paying the specialty, the more competitive the residency. Surgical specialties like cardiac, plastics, and ophthalmology are the hardest to get into. Chronic care, psychiatry, and pediatrics are less competitive."

"Okay." Scott incorporated the information. "So, assuming I was right about you both being at the top of your class, you could have become a surgeon, too."

"Sure." Jewett tried to anticipate Scott but could not guess the direction of his argument.

"Did it ever occur to you to go into one of the higher-paying specialties?"

"Of course." Jewett shrugged. "I considered all the possibilities and decided chronic care suited me best."

"You decided? Kaign had nothing to do with it?"

Jewett went on the defensive. "Well, of course Kaign helped. He pointed out that I really didn't have the drive to compete with a pack of aggressive surgeons. Also, if we got married we'd never see each other because of the long hours surgeons keep." She added quickly, "And I agreed with him."

"Uh-huh." Scott took the last with a grain of salt. "And once you were no longer competing with him, but standing behind him, that's when your relationship got serious. Right?"

"It was about that time, yes," Jewett shot back. "But not for that reason."

"You promised you wouldn't get mad," Scott reminded.

"I'm not mad!" Jewett snapped. Realizing how ludicrous that sounded, Jewett calmed herself. "Sorry, you're right."

"Do you want me to finish?"

"There's more?"

Scott nodded.

"All right. Go ahead." Despite her irritation, Jewett could not help feeling impressed by Scott's insight.

"Gradually, all your friends disappeared." Scott returned to his reclining position. "At first, they'd ask when Kaign was free; but, somehow, their social functions always occurred at times he couldn't make it. Then, Kaign wouldn't let you go to them alone. Or he'd let you, but he'd make you feel guilty if you did. Soon, your friends stopped asking, and you all grew apart."

Jewett's first reaction, denial, passed quickly. Called to settle friends' disputes, she had long ago learned no side of any argument was ever wholly correct, and she had trained herself to consider both sides. *Maybe some of my friends really did break away because they didn't like Kaign.* "Look, Scotty. Kaign's not perfect, and he can seem abrasive to people who don't know him as well as I do. But everyone has a few annoying habits."

"Annoying habits?" Scott laughed. "Leaving the cap off the toothpaste is an annoying habit. Shouting at strangers in public places is a personality defect."

Jewett scowled. "I can live with it."

Scott's smile disappeared. "You've shown that adequately enough. The question is: Why should you have to?"

Scott's inquiry seemed ridiculous to Jewett. Her mind drifted back to the passionate session of love-making with Jones that had soothed her frazzled nerves, at least for an hour or two. "Because Kaign and I have a strong and special relationship."

"Do you?"

"What's that supposed to mean?"

Scott sat straighter, draping his hands in his lap. "If your relationship is so strong and secure, how come you're both afraid of a stranger who tried to pick you up in a bar?"

"Afraid." Jewett snorted. "I have news for you, Scotty. We're not afraid of you. We just don't like you." Having blurted the words in anger, Jewett winced. *That's right, stupid. Insult the one cop who's trying to help you.* "I'm sorry. I didn't mean that."

"That's all right. I didn't buy it." Scott inclined his head toward the site where he and Jones had exchanged words. "If your parents had followed you on a date, instead of Kaign, what reason would you assume they had?"

Jewett pictured her father secretively trailing a high school date. She gave the obvious answer without consideration. "I'd think they didn't trust me."

Scott smiled in silent triumph.

Jewett realized she had made Scott's point for him. *Oh, damn!* Hearing it from her lips made the argument that much more difficult to deny.

"As for you," Scott continued, "when we went out, you

decided in advance you weren't going to have a good time no matter what happened. Because, if you did enjoy yourself, you'd have to make a choice."

"A choice?" Jewett shook her head in disgust. *You arrogant little jerk!* "Between Kaign and you?"

"No," Scott corrected. "Between Kaign and the rest of the world. If I find you attractive and interesting enough to compete for, other men will, too. Others, that is, who won't try to control your every move and whittle away your self-confidence. Do you really believe there's only one person in the world you can love?"

"Give me some credit." Jewett's thoughts slid back to the year between her childhood sweetheart and Kaign Jones, a lonely period of broken dates and shattered hopes.

Scott tilted his head into a position where he could see Jewett and the passersby. "Why tie yourself to someone who makes you miserable as often as he makes you happy without, at least, finding who else is out there? Why spend your life wondering how it would feel to make love with someone else or to go to a restaurant without worrying about your husband throwing a tantrum over the menu. If your relationship is really as special as you say, it'll endure some time apart."

Jewett lowered her head. "Kaign would never let me see other men." *And if I lose Kaign, I have nothing.* "I don't want to see other men. I love Kaign." Another thought struck her, and she voiced it aloud. "How did you know about the menu incident?"

Scott smiled again, and Jewett noticed how the expression gentled his gaunt features until they looked almost handsome. "When I went to settle credits at Webster's Convention, the waiter told me about it." He sighed, his tone sobering. "I wanted a chance to sit in the spring air and talk about you for a while, not Kaign. Personally, I think if you lose him, good riddance. But I'm not in love with him, and I have a biased interest in getting you away from him. Still, I hate to see you fall victim to this inferiority complex he's given you. Neither of you knows it yet, but he needs you more than you need him. There aren't a lot of women who will put up with public humiliation, even in exchange for Kaign's looks, wealth, and power. Eventually, he'd come back to you." Scott shrugged. "If you didn't find someone better in the meantime, at least your relationship would have changed for the better. You've got nothing to lose."

Nothing but a nine-year relationship and a handsome, competent, loving man. Jewett did not express the thought. "Take me home." Her gaze followed a homely man as he trotted toward them from one of the walkways.

Scott adopted a medieval accent. "As you wish, milady." He jumped down from the fountain and gave an elegant bow as if from an old Errol Flynn movie. "My deepest apologies for speaking ill of the lord of the castle."

The passerby stared as he passed, then took one last surreptitious glance from over his shoulder.

Jewett rose.

"Thence, milady . . ." Scott jabbed his thumb at the stranger's retreating back. ". . . goes a man with a pet rock."

Apparently feeling guilty for his tirade against Kaign Jones, Scott did not broach the topic on the drive to Jewett's home. Instead, he chatted about current affairs, seemingly oblivious to the inner turmoil he had inspired.

Jewett spoke little, ideas swirling through her mind. *If I lose Kaign, I may never find another man.* The argument had convinced her so many times before, but now she added logic. *True or not, it's a stupid reason to continue a relationship. I'm staying with Kaign because I love him and he loves me.* Confusion turned to indignation and back to confusion, the cycle broken only by the jokes Scott interspersed into a conversation Jewett's deliberation turned into a monologue. *I do love Kaign.*

Soon, Scott pulled the timeworn Dart into Jewett's driveway and cut the engine. "Will you be all right?"

Jewett opened the passenger door and stepped out. "I'll be fine." She leaned on the frame, fumbling for her wallet. "Thanks. Kaign will be by after work."

"Listen, if anything else strange happens, call the police. I'll be sending an officer around to take a full statement on the two incidents we discussed earlier."

Jewett nodded. Wallet in hand, she slammed the car door and headed up the walkway. Once on the porch, she freed the key card and reached for the door handle. It yielded easily to her touch. *Darn it, I left the door unlocked again.* She replayed leaving the house in her mind, trying to recall whether she had hit the lock on the way out. The detail eluded her. *You'd think I would have learned from this afternoon.* Jewett replaced the card in her wallet and pushed open the door.

The familiar odors of furniture polish and the grilled cheese sandwich she had eaten for lunch met her, the air stale without the circulating breeze. In the darkness, the silhouettes of her furniture formed their welcoming line of customary ridges and valleys. *One of these days, I'm going to get robbed, and it'll be my own fault.* Closing the door, she reached for the panel of lights.

Before Jewett could punch the buttons, a hand clamped onto her arm. Cold metal pressed into the base of her neck, and a male voice hissed into her ear. "Be quiet. Don't move."

Jewett gasped. Her throat squeezed shut, and her chest clenched tight over her pounding heart. She froze.

"Get away from the window." The man flung her from the line between the door and the window.

Jewett stumbled toward the television. The stranger twisted her arm, shoving her, face first, into the wall. She caught a glimpse of the gun, the thin line of sunlight through the curtains' crack glimmering from the barrel. In the moment, she recognized it as a machine pistol. Then, he jammed the muzzle back against her skull.

Jewett shuddered away, her nose crushed against the wall. She bit her lip, trembling. *Please just want my money. Please, please don't hurt me.*

The man waited, his free hand hard and professionally steady against her spine. He went as still as Jewett.

He's listening for something. Jewett tried to draw her scattered wits together long enough to figure out the reason for his hesitation. *The sounds of Scotty's engine.* She felt suddenly cold. *He's waiting for Scotty to leave so he won't hear the gunshot. He's going to kill me!* Jewett tensed.

The gun ground deeper into her flesh. "Don't move." Even whispered, the tone of his words implied his next warning would be a bullet through her head.

Jewett stifled a whimper of pain. *Can't scream. He'll shoot me for sure.*

A knock on the door startled her. She stiffened against the gun; the ache in her head intensified.

The stranger swore.

Scott's voice wafted through the door, its calmness sounding out of place. "Pat, you forgot your purse."

Jewett traced the distance to the door in her mind and

knew the gunman could kill her faster than Scott could get inside. *Wait a second. I didn't bring a purse!* Hope spiraled through her. *But how could Scotty know I need help?*

The gunman spun Jewett toward the door. "Get rid of your boyfriend. Fast." He steered her to the door and jabbed her to the side that opened. Ducking behind the door, he pulled it ajar, the automatic pistol aimed, unwaveringly, at her head.

The lights! That's what cued Scotty. Who enters a dark house without switching on the lights?

Daniel Scott stood on the recessed porch, his stance casual, his right hand tucked behind him. "You left your purse," he repeated, making no attempt to pass her anything. He avoided her stare, looking instead at the door.

Catching the hint, Jewett rolled her eyes toward the gunman. "Thanks." She reached as if to take something, her voice steadier than she expected.

As soon as she moved, Scott's right hand flicked up to reveal a hand gun. He fired twice, blindly, through the door. Missed, the stranger dropped back and to one knee, redirecting his machine pistol. Before Jewett could shout a warning, Scott seized her wrist, snapped her through the doorway, and hurled her toward the yard. "Run! Call for help!"

Jewett staggered onto the grass, slipped, and crashed to the ground. A round of bullets strafed through the door from the inside.

"Shit!" Scott leaped back, flattening against the wall just outside the door. "I'm a police officer! You're under arrest. Come out with your hands up." As soon as he finished speaking, he crept further from the door to a new position against the wall.

Jewett half-stumbled, half-crawled toward Scott's car,

cursing the loss of her beeper/phone. A short silence ensued as Jewett pulled open the door and groped for the car's cell. She snatched up the receiver, discovered the keypad under the radio, and poked out 911. The line buzzed.

A shrill clatter of breaking glass sounded clearly through the open front door to the house. *The window! He's getting away.* Jewett heard the connection from the other end of the telephone.

Scott sprang for the entrance. "Police! Freeze!"

Scott's shout blotted out the speaker on the phone line. Jewett responded anyway. "We need help! It's an emergency. The address . . ."

A single gunshot rang out, followed by a wild blur of automatic fire and a single scream.

Jewett whimpered. ". . . 1315 Morgan Hill," she managed. Back-lit by the now open window, Scott still stood in the doorway, no longer attempting to hide. *Thank God.* "We need police. And an ambulance." She slammed down the receiver and rushed to the house.

As Jewett sprang onto the porch, the scene became clear through the open door. Scott stood near the entryway, the pistol still clutched in his hand. The gunman sprawled, unconscious, beneath the shattered window, his gun several feet from his limp hand. A red-edged entry wound stained his dress shirt in the center of his upper chest. A row of holes in the ceiling demonstrated, in vivid clarity, where his finger had spasmed on the trigger as he fell.

While Scott glanced carefully into the other rooms, Jewett stared in horror at the gunman, assessing his injuries from long habit. His chest rose and fell rapidly and unevenly, indicating lung compression. *Must have missed the heart and great vessels or he'd have bled to death by now.* The memory of the gun barrel grinding into the base of her neck sent a shiver of outrage through Jewett. *The bastard came to kill me, and I'm going to save his worthless life.* The irony seared. Sweat dried on her limbs, an uncomfortable reminder of her fear. Her fingers were still trembling. The urge seized her to surrender to the rising storm of violence, to kick the fallen man, again and again. *The law says I have to help him and, damn it, he's going to live.*

Shoving past Scott, Jewett grabbed her emergency kit from a drawer in the bedroom and returned to the gunman. Kneeling, she jabbed her fingers against his neck. The pulse felt rapid and thready. *May have nicked the pericardial sac after all. Or else he has a bad pneumothorax.* Jewett awaited the usual rush of sympathy followed by a natural progression of treatment options, but only one thought came to her mind. *A little lower and he'd be as dead as Krystal Fantella.*

Scott stood over the gunman. "What the hell are you doing?" He sounded incredulous.

"What's it look like I'm doing?" Jewett snapped. Not bothering to meet his gaze, she rummaged through the kit for a stethoscope and a mask through which she could supply breaths to her patient if needed. *I'd die before I'd give this murderer mouth to mouth.*

"It looks like you're helping a professional assassin. Either that, or you're going to dissect him alive." Scott paused while Jewett wrestled her stethoscope from the pack. "If you're half as smart as I think you are, you're dissecting."

"Shut up!" Jewett flicked the earpieces in place and pressed the diaphragm of the stethoscope to the gunman's chest. Years had passed since she managed any patients on an emergency basis, and the threat to her life had already shattered her concentration. The breath sounds seemed distant, the throb of the heart deeply muffled and shifted to the left. *Free air in the chest cavity. Possible bleed. Definite spinal shock—bullet went through to the spine, at least. This guy needs a tap right now; and even if he makes it, he may be quadriplegic.* Realization hit as hard as a physical blow. *On my ward.* Helpless rage drove tears to her eyes. She threw the stethoscope to the floor and ripped open her emergency kit. "I don't like it any more than you do, but I'm a mandatory Good Samaritan. You have to warn reckless drivers; I have to help injured people no matter how disgusting they are."

"Really." A strangled tone entered Scott's voice. "Are you good at it?"

Without looking up, Jewett continued shuffling through equipment, vision blurred by a hot curtain of tears. "It's what I do for a living."

Scott mumbled something beneath his breath.

Jewett struggled to decipher his words. She had just come to the conclusion he had said, "Let's see what you can do with this," when two gunshots roared at close range.

Screaming, Jewett curled into a fetal position. Her heart pounded, and her ears rang painfully. When she dared to peek around her protective arm, she found Scott in the same position, the pistol dangling at his side, his hand clenched around the barrel like a child afraid to surrender a doll. Two new entry holes had appeared on the gunman's chest, and a rapidly spreading puddle of blood on the carpet made it clear at least one had penetrated the heart.

"Why . . . ? How . . . ?" Uncertain how to finish her question, Jewett gaped, aware she did not have the necessary equipment or experience to repair a damaged heart. Despite her shock and horror, she could not dispel a growing feeling of relief. She opened her mouth again, and this time words came out. "Why the *hell* did you do that?"

"I saw him reaching into his shirt." Scott tried to sound matter-of-fact, but a quaver in his voice betrayed him. He searched the corpse briefly. "I thought he was going for another gun. I guess I was wrong."

"He was unconscious . . ." Jewett started.

"I saw him move." Scott jabbed his pistol back into its shoulder holster. He dodged her stare.

"He was in spinal shock." The too-familiar odor of blood amid the normal smells of her home made Jewett queasy. She turned away.

"Look." Scott used the same defensive, agitated tone as a young resident accused of mismanaging a dying patient. "When this case comes up for review, I'm going to tell them he moved. You can say whatever you want, but you and I both know you were looking the other way when it happened."

Suddenly, the situation became clear to Jewett. *If Scotty can't prove he fired in self-defense, he's up for murder.* Her stomach lurched. *He's feeling bad enough about what he just did. Why am I making it worse?* "Now that I think of it, I did see him move."

Scott's muscles seemed to uncoil slightly.

"Just tell me you didn't do it for me." Jewett met Scott's gaze, finding a deep, solid emotion she could not read.

"Pat." Now familiar, Scott's sharp, crooked features no longer seemed dangerous, just characteristic and, in a strange way, becoming. "Have you ever had a patient die and wondered whether something you did or didn't do killed him?"

Jewett nodded vigorously. "Sure. We all do."

"Did you ever get a morbid urge to intentionally repeat the mistake on other patients?"

The idea horrified Jewett. She glanced at the corpse,

concerned for where this conversation appeared to be leading. "Never. I would never do anything I didn't believe was in a patient's best interests."

"That's because you're normal." Scott glanced out the open front door. "When most people kill, by accident or necessity, they feel guilty. If forced to kill again, they feel just as guilty. I think it's a species survival instinct." He turned back to Jewett. "Every once in a while, you find a man-eater."

Jewett rocked, fighting down waves of nausea. "You mean like lions."

"Right. A lunatic who gets a taste for blood *and likes it*." Scott's tone went dry with contempt. "The type who murders for pleasure, who makes a career out of slaughter and prides himself on his ability to attack silently, to kill quickly and painlessly or as agonizingly slowly as human endurance can stand."

Jewett shivered.

"In jail, the man-eaters kill other inmates. Put them in solitary, and they sit and plot alone. Get them involved in social programs, they go through the motions. Release them, and they kill again and again and again. It's a disease, a madness with only one proven cure." Scott rolled his gaze to the corpse. "And every rare once in a while, the common good takes precedence over a rabid animal."

The memory of the gun barrel and the man's coarse threat brought a metallic taste to Jewett's mouth. She took another look at the gunman, studying his face for the first time. "Wait a second, Scotty. That's him!"

"Who?" Scott sounded as excited as she felt.

"The janitor in the basement. That's him."

"That explains why he's here." Scott gestured toward the bedroom. "Is this the same one you saw leaving

Schober's room after the murder?"

"No," Jewett said hesitantly, then more certainly, "No."

"Whoever paid this creep has enough credit and contacts to hire professionals. He isn't finished with you yet. Pack your things. You're going to disappear for a while."

Jewett started toward the bedroom, then stopped. "No," she said without turning.

"No?"

Jewett doubted Scott could understand. "I have patients to take care of, and I all but forced the head administrator to let me keep working."

From the sound of Scott's voice, Jewett could tell he was moving, probably searching the corpse more thoroughly for identification. "Pat, didn't you hear a word I said? This guy didn't come for your silverware; he came to kill you. You're no good to your patients dead."

Jewett spun to face Scott, her sense of duty warring with common sense. "You weren't there. You didn't hear the things I said to Dr. Cambridge."

Scott looked up from his inspection. "No. But I was here when a man-eater with an automatic weapon tried to blow your brains all over the carpet."

Jewett forced the incident from her mind. *When's that ambulance going to get here?* "I have to call, at least." She headed for the telephone.

Scott sprang for the device first. "Not on this phone, you don't. The killer had plenty of time to tamper with it." He tapped a finger on the coffee table. "Tell you what. If we leave right now, I'll take you to the hospital in person. I'll call my people on the way in and have them take care of your house and this mess. They're not going to like me leaving the scene much, but that's life."

Jewett considered. "You'll let me talk to Kaign, too?"

"Over the hospital phone. And no details about where we're going."

Jewett recalled the earlier conversation. *Perhaps Kaign really is unintentionally giving away information.* "Deal," she said slowly.

They headed for the door.

CHAPTER 11

After a walk down stuffy pathways crammed with the moist pollen aroma of April flowers and hot, crowded hospital corridors, Dr. Cambridge's air conditioned office felt comfortable to Lieutenant Daniel Scott. Behind a magnificently carved, antique desk, Cambridge waited patiently, dwarfed by his furniture. Jewett sat, stiff and tall, in a wooden chair on the opposite side of the desk, arguing with Kaign Jones' receptionist over the telephone.

The nurse-receptionist's voice wafted clearly over the intercom. "I'm sorry, Dr. Jewett. Dr. Jones said he was not to be disturbed for any reason."

"But this is an emergency." Jewett's voice held the flat tone of a person who has endured too much, too quickly.

Scott paced, masterfully controlling his annoyance. He glanced at his watch for the third time in six minutes. *We don't have time for this nonsense.*

"I'm sorry," the receptionist repeated, rearranging the emphasis, as if this might help Jewett to understand. "Dr. Jones said he was not to be disturbed for *any* reason."

Jewett's cheeks gained a pink tinge, and she opened her mouth suddenly, as if to speak in anger. But her words emerged calm and defeated. "Okay. Sorry to bother you." She punched the disconnect with a violence more suitable to her mood. "Darn it! I know if she'd just get Kaign, he'd listen."

The thought of abandoning Jewett did not appeal to Scott, but he doubted the killers would barge through a hospital in broad daylight, past wards, offices, and Cambridge's secretary to murder Jewett in front of witnesses. *These guys are professionals, and they're not that desperate. Yet.* "Pat, we don't have a lot of time to waste. Why don't I go down to Kaign's office and talk to him while you take care of your business here?"

Jewett tented her fingers on her lap, looking miserable. "Thanks, but I don't think that's a good idea."

Scott caught her shoulder and squeezed it gently. "I won't cause any trouble. I'll just find him and have him call you here. All right?"

Jewett stared at her fingers. At length, with reluctance, she said, "All right."

"Don't go anywhere." Scott headed for the door. "And don't worry. Kaign and I'll get along fine." He gave Cambridge a two-fingered parting gesture, between a wave and a salute, slipped through the door into Cambridge's secretary's office and out into the hallway.

Recalling the location of the surgery offices from his investigation, Scott traversed the corridors, alone with his thoughts for the first time since the shootout. Remorse clung like a lead-weighted shroud. He could not escape the realization that he had, in his own way, played God, meted justice by killing an assassin in cold blood. Other thoughts balanced it: the hunted deer look of Patricia Jewett when she realized she would have to save the life of a vicious killer whose only redeeming quality was that he had been lucky enough to be born human, the understanding that he had rescued future innocent victims from a system that thrusts man-eaters back on the streets in the name of justice. *If it was the right thing to do, why do I still feel as evil as the man I killed?*

As Scott turned onto the surgery wing, he cast aside this

jumbled maze of thought for another. *I can't believe I just talked myself into another confrontation with Kaign Jones.* He considered what he had seen of the surgeon. *An outwardly arrogant, inwardly insecure, egotistical jerk who makes himself look important by sneering down at everyone else.* Scott shook his head in incomprehension. *What does Pat see in him?* No answer came, but he did reach a conclusion. *I'm missing something. But, if Pat really loves him, what right do I have to interfere? I've given my best. I lost. Now it's time to concede the battle to the . . .* Scott winced, unable to use the term "better," even to himself. *. . . other man.*

Jones' waiting room was empty when Scott arrived. He discovered the nurse-receptionist behind the simulated marble desk, reading a romance novel. She set the book aside as he entered. "Can I help you?"

Beyond the desk, Scott could see the rows of examination rooms. "Lieutenant Daniel Scott, Des Moines police. I need to talk with Dr. Jones."

The receptionist stared as if in deep thought. "I'm sorry, sir. Dr. Jones is back in the examination room. He was very explicit that I not disturb him for any reason. Can I have him call you?"

Scott hesitated, not wanting to create a scene. "Is he with a patient?"

The receptionist glanced at the computer screen, but she certainly knew the answer without looking, and her effort seemed more from habit than necessity. "No, Lieutenant. He's got no patients scheduled for the next half hour."

"Thank you." Scott side-stepped around the desk and headed for the examination hallway.

"Wait, you can't go back there!" The receptionist's voice trailed him, but she did not abandon her post.

Scott gave a warning knock and opened the door numbered one. Finding only a room well-stocked with examination equipment, he moved on to the second. He tapped, twisted the knob, and pushed.

The door swung ajar to reveal a pale tangle of two naked bodies on the examination table. The woman on the bottom had her face turned from the door, her hair hanging like a golden curtain over the edge of the too-small table. Her pink, surgery nursing scrubs lay, slung in a rumpled pile across a chair. On top of the nurse, Jones had not bothered to remove his shirt. Apparently cued by Scott's knock, Jones' eyes flared open, as dark and menacing as a rising tempest.

Scott stood for a moment in blank disbelief. Outrage followed, sweeping through him as if to touch every corner of his being. Without a word, he gently pulled the door until it clicked closed, cutting him off from the ugly reality of examination room two. He wanted to put as much distance as possible between himself and Jones, aware leaving would be the only sure way to keep him from damaging the surgeon's pretty face. *But, damn it, I have a message to deliver.* Scott moved out of the path of the door, waiting.

Shortly, the door wrenched open. Now fully dressed in his operating room scrubs, Jones blustered out so fast, he overran Scott by the door. The surgeon whirled, his face red to the edge of purple, his brown eyes blazing. He jabbed a finger at examination room one.

Scott nodded.

Jones slammed open the door to the unoccupied room, and stomped inside. Scott followed, keeping his judgments and emotions to himself. *I can't believe I nearly gave up Pat to this cheating, self-important piece of scum.* He closed the door behind him.

As soon as the latch clicked shut, Jones turned on Scott.

"Who the hell do you think you are? Just because you're a cop doesn't mean you can come bursting into private examination rooms!"

Scott kept his manner calm, knowing Jones must eventually realize he, not Scott, was the one in trouble. "Yeah, Kaign. Real thorough examination you were giving there. What do you call that instrument you were using?"

The sterile array of table, sink, and cabinets behind Jones made an odd background to the ranting surgeon. "Don't give me any of your smart-ass remarks. I've had it with you. I'm getting you thrown off the case." His hands clenched to fists. "Better, I'll get you thrown off the force!"

Compared with the knowledge that he might get tried and convicted of murder, Scott assigned Jones' threat no more significance than a single whisper of wind in a thunderstorm. "Thrown off the force? For what? Conduct unbefitting an officer?"

"Illegal search and seizure!" Jones was screaming now, and Scott hoped, for the nurse's sake, the rooms were sound-proofed. "You didn't knock. You didn't announce yourself as the police . . ."

I did knock. Scott interrupted, not bothering to correct the inconsistency in Jones' story. "Fine. If I'm getting fired, then I have nothing to lose." He headed for the door.

"Wait!" Jones called after Scott, his voice drained of some of its resonance.

Scott reached for the knob.

Jones' hand clamped down on Scott's shoulder, restraining. "Wait. What are you doing?"

Jones' touch sent a shiver of revulsion through Scott. He turned deliberately, wanting to physically remove Jones' hand. *At the wrist.* But Scott maintained his composure and dignity, limiting himself to a threatening glance at the fingers on his shoulder. "Just calling for witnesses before she leaves." He jerked his thumb toward the examination room next door. "I'll lose a job where people shoot at me. You'll lose one where you get paid more money than I can imagine for hiding in examination rooms and screwing women who are supposed to be your subordinates. Which one of us is going to be sorrier?"

Jones' features faded to red, and his fingers trailed from Scott's shoulder. "Fine. You win. You don't tell; I won't tell."

I don't work that way. Scott said nothing, nor did he make any gesture of agreement.

The silence lengthened and quickly grew uncomfortable. Jones shifted from foot to foot, his hands tensing and loosening at his sides. "What the hell did you come for anyway?"

"I'm taking Pat into protective custody."

Jones' features darkened again. "What?"

It was obviously a rhetorical question, so Scott went on. "Someone's trying to kill her." *One of us has Pat's best interests in mind.* Not wanting to further antagonize Jones, Scott kept the snide comment to himself.

"Nonsense." Jones downplayed the issue. "I heard the stories, and they were coincidences."

Great. A surgeon playing cop. "I don't believe they were coincidences. I . . ."

Jones jumped in, his tone rising again. "Pat's understandably scared. You're just playing on her paranoia." His eyes widened, apparently in response to a sudden realization. "You're trying to get her alone! Aren't you?"

Scott ignored the ridiculous accusation. "Kaign, I killed one of Pat's paranoid hallucinations this afternoon."

"What?"

"I shot a man in her apartment. He had a gun. Hallucinations don't use real bullets."

Jones' face dulled to pink, and his fingers uncoiled. "Is she all right?"

To Scott, Jones' question sounded like the only logical thing he had said so far. "She's fine. But I'm taking her into protective custody."

"Where?"

"I can't tell you."

"For how long?"

"As long as it takes to keep her safe."

Jones' frustration reverted back to anger. "I demand to know. I have a right to know."

"You don't have a right to anything!" Scott refused to be bullied. "She's going away for her protection. The less you or anyone else knows, the safer she is."

Jones scowled. "She's not going off with you. I forbid it."

"You forbid it? You *forbid* it?" Scott snorted. "What am I, a suitor in eighteenth-century England? I'm not asking your permission. I'm just telling you, and I'm only doing that as a favor to Pat. She asked me to speak with you and have you call her in Dr. Cambridge's office. Consider yourself speaked to."

"Spoken to," Jones corrected.

Scott reached for the knob, but Jones sprang between him and the door.

"Wait." Jones wrung his hands in agitation. "You can't tell her about this." He tossed his head to indicate the incident in the other examination room.

Scott knew Jones was right, and it irritated him. *After the things I said about Kaign, she'd never believe me. And this is not the time to hurt her.* Despite his realizations, Scott would not let Jones off so easily. "Why not?"

"It'll shatter her. With all the stress she's under, she couldn't handle this. If you tell her, she'll break down. She's not that strong."

Scott's disdain for Jones took a quantum leap. "She's a lot stronger than you give her credit for."

Jones remained between Scott and the door. "I could see how she might seem that way to someone who hasn't known her long." He seemed to be attempting to sound diplomatic, and, to Scott's impression, failing miserably.

Scott waved for Jones to move away from the door. "You're pathetic. You don't even know what you've got." *And she's more than you deserve.*

Jones did not budge. "How much do you want?"

"What?" Scott could feel the warmth of his own rising anger.

"How much money do you need to keep quiet?"

Scott lowered his head, wrestling his rage, his mouth clamped shut. He concentrated on keeping his hands low and his fingers spread. Holding all emotion from his words, he said simply, "Move aside."

Jones' speech quickened. "You won't tell her. You can't tell her, you know. You'll break her up. You'll lose a witness—"

"*I* shouldn't be the one who has to tell her." Scott reached his breaking point. He spoke slowly, every syllable distinct. "If I have to move you, we're both going to be sorry."

Jones moved.

Perched in a padded chair on the opposite side of Dr. Cambridge's desk, Jewett had scarcely finished her business when the administrator's phone beeped, indicating a message from his secretary. He poked the intercom button. "Yes, Aaron?"

The secretary's strong voice came over the speaker with life-like clarity. "There's a woman here. A wife of one of the patients. She wants to talk to Dr. Jewett. Oh, and Dr. Jones from surgery's on line one."

"Dr. Jewett's on vacation. And we'll take the call. Thanks." Cambridge disconnected, isolated line one, and passed the receiver to Jewett.

Jewett frowned, concerned for the woman in the secretary's office. *If one of my patients' relatives needs me, I should be there for her.* Realizing it was too late to argue, she spoke into the mouthpiece. "Kaign?"

"Pat, thank God you're all right." Jones' voice held a strange tone Jewett attributed to concern for her. "You are all right?"

"Yes, I'm fine." Jewett watched Cambridge become engrossed in his paperwork, discretely ignoring her conversation with Jones.

"My God," Jones continued. "Someone really was trying to kill you. I can't believe I passed it off. Is there anything I can do? I want to help."

Jewett tried to answer in the negative, but Jones rambled on.

"Let me take you away. That cop's an idiot. He doesn't really care what happens to you."

"Kaign, please." Jewett swiveled her chair away from Cambridge, embarrassed by the turn of the discussion. "Scotty's a professional."

"A professional asshole," Jones finished. "Pat, that cop just came down here. Out of the blue, he started fighting with me about taking you away." Jones sounded agitated, almost frightened. "He said whenever you got done spending a week with him, you'd never come back to me again." He swallowed. "Pat, honey, they are trying to kill you, and we've got to do something about it. I mean, my God, if anything happened to you, I don't know what I'd do." He was pleading now. "But don't go away with him. Let me take you someplace. We'll fly to France."

Jewett had never seen this side of Jones before, and it confused her. "Kaign, I'm not sure. I have to think about it. I'm not supposed to leave the state, and I don't want to get in any more trouble. The guy who tried to kill me was a pro. The police are trained to handle people like him." *Scotty promised not to antagonize Kaign. Damn it, I've got enough to deal with without those two acting like children.*

"Whatever you think is best."

Jewett all but choked on her saliva, not daring to believe Jones credited her judgment.

"You just watch that cop. I don't trust him. Pat, he kept threatening to steal you away from me. He's going to lie to you, I just know it. He's got to have some story cooked up." Jones' voice became more characteristic and demanding until only a trace of uncertainty remained. "He acted like he was planning something devious. He said after he got done talking to you, you wouldn't believe a word I said. And he swore that, by the end of the week, he'd have you in bed."

Jewett hesitated, uncertain what to think or say. The man Jones was describing bore little resemblance to the Scott she knew. *But I've never been all that good at analyzing people. Scotty seems sincere, but why would Kaign lie? It makes sense for Scotty to show me his best side and Kaign his worst, and he has been talking down Kaign since the moment we met.*

"I'll be careful," Jewett promised. "I'll page you if anything changes. Okay?"

"All right," Jones said reluctantly. "And Pat?"

"Hmmm?"

"Remember, I love you very, very much. After this is all over, I still want to marry you."

This time the proposal sounded heartfelt, and Jewett felt warmed and relaxed. "I love you too," she said.

Another light on Dr. Cambridge's phone flashed, and he worked the buttons to address his secretary without cutting in on Jewett's private call. "What is it, Aaron?"

"Lieutenant Scott's back. And that patient's wife of Dr. Jewett's is still here and getting very . . . um . . ." The secretary minced words, apparently within earshot of the woman he discussed. ". . . insistent."

Cambridge glanced at Jewett for confirmation.

"I have to go now," Jewett told Jones. "I'll get in touch as soon as I can." Answering Cambridge's unspoken question with a nod, she waited for Jones to say the last words.

"Take care." Jones' warnings gave the words an importance beyond the usual, blind platitude. "Bye." He disconnected.

"Let Scotty in." Cambridge avoided his secretary's other dilemma for the moment.

Jewett pursed her lips in apprehension. Jones' words conjured mental images of a Lieutenant Scott/Mr. Hyde who would come bursting through the doors, disheveled from his battle with Jones, his grin cold, his eyes tiny and darting, hiding a mind plotting evil.

But Scott came through the door with his usual brisk composure and friendly, crooked features. He might have returned from a walk to the supermarket. As he closed the door behind him, he glanced at Jewett, and something in her expression must have given away her concern. "Did Kaign call?"

"Yes. How did you know?"

Scott blinked, staring as if she had just asked the most obvious question in the world. "I told you I'd have him call you." He asked with sudden caution, "How are you doing?"

Ah ha! Scotty knows Kaign might have told me something upsetting. Jewett hesitated, doubts raised by the thought. *Why would Scotty threaten Kaign knowing Kaign was going to tell me about it right afterwards? The whole situation makes no sense.* "I'm fine," she said suspiciously. "Why do you ask?"

Scott turned his gaze to Cambridge as if to confirm that his simple query had elicited Jewett's hostility. "Why did I ask how you're doing? You mean other than because some cannibal stuck a machine gun in your back, and you had to come to work and beg for a vacation you refused earlier today? I don't know. I'm taking a survey?" He kept his tone so amiable, the gibe did not sting. "Seriously, Pat, if I wasn't trained for this stuff, I'd be a nervous wreck."

Despite Jones' warnings, Jewett found it nearly impossible to remain mad at Scott. He had mastered sarcastic wit to the point where he could modulate his voice to make even bitter comments sound funny. On the surface, he reminded her of a hard-nosed detective from an old mystery movie; if not for the Secret Diagnosis sessions, she would never have known he had hidden a softer, less secure side she found attractive.

When Jewett did not respond for several seconds, Scott continued. "Mrs. Schober's out in the other office. She seems upset about something. I'd rather not lose more time, but I think we ought to hear her out, if you're up to it."

Jewett nodded, glad she would not have to argue with Scott about seeing the patient. *Scotty's got enough to worry about. Killing that assassin. Leaving the scene. Taking off with a murder suspect to some unauthorized place. Rank or no rank, he's going to be lucky to have a job tomorrow.*

Dr. Cambridge sucked air through his teeth. "Elaine? Dr. Schober's wife is the insistent woman Aaron was talking about?" His long face revealed his mortification. "I'll talk to her."

Jewett waved him off. "Me first. It's certainly patient-care related. No need to compound the error by putting you in the position of trying to handle something blind."

Cambridge bobbed his head. He could smooth any ruffled feathers after Jewett handled the initial problem bothering Mrs. Schober. "Please tell her I'm very *very* sorry. I'll speak with Aaron later about not referring to the former dean's wife as 'some woman.' "

Jewett followed Scott through the connecting door into Cambridge's secretary's office. From behind a sleek desk, Aaron followed Elaine's frantic pacing with his eyes. Apparently spotting Jewett, Elaine froze in the center of the room, her gray hair swept back into a hand resting on the top of her head.

Elaine lowered her hand to her side, letting the strands fall randomly around her face. "Pat, thank goodness. I need your help with Stanley."

Jewett gestured at the door to the hallway to indicate they would talk on the way. "What's wrong?"

Scott opened the door, ushered the women into the corridor, and trailed them through. They headed toward the chronic care ward, traversing the familiar hallways as they discussed the situation.

"Stan's blinking again," Elaine explained. "The nurses keep giving him extra doses of medicine, and he sleeps for a while. When he wakes up, he goes right back into it." She opened and closed her eyes deliberately to demonstrate.

"It's been going on all day."

They came upon an intersection, and Jewett took the left fork. "Has the resident seen him?"

"He looked at the monitors but didn't seem to know what to make of the brain wave patterns. I heard him and that new staff physician, Dr. Bartram, mumbling something about it not looking like any seizure pattern they ever saw. But they just told me it was worsening brain damage." Elaine took the lead as they swung onto the main corridor. "So I tried some things. I talked to Stan, trying to get him to answer questions. You know, one blink for 'no,' two for 'yes.' "

Jewett nodded. It was standard procedure to measure brain function and communication skills in this manner; she and the nurses had already tried it for Schober without success.

"So then, I thought maybe he couldn't hear. So I wrote the instructions on paper."

The brain waves indicated activity in the aural areas, and Jewett doubted the stroke could have affected Schober's auditory nerves. "And?" she encouraged.

"It didn't make any difference," Elaine admitted. "But I still think he's blinking on purpose. As far as I can tell from the timing of his medication doses, he never does it when no one's in the room. And, when I blinked back at him, he copied my patterns."

Intrigued, Jewett looked up quickly. "What do you mean?"

Elaine clarified, "I'd blink twice, so he'd blink twice. I wasn't sure, so I kept doing more complicated patterns. By the end, we were blinking in time to our song. Together."

Jewett was excited now. The neck trauma would keep Schober paralyzed forever, but nearly all stroke survivors regained some mental functions over time. Aphasia, the inability to use language, came in many forms; and damage to specific areas of the brain could lead to odd results. In some cases, the stroke patients would understand speech perfectly but could not find appropriate words to respond. In others, the patients could speak and write fluently but could not comprehend others. There was a wide range of possibilities. Jewett had once read a reported case in a medical journal of an aphasic musician unable to speak or understand words. That patient knew musical notes so well, they had become symbolic pictures; his mind no longer needed to convert them to letters to understand them. His doctors established a limited form of communication using written symbols and a student with perfect pitch. *If sometime in his past Schober learned to use eye blinks as a substitute for speech, he might be able to communicate with them and still not understand verbal or written speech.* The idea seemed ludicrous. *But why would anyone learn to use eye blinks as a form of speech?*

Elaine pressed, "Do you think it means anything?"

"I don't know," Jewett admitted. "It certainly might."

The trio arrived at the chronic care ward and slipped into Schober's room. He lay still amidst the portable screens and monitors, staring toward the television where the all-news station paraded silent pictures of a burning apartment building.

Elaine placed a warning finger to her lips, pointing to indicate her husband's apparent absorption in the show and his lack of blinking. Jewett stepped within Schober's view. As if it was a cue, he started opening and closing his eyes, wide and deliberate, then faster and slower again.

Scott came up beside Jewett, watching in quiet fascination while Jewett tried to establish a pattern. "Dr. Schober, can you understand me? Blink once for 'yes,' and stop."

Schober hesitated, but continued blinking.

Scott continued to stare.

"What do you think he's doing?" Elaine gazed intently, hopefully, at Jewett.

"It's possible he's trying to communicate," Jewett said, her eyes locked on Schober in frustration. "He might just be trying to demonstrate that he's aware, but he's awfully persistent for that alone. He doesn't seem to understand speech, so he has no reason to believe we don't already know he's conscious. The only way I can figure it, he's got to know some sort of eye blinking code. And he's got to know it so well, he doesn't need to think of it as speech any more." Jewett turned, recalling the musician and trying to explain the concept in a way that made more sense. "It's like learning a foreign language really well. At first, you have to translate into English before it makes any sense. After a while, the foreign words stand on their own. You learn to think in both languages. Do you know what I mean?"

"Yes." Though she answered in the positive, Elaine's voice betrayed uncertainty. "But why would Stan know a blinking code?"

Jewett shrugged helplessly. "I was hoping you could answer that."

Elaine shook her head.

Scott inched forward until he stood directly over Schober. Without turning, he addressed the women. "Mrs. Schober, was your husband in the military. Maybe a long time ago?"

Elaine rolled her eyes questioningly toward Jewett. "Way back in the early 1970s. Stan figured he'd get drafted into the Army, so he enlisted in the Navy instead. He was a communications technician." The logical question followed. "Why do you ask?"

Scott turned, his expression more somber than Jewett had ever seen it before. "Mrs. Schober, I'm going to have to ask you to leave. Police business."

"What?" Elaine shuffled backward, her voice mingling anger and doubt.

"I'll explain later. The less you know, the safer you are. If you refuse to leave, you'll be obstructing an investigation."

Scott's intensity concerned Jewett. "It's for the best," she reassured.

Elaine Schober gnawed her lip in consideration. Soon, she came to a decision, heralded by a sudden toss of her head and a fixing of her sharp, green eyes on Scott's face. "Lieutenant, I've spent the last two days tracking down eleven lawyers, not one of which would touch Stan's Living Will agreement. If Stan can communicate, I want to know what he has to say. If he still wants to die, I'll see every idiot partner in every idiot law firm in Des Moines, but I have a right to know Stan's wishes before I torture myself talking to idiots any more."

Jewett held her breath, knowing Scott's investigation would have led him to question Schober's wife, but ignorant of whether Elaine had told Scott the depth of her promise to aid her husband's right to die. Jewett waited until Scott gave a stiff, reluctant nod before addressing him. "Are you saying Dr. Schober *is* using a code? And you might know it?" It seemed impossible, yet Scott's implication, that he was about to talk with Schober, remained clear.

"Morse code," Scott said simply, as if that would explain everything.

The words meant nothing to Jewett.

Apparently reading Jewett's consternation, Scott continued. "It was an easy substitution code. Letters were represented by dashes and dots on paper or short and long noises or flashes of light. Back before satellite radio transmissions, people used to use Morse code because it would carry over radio waves without difficulty. Static and interference didn't affect the signals much." Scott looked back at Schober. "Satellites eventually made it obsolete."

Torn between curiosity for whatever message Schober might convey and Scott's knowledge of an archaic code, Jewett asked the latter first. "How do *you* know it then?"

Scott never took his eyes from Schober. "I was a Boy Scout. They taught us the Morse code distress signal. In case we ever got lost in the woods, we might be able to rig up a flare or a halogen light." He leaned closer to Schober, his answer to Jewett becoming more off-hand. "My neighbor and I got a book and learned the whole code so we could flash messages after bedtime . . . Holy shit!" The exclamation seemed unrelated, in response to something Schober had done.

Alarmed, Jewett came to Scott's side. "What is it?"

Scott raised a hand to silence her. "My memory is sketchy at best, and he's throwing in nonsense words."

"Neologisms." Jewett used the technical term. "That's part of the stroke. Ignore them." Excited now, she sat on the edge of the bed in a position where she could see Schober's and Scott's faces. "What's he saying?"

Elaine stood at the foot of the bed, her hands sliding up and down the board.

Scott turned his gaze to the television screen, and Jewett followed suit. An image of Benjamin Nash had replaced the burning building sequences. The President stood by his limousine beside the newscaster, his lips moving in the silence contrived by the volume control being turned off. Occasionally, the cameras cut to the crowd.

"Take the remote." Scott returned his attention to Schober as Jewett unclipped the plastic square from the siderail. "When I tell you, hit pause."

Jewett watched as the camera angle changed, catching Nash's profile and a corner of the throng.

"Now," Scott said, his eyes still fixed on Schober.

Jewett thumbed the pause, holding the picture on the screen.

Scott looked up. "Good. Now bring it in closer."

Jewett turned the dial, narrowing the view toward Nash's face.

Scott caught her hand. "No, no. Stop. Focus in on the guy in the suit."

Jewett scanned the picture. The only other person in a suit she could locate was Nash's Secret Service man, the one who had jostled her the day Nash had "healed" Schober's seizure. "The bodyguard?"

Scott nodded.

Jewett rolled the dial, enhancing the close-up onto the guard's face.

"Closer," Scott instructed.

"Closer?" The order confused Jewett. "If I get any closer, all I'll have is his nose."

"Eyes. Center the eyes."

Obediently, Jewett concentrated the image. She had just cut off the broad chin and close-cropped, brown hair when Scott's intention become abruptly, horrifyingly vivid. "That's him!" The remote slipped from Jewett's hand. She bobbled it twice, missed, and heard it fall to Schober's covers. "That's the murderer."

Elaine Schober gripped the footboard tighter. "Oh God."

"Are you sure?" Scott pressed Jewett.

"No," Jewett had to admit. "How could I be? The killer wore a surgeon's cap and mask. It's hard enough recognizing nurses I know from the operating room without their masks."

"But someone who spends most of his life in the operating room, say an aging obstetrician, might be better at recognizing people than you. Especially if he witnessed the mask slip during a brief struggle with the victim."

Jewett's gaze went naturally to Schober.

Elaine stared also. "Stan told you that?"

"Not in so many words." Scott retrieved the remote and returned it to its clip. "He indicated the murderer, and I used Pat to corroborate. And he said something else you should know about."

Before Scott could elaborate, the bedside telephone buzzed. He caught the receiver between two fingers and brought it to his ear. "Hello?" He paused, listening. "Dr. Cambridge, hi. She's fine. Her, too. Yeah, patch him through." Scott explained to Jewett. "One of my men."

Jewett and Elaine shifted uneasily, too interested in Scott's call to exchange conversation of their own.

"This is Scotty. What'd you find?" Scott stared at the ceiling, listening, then cringed. "Yeah, I know. I know. Stall him. I got a lead here that just couldn't wait." He paused again. "We'll talk about it later. Tell me what you found out about the man-eater. No I.D., right?" Scott listened in silence for several minutes, his brows raised in interest. "Good idea. Try legal, undercover stuff, too. Don't push too hard yet. We're going to need to set up a guard for Dr. Jewett. Maybe a safe house. Can you get to work on that?"

Apparently receiving confirmation, Scott finished. "I'll get back to you." He returned the receiver to its cradle.

Jewett stared expectantly. "Well?"

"According to his genetic screen, your . . . um . . . visitor died some five years before I killed him." Scott paced. "And somehow, most of his computer files just happened to disappear."

"Secret Service, too?" Elaine ventured, apparently piecing together Scott's vagaries.

Scott frowned disapprovingly. "I'd bet on it."

The whole thing still seemed implausible to Jewett. "I don't get it. Why would Secret Service men be running around killing people?"

Scott's features twisted into a grim parody of amusement. "I hate to dispel the myth of Santa Claus, but running around killing people is what Secret Service men do. Sometimes. What bothers me is who these particular Secret Service men have to be working for."

Scott's insinuation rang through loud and clear, and Jewett felt it muddled rather than clarified the issue. "Nash? But that makes no sense. His entire campaign is based on wiping out death. Why would he order his men to kill Krystal . . . or me? Why would anyone obey such an order?"

"You're underestimating the loyalty of Secret Service men to their agencies and leaders." Scott addressed Jewett, but his gaze remained locked on Schober's blinking eyes. "To a secret organization, blind loyalty is more than an asset, it's a necessity. History's full of examples of people who murdered, lied, cheated, stole, or killed themselves for a cause, even one they didn't believe in, out of allegiance to a country or a leader. Nazi Germany. Watergate. The Branch Davidians. Hell, Clinton ensured we can't even question the guys about their clients, and that was just over a stupid affair." He nodded, apparently in response to Schober. "And you're forgetting Secret Service men are trained and committed to throwing themselves in front of bullets aimed at the President. If they're willing to sacrifice *their* lives for his causes, why not the lives of strangers?"

Jewett awaited an answer to her other question, and Scott complied.

"As for Nash's motive, I'm guessing blackmail. Remember the baby? The money we found in Fantella's account?" Scott paused to return several slow winks to Schober. "I'd bet Nash and Fantella got real close during his campaign. After all his moral rantings, a scandal like that would destroy his credibility. She must have demanded more money, perhaps threatened to expose him; or maybe she just wanted her baby to know its real father. We'll never know, and it really doesn't matter. What does matter is he silenced her with murder. Then, he tried to silence the only two witnesses." Scott indicated Schober and Jewett. "He gave up on Schober when they discovered he was essentially brain dead. And, if you hadn't seen the disguised janitor in the basement, they probably would have given up on you, too."

"And all that talk about ending death by 2030?" Jewett asked.

"Hypocrisy," Scott supplied. "Does that surprise you?"

"A little," Jewett admitted.

"Now what?" Elaine's voice startled Jewett. She had nearly forgotten the older woman's presence. "You arrest the President?"

Scott's face lapsed into harried wrinkles. His cheeks appeared more gaunt than usual. "No. That's the problem. Pat's identification of the Secret Service agent is iffy at best." He gestured at Schober. "The other doctor's only intermittently coherent, and I'm willing to bet no amount of digging is going to directly connect Nash to Fantella's money. Even if we pin the murder on the Secret Service guy . . ." He waved at the bodyguard on the television screen. ". . . he'll deny any connection between the murder and the President."

"You're saying it's hopeless?" Jewett said.

"No. I do have an idea, but . . ." Scott glanced from Schober to Elaine to Jewett. ". . . it'll involve lying." He added hastily, "Not perjury, but lying. My job's already hanging by a thread. If this doesn't work, it's lost. I can't vouch for your job, either. And every life in this room will be in jeopardy. I won't proceed unless I have your complete cooperation and permission."

Jewett considered, her thoughts in a whirl. It seemed impossible for a man so dedicated, so verbally committed to life to authorize murder. Yet Jewett had seen people's attitudes toward life, abortion, and illness reverse when it involved the welfare of themselves or their loved ones. *My life's already on the line, and I'm a lot safer if Scotty corners the real killer. Besides, why should a hypocrite get away with murder just because he's wealthy and powerful?* "I'm with you."

Scott's head turned to Elaine. The older woman ran her hands along the ledge of the footboard in progressively quickening motions. "First, I need to know what Stan told you."

Scott nodded. "He kept repeating the same thing again and again. He was saying, 'Please, let me die.'"

Understanding sparked through Elaine's green eyes, and she turned her husband a tight-lipped smile of promise. "I'm with you, too," she said.

Chapter 12

Dr. Patricia Jewett shoveled dirty plates into her dishwasher, flipped the metal-rimmed plastic door shut, and turned back to the kitchen table and her guests. Officer Halstead swirled the last mouthful of coffee in his mug. His lowered head gave Jewett a view of dark blond stubble and the edge of hard, gray eyes that never seemed to focus on her. His synthetic cotton dress slacks and polo shirt fit his meaty frame without a stretch or wrinkle, as if tailored. Smaller, thinner, and quieter, Officer Winterstein met Jewett's gaze with a mild grin, his brown eyes large and friendly.

"Just pretend we're not here," Winterstein said.

Easy for him to say. Jewett met the words with a shy half-smile. *If they weren't here, I wouldn't dare be here either. I can't believe I talked Scotty into letting me stay at my house.* At the time, it had seemed like a good idea. If the newspaper story came out the way they planned it, the President's men would find Jewett too useful as an information source to kill. Scott had told her to expect a telephone call about Schober's medical needs, perhaps from the Surgeon General himself; and Elaine had signed the necessary papers to allow Jewett to violate patient confidentiality.

Jewett headed for the living room. As she walked through the doorway, the faint odor of enzyme cleaners pinched her nose. She swallowed hard, feeling dinner churning in her gut, and glanced across the room to the window. A board replaced the glass the gunman had shattered. Without a breeze to stir them, the patterned curtains lay flat and still. Before Jewett could look at the site where the gunman had lain, her eyes jerked away as if of their own accord. She gazed over the familiar arrangement of archways and furniture: the blue couch sandwiched between plush matching chairs and the opening to her bedroom behind the couch, beside the entry to the kitchen. Directly opposite the window, the front door stood, securely locked. Across from the couch, the blank screen of the entertainment center seemed to stare back at her. The central coffee table held the policemen's tiny computer attached to the telephone. The device would identify the exact location of any caller in seconds and flash it on the display. The television remote perched in its usual location on the arm of the couch.

With no place left to look, Jewett forced her attention to the area of carpet beneath the window. For an instant, her mind replaced the corpse there, his blood still fresh and brilliantly scarlet. The image disappeared swiftly, leaving her staring at a spot so well cleaned, it made the rest of the rug appear dingy. Neither a single splash of blood nor light dusting of chalk remained, and Jewett breathed a relieved sigh. *This is Scotty's doing. He must have called ahead while his men took me home and told them to clean up before I got here.* She found the small favor thoughtful, a courtesy that could easily and understandably have been forgotten amid more important details.

Someone tapped on the door. The sudden noise startled Jewett. Stiffening, she backed toward the bedroom.

"I'll get it." Officer Winterstein trotted to the door and flicked the peephole. He glanced around for several seconds before releasing it. "It's the paper Scotty promised."

Jewett nodded, still jumpy and restless. She sat on the

couch while Winterstein opened the front door and retrieved *The Des Moines Register* from the porch. Closing the door, he crossed the room and offered the newspaper to her.

Jewett accepted the *Register* with trepidation. As a chronic care physician, she had grown accustomed to assessing and revising patient care plans daily, but Scott's scheme required constant reevaluation and possibly modification on a moment's notice.

The headline glared at Jewett from the front page: *Comatose Doctor Becomes Murder Witness.*

Winterstein sat in the chair nearest the kitchen entryway, his back to the front door, and fiddled with the computer on the coffee table.

He's bored. Jewett passed Winterstein the television remote, then settled back into the cushions to read.

"Thanks." Winterstein snapped on the picture, keeping the volume respectfully low.

Halstead's gruff voice emerged from the kitchen. "Mind if I make some more coffee?"

"Go right ahead," Jewett called back. Returning her attention to the article, she read:

> Unidentified sources at C. Everett Koop Memorial Hospital revealed a major break in the case of a nurse murdered in a patient's room early last Tuesday. Krystal Fantella was found stabbed to death in the room of former staff obstetrician, Dr. Stanley Schober, a chronic care patient comatose since a stroke-induced car accident earlier in the week. Completely technologically dependent, Schober was considered brain dead until staff members discovered a means of communication earlier today.

Through a series of eye blinks, Schober was able to convey his needs and indicate that he had witnessed the murder. Shortly after police questioning began, Schober lapsed back into a coma without having revealed a full description of the killer.

Police Lieutenant Daniel Scott refused to confirm or deny the information, saying only that Schober would be placed under strict police protection. According to Schober's physician, brain wave expert Dr. Patricia Jewett, "Dr. Schober has a convulsive disorder as a result of his injuries. We had reason to believe the blinking was a manifestation of these [seizures], so he received a larger than normal dose of his [seizure] medications. That, combined with the excitement and effort of communication, caused him to lose consciousness . . . I would expect him to return to his previous state of awareness within twelve to thirty-six hours . . . I have every reason to believe Dr. Schober should be able to testify."

The first to arrive at the scene of Fantella's early morning murder, Jewett was herself the primary suspect at one time. Police sources refused to explain why she was no longer considered a suspect, explaining only that "new evidence has come to light that clears her completely." Other hospital employees, who declined to be identified, added that the police protection is adequate or excessive. One said, "No one's allowed in the room, not even family. They've put a lock on the computer file so only Pat [Jewett] and one nurse can access it."

Dr. Schober's wife, Elaine, is upset by what she considers "overblown precautions." She told this reporter, "For days I've been trying to tell them Stan can communicate, and no one would believe me. Now, they won't let me in to see him, won't tell me how he's doing, or even what they're doing with his medications. It's not fair . . ."

The chime of the doorbell interrupted Jewett's reading. She lowered the newspaper and glanced at Officer Winterstein. The creases across his forehead warned her that, this time, he was not expecting company. She waited, tracking Winterstein's walk to the peephole.

Winterstein looked out. "Man in a delivery uniform. He's got a basket of flowers."

Jewett relaxed. *From Kaign, no doubt. He was so upset, and Scotty must have told him I came home instead of going to the safe house.*

Winterstein was less trusting. He called loud enough to be heard through the door. "Who is it?"

The reply sounded faint. "I've got a delivery for a . . ." He paused as if glancing at a card or paper, ". . . Pat Jewett. From 'Flowers Are Us.' "

"Thanks. Leave them on the porch." Winterstein continued to watch the deliveryman.

"I can't do that." Though still muffled, the ire in the stranger's voice came through clearly enough.

"Why not?"

"That's one of our priciest arrangements. If I don't get a signature, I'm responsible."

"Refuse it," Halstead said, apparently watching from the kitchen window.

Jewett stiffened, imagining Jones' reaction. "No."

Winterstein glanced in her direction, and she imagined Halstead did the same. Neither said anything, though, so Jewett explained.

"You'll wind up with a frantic surgeon on the doorstep next." When the officers still remained silent, she finished with, "Believe me. You don't want that." She cringed at the image of Kaign Jones ranting on the front porch while the police refused him access.

Winterstein turned back to the door. "Can I see some identification?"

A long pause followed.

"What's he got?" Halstead asked from the kitchen.

"Driver's license." Winterstein studied it through the peephole. "Can't read the name, but it's got his picture. And a business card from 'Flowers Are Us.' Looks legit." He cleared his throat and spoke louder, so the man on the other side of the door could hear. "Put the basket and whatever you want signed on the porch. Step back, and keep your hands where I can see them."

Another long pause, then, "What the hell is this place?" A hint of discomfort entered the flower man's tone, perhaps fear. "A drug house?"

"You want to deliver those flowers, do what I say."

"All right! But I'm keeping my cell phone in my hand, preset to 911. I'm not becoming no statistic."

Jewett shook her head at what seemed like a paranoia showdown, but she did not interfere. The officers knew their job, and her insistence on accepting the delivery had caused the standoff. They had every right and reason to remain cautious.

Halstead called from the kitchen, "No. Nothing in his hands."

Winterstein paused. "I'm a cop. You're not in any danger. Just keep your hands empty and high."

For a moment, Jewett thought the delivery man would refuse, and she could hardly blame him. It seemed the best compromise. At least, Jones would not get the message she had refused his peace offering. He might give the flower shop an earful, but he would not likely come to her home to argue with the police.

Finally, the man said, "All right, officer. Just sign, and I'll be on my way."

Halstead's voice wafted from the kitchen. "He doing what you said?"

"Yup." Winterstein glanced over his shoulder at Jewett. "Ma'am, you need to stay out of the way."

Uncertain what that required, Jewett hunkered down on the sofa.

Winterstein opened the door to reveal a brown-haired man of medium build, dressed in delivery whites and innocently holding out empty hands. A huge basket of multicolored flowers stood on the porch behind an old-fashioned clipboard.

Never taking his gaze from the delivery man, Winterstein picked up the clipboard, released the pen, and scribbled on the paper. "Don't you have a computerized signing system?" He returned the pen and offered the board to the delivery man.

"We're a small outfit, officer." He accepted the clipboard. "We go cheap and easy where we c—Hey! Is this a joke? There's nothing written here." He shoved it back toward Winterstein.

Winterstein took back the clipboard, glancing at it for a fraction of a second before returning his gaze to the delivery man. "You're right." He unfastened the pen again and pressed the tip more carefully against the signature line. He risked a look as he scribbled his name, then shook the pen stiffly. "Something wrong with this pen."

"Sorry, I got another." The man stuffed a hand into his right hip pocket.

"No!" Winterstein dropped the clipboard, which clattered against concrete as he reached for his gun.

The stranger's hand emerged first, clutching a small pistol. A soft pop sounded.

Winterstein shrieked. His hands clutched at his lower abdomen, and he crumpled to the carpet.

Jewett screamed. She made a dive for the entrance to her bedroom, half-rolling, half-vaulting over the back of the couch. Its front legs rose from the ground. The couch teetered dangerously, then slammed back into position, flipping Jewett to the floor behind it. The fall jarred the breath from her lungs. She caught a glimpse of the stranger snatching a pistol from Winterstein's writhing, screaming form before she managed to funnel air to her lungs. Gathering her legs, she made a crouched sprint into the bedroom.

Gunshots sounded from the kitchen as Halstead fired at the stranger near the front door. Winterstein's pained howls obscured the noise of the gunman's silenced return fire. Jewett huddled near her bed, uncertain what to do. The array of clock/stereo and knickknacks on her dresser would prove useless against bullets. Her carefully made bed seemed alien, as if she had run into another world rather than her own room. As instructed earlier, she avoided the two windows.

Winterstein's screams died to pained gasps, and the exchange of gunfire became clear, a wild volley of single and double shots. As chilling as Winterstein's moans sounded, Jewett appreciated the noise; it assured her he was still alive. *It's my fault, all my fault. I should have let him refuse that delivery.*

Winterstein's voice sounded thin as a whisper. "There's another—" He grunted and broke off suddenly, apparently kicked by the gunman.

A Time to Die

A moment later, another man strode boldly into the living room, apparently trusting his companion's covering fire to pin Halstead in place. From the bedroom, Jewett could see he carried a machine pistol like the one the "maneater" had used against Scott. Heart pounding, she slipped between the bed and window, out of sight. *I can't believe this is happening. Scotty said they wouldn't come after me any more.* Tears of fear and anger sprang to her eyes. She backed toward the wall, forgetting in the encroaching panic that Scott had made no such promise. He had expected the Secret Service to act more professionally subtle, to get the information they needed from her using peaceful, legitimate channels. *Maybe he's wrong. Maybe the President's not involved at all. Maybe they're just killers.*

The man with the automatic weapon sprayed a sloppy line of bullets across the kitchen entryway. He moved toward the bedroom and Jewett, blasting another line of fire to keep Halstead hemmed in the kitchen.

Despite the gunfire, Halstead's bass rumbled placidly. "Pat, run! Get out the window! Go!" He returned one desperate shot, immediately answered by the machine pistol.

Jewett seized the moment. She unsnapped the clasp and wrenched open the glass. Not wanting to waste time removing the screen, she rammed through it. The thin steel folded around her. She dropped the four feet to the grass, rolled and ran. Her first thought was to fly in wild, directionless panic. Common sense intervened. *A car. I need a car.* She raced around to the front of the garage.

Once there, she seized the handle and jerked upward. For the first time, her carelessness with locks was rewarded. The door lifted. She dove beneath it, letting it fall back into position, too concerned about getting to her Ford Pegasus to concern herself with the door. *Safe. Oh God, safe. Got to get help.*

Hands trembling, it took an effort to fumble the wallet from her pocket. She reached for the key card. Grasping it, she pulled. The quick motion loosened the others, and cards scattered in a frenzied, plastic spray. Still clutching the car key, she dropped the wallet amid the strewn credits. She ran the magnetized strip across the lock until she heard the opening click. Sliding behind the wheel, her shaking fingers guided the card twice before the ignition button operated. From habit, she locked on her seat belt, snapped the switch from charge to drive, and caught herself reaching for the hospital pre-set. *I'll have to drive manual in case I'm followed. Or tracked.* She hit the garage door opener instead, worked the lever by her left knee into manual, and reversed. She flicked on the headlights.

Just as the car started rolling, Jewett heard a click to her right. The passenger door whipped open. She screamed. Before she could think to act, a stranger sprang into the seat, waving a pistol. "Keep moving," he commanded as he slammed the door closed.

It took all of Jewett's concentration simply to obey. Dizziness swam down on her. She felt weak and tired, defeated, as if her mind and heart had stopped, leaving a blank automaton. She reversed onto the main road.

"Forward." The man slid the gun under his shirt unobtrusively, the barrel still pointed at Jewett.

She complied, forgetting the name of her own street, uncertain who or where she was, knowing only the slim, firmly-muscled, gray clad man beside her. Easily six and a half feet tall, his head nearly touched the car ceiling. His legs folded into the roomy floor space set for Jones' long limbs.

"Keep your eyes on the road, and tell me about Stanley Schober."

The stranger's demand jarred Jewett back to reality. Scott had been vague, explaining only her role in his trap for Fantella's murderer. He had told her that, for the safety of all the players, each would know only the parts involving him or her. Then, Jewett had not been able to shake the feeling he had hidden some important fact, one she would not approve of. Now, she was glad he had concentrated so hard on her piece of the plan. She knew her lines so well, they bubbled to the forefront despite her terror. "What?" she managed. "What about Dr. Schober?"

"What's his condition?" The car came to the end of the road. "Turn left here."

"He's in a coma." Jewett had gone over the scenario so many times, the lie came easier than the truth. She turned without bothering with the signal. "But he'll wake up any time now."

"Is he competent to testify?"

"Definitely." It was another lie. Schober's inability to understand speech and use of repetitive and nonsense words might invalidate his testimony.

"What did he see?"

"I don't know. We think he's got a full description of the murderer. I hope they catch you," Jewett added to throw the gunman off-guard and make him think she had no vague idea of the killer's identity herself.

The man smirked. "What medications is he on?"

The list included the standard chronic care prophylactics to stimulate the bowels and oxygen exchange, antibiotics, and his anticonvulsant. Jewett rattled them off individually.

"Take a left here." The man gestured deeper into the city.

Jewett obeyed. Rationality seeped into her brain, and she suddenly realized her predicament. *Now that I've given him all the answers he needs, he has no reason to keep me alive. And he let me see him clearly, so he has no choice but to kill me.* Her hands clenched on the wheel until her knuckles blanched. She forced herself to concentrate on the roads. *We're headed northeast, the bad side of town. There's a murder there every day. No one will even notice. Or care.*

"What kind of protection does Schober have?"

Jewett answered automatically. "The ward is crawling with cops." She added quickly, hoping it would provide a reason to keep her alive, "Only me and the police lieutenant can go in the room."

"Turn right up ahead." The stranger gestured an alley.

Jewett's mouth went so dry it hurt. *That's where he's going to gun me down.* "What are you going to do with me?"

His voice never changed from its gruff monotone. "Just do as I say, and you won't get hurt."

Jewett bit her lip as the car approached the alley. She slowed. *The bastard doesn't even have the decency to admit he's going to shoot me!* She revived an image of a ten-year-old pulmonary patient from her pediatrics rotation. The boy had a rare, fatal lung disease, not yet approachable by genetic surgery or medications. The parents had forbid Jewett and her attending physician from explaining the child's fate to him, afraid it would upset him. But, like most intuitive patients, the boy knew. As he fought for every breath, he knew and he feared alone, feared what fate awaited him that was so awful, so much worse than death that his parents and the doctors refused to tell him. Jewett's anger flared.

Jewett removed her foot from the pedal, and the car slackened to a crawl. Her rage chipped away at her panic, but it was not enough. She needed a hole, an opening large enough to smash through her natural timidity and bridge the terror holding her in thrall. *Secret Diagnosis.* Jewett forced herself to picture the gunman in his underwear; but he remained six-foot-six, a brawny, armed man-eater in his boxer shorts. The alley approached. Jewett stared until her eyes blurred, adding bright red hearts to the image, then an abdominal tattoo reading, "Mother." *Nothing. Oh God, nothing.* She shivered, feeling wrung out and nauseated. Her mind sped, as if drugged. *He wears women's clothing.* Quickly, she redressed her vision, in black lingerie and red high heels.

Jewett still felt coiled in knots, but the tear in her panic widened. The car glided toward the alley. Swiftly, Jewett added a pet rock to the image, a veritable boulder perfectly suited to a man of his size. She felt the rip increase. *One more, and I got him.* She screwed her eyes closed and envisioned the gunman pulling a skirt and blouse onto his rock.

Jewett broke into savage, hysterical laughter. *I'm going to die anyway. This jackass is going with me.* She kicked the pedal to the floor, and the car leapt forward like a thing possessed.

"I told you to turn right!" A trace of emotion entered his voice.

Jewett's scattered wits interpreted his anger as fear. "I'm going straight." She suffixed it with a laugh as crazed as a movie witch.

"I said turn! I've got a gun." The stranger whipped the pistol into view, jamming the barrel into her side.

Jewett slammed the wheel into a wild left turn away from the city, jarring the gunman against his door. "You've got a gun. I've got a Ford!"

He grabbed for the wheel.

Jewett spun the car into another left, hoping he would hold his fire until she completed the turn. *Three seconds and I'm on the straightaway to the highway.*

The stranger's head thunked against the window. "Lady, I don't know what you think you're doing. I'm going to blow you away!" He reached for his seat belt, but it was tucked beneath him. "Slow down!"

Now on the open road, Jewett watched the speedometer climb to eighty, then she hit cruise. She locked her gaze on the approaching entrance ramp.

"I'll shoot you!" he threatened.

"Be my guest." Jewett gunned the motor, in an adrenaline-inspired frenzy. The speedometer edged to a hundred, then one hundred twenty. She relocked the cruise control. "Now, throw the gun out the window!"

"What the fuck!" He stabbed the gun barrel into her side. "Are you insane?"

A car appeared suddenly in front of her, as if from nowhere. Jewett swerved. She looked out the rear view, glancing across the computer controls by her left hand, and suddenly realized she had override of every system in the car. "You have a choice, buddy. Pitch the gun and live, or shoot me and try to gain control of a careening car at one hundred twenty on a highway surrounded by poles and bridge abutments. Or, we can just wait for one of the tires to rip away from the rim because we're going faster than they were made to stand."

The stranger leaned forward, grabbed the emergency brake, and yanked it up. Surprise flashed across his features.

Jewett loosed another burst of hysterical laughter. *Well, that answers that question. They didn't sabotage the brake; it was an accident.* "That's broken," she stated the obvious, inspired by the comically wide-mouthed expression on his face. She swerved around another car. Once back in control, she jabbed the passenger seat setting. The seat slid forward, cramming the gunman's huge frame beneath the dash. "Throw out the gun!" she screamed. She let the passenger seat rock back into position, then slammed it forward again. "Throw out the gun!"

The gunman flicked the adjustment on his own side into place, and the seat returned to its correct position.

Aware she had the override, Jewett jarred the seat forward. "Throw out the gun!" She reached for the lever again.

"You're a fucking lunatic!" The pitch of his voice rose.

Jewett found a concrete bridge abutment in the distance. "Look! About a mile up ahead. There's a bridge coming. If your gun's not out the window by the time we get there, I'm just going to turn the wheels to the left as hard as I can. The car's going to spin. Your side will hit first, so if one of us lives, it sure isn't going to be you. I want that gun out the window. Now!"

"You won't do it. You'll die, too."

"What have I got to lose?" Jewett hunched over the wheel. She veered left.

"All right. All right." Opening the window, he flipped the weapon toward the shoulder.

The bridge whizzed by.

The cramped position muffled the gunman's voice. "All right, lady. You think you're smart. What are you gonna do now?"

The answer came without thought. "I'm going to slow down to thirty. You're going to follow your gun."

"What the hell are you talking about?"

Jewett explained deliberately, as if to a young child. "I'm

going to slow down. Then, you're going to jump out of the car." Jewett punched off the cruise and let her speed drop. The radar detector started pulsing soft shrills above the whoosh of air through the open window.

"Are you out of your fucking mind?"

Jewett jammed down the pedal. The car accelerated.

"All right! You're out of your fucking mind."

Jewett released the pedal again, allowing the car to slow gradually to forty.

The stranger made a desperate grab for the wheel, ripping it free of Jewett's control. The car swerved toward the guard rail.

Jewett rammed down the pedal, aware her only weapon was speed. The car sprang forward, tires squealing. A pickup appeared from the opposite direction. The driver reacted quickly, whipping to the wrong side of the road. The truck whisked by, horn howling. Then it disappeared behind her.

Jewett tried to transform her panicked frenzy into rage. As the Ford Pegasus jolted over the seventy-mile-an-hour speed limit, the stranger backed off and the radar detector sang again. "That was stupid!" Jewett screamed. She slapped at him. "Get out of my car. Get out, or we're going to get stopped for speeding, and you're going to get arrested for kidnapping. Get out!"

"All right, slow down."

"No! I tried that, and you misbehaved. Jump out! Now!"

"I'd rather get arrested than die."

"Fine!" Jewett just wanted the stranger as far away as possible. She slowed to fifty-five. "Get out!" She punched him. "Get out!" She hit him again with the frenzied violence of a toddler in a tantrum.

The gunman threw open the door and dove out.

Jewett watched him through the rear view mirror as he hit the shoulder and rolled. Still half-crazed, she dashed in the brakes, slammed the car into reverse, and rolled toward him.

The stranger glanced up, looking stiff and dazed. His eyes widened in understanding, and he sprang over the guard rail to safety.

That ought to give him something to think about. Jewett had no intention of actually hurting the man, only scaring him. *Go back and tell your friends I'm crazier than they are.* She yanked the door closed, went back into gear, and whisked down the road, seeking the source of the radar.

As adrenaline ebbed, sapping Jewett of her rabid, hysterical rage, her limbs began to jerk and shake erratically. The tears fell in a steady stream, yet an exultant aura of triumph trickled through beneath her fear. She thought of all the old movies where gunmen forced drivers to their will and wondered why no one ever seemed to realize a car can make a far more powerful weapon than a handgun. She wondered how she had found the will to stand against a professional killer. And wondered what could possibly go wrong next.

CHAPTER 13

Escorted to C. Everett Koop Memorial Hospital by the highway patrolman, Patricia Jewett regathered her self-composure in the car. During the trip, the struggle on the road seemed hazy and distant, a drug-inspired nightmare fading into drowsiness. In the wake of the excitement, she felt drained and awkward, sweaty, trembling, and enveloped in goose bumps.

As Jewett gradually regained enough awareness to function, she found gaps of time missing. The incident with the gunman leapt to the forefront of memory, intense and graphic in its clarity. The loss came afterward. She could not recall the words she had babbled to convince the policeman to deliver her to the hospital, his name and description, nor most of the ride in the car. Scott's half a dozen subordinates in the main hallway near the chronic care ward greeted Jewett with relief rather than the surprise she had anticipated and ushered her into Schober's room.

Schober lay with his eyes closed, but the waking pattern on the brain wave monitor told Jewett he was feigning sleep. Elaine sat on one of the three chairs in the narrow aisle between the bed and the farthest wall, stroking her husband's blanketed arm absently. Daniel Scott caught Jewett's arm as she came through the door.

Finally feeling truly safe, Jewett turned the quiet welcome into an embrace. It seemed strange. Many years had passed since she had hugged any man but Jones; and, though she made no attempt to consider the differences, they became instantly apparent. There was so much more substance to Scott; his chest was a thick, reassuring presence against her. Though hesitant and uncertain, his careless strength made Jones' most passionate touch appear light as a bird's.

"Are you all right?" Scott asked. Only then Jewett noticed he competed with the television volume, soft but discernible over the ventilator and vital signs monitors. "What happened?" He pulled away, retrieved the extra chairs, and placed them in the center of the room.

They both sat. Jewett's mental state had returned to normal, and she told the story with as much detail as she could recall.

Scott listened in interested silence. When Jewett described using Secret Diagnosis to control her anxiety, he smiled. The image of a long-legged gunman stuffed beneath the dash sent Scott and Elaine into peals of laughter.

Now, even Jewett could see the humor in the moment; but, worried for Halstead and Winterstein, she found Scott's mirth callous and misplaced. As she came to the end of her story, she verbalized her concerns. "What about my guards? We need to check on them. They might have been killed." Jewett harbored little doubt. *Those men would have murdered me without a pang of remorse. Halstead and Winterstein didn't stand a chance.*

"I got a call from Halstead fifteen minutes ago. They're both fine. They were worried about you."

Jewett hesitated, wondering if she had misheard Scott over the noise from the television. "What do you mean they're both fine? I saw one of them shot."

"In a nonvital area. He's in surgery now, and they expect him to recover fully."

Excitement plied Jewett, but she quelled it, certain Scott

must be lying to comfort her. "But I must have heard four hundred gunshots. What happened?"

Scott looked at his hands, his uneasiness incongruous with his words. "Apparently, they were just shooting to keep the boys out of the way so they could get to you."

"Don't lie to me." Jewett glared. "I can handle it, Scotty. What you're telling me doesn't make any sense."

Scott picked at a callus on his palm, gaze still locked on his hands. "Yes it does. The people we're dealing with aren't just assassins. They're Secret Service, glorified police officers essentially. Nothing goes more against a cop's grain than shooting another cop." The pause before his next words went just a bit longer than natural, cuing Jewett that something serious troubled him. "They wanted you. There was no need to kill anyone else."

An idea brushed Jewett's mind; but, upset by the recent turn of affairs, she could not immediately fathom it. "You mean all the killers who came after me were Secret Service agents?"

Scott nodded, still avoiding Jewett's gaze. "The one who tried to run you over." Another stiff pause. "And the one I blew away in your apartment."

Understanding struck Jewett with abrupt and bitter finality. *Oh God. Scotty thinks he killed a cop, not in the line of duty, not by accident, but in cold blood and without just cause.* She shivered, deeply guilty for her own hand in the slaying. *I didn't pull the trigger, but he did it to save me from the same pain he's feeling now.*

Jewett knew Scott's remorse needed sharing, and she also realized he could never tell anyone what he had done without confessing to murder. *I'm the only one who can work this through with him. And I owe him that, at least.* She recalled the blind volley the gunman had fired through her door, the bullet holes across her walls and ceiling. *Whatever the compunctions of the man who shot Winterstein, the one who confronted Scotty would certainly have killed him.* Another thought came to Jewett, and she spoke this one aloud. "The fact that they're 'like cops' doesn't excuse them from killing innocent people any more than being the President should. Those men are assassins, pure and simple. Hiding under the words 'patriotism' and 'loyalty' doesn't make what they tried to do any less evil."

Scott made no reply.

Not wanting to lose track of their current purpose, Jewett changed the subject. "All right. So what happens now? Did I wreck the plan?"

"Wreck it?" Scott looked up. "You did great."

Jewett got a sudden, nagging suspicion she had been set up. "You mean that was supposed to happen?" *I could have been killed.*

"Oh God, no." Scott took Jewett's hand. "I knew it was a possibility, which was why I put you under guard. But I figured Halstead and Winterstein would scare them off. Why attack two cops and risk recognition and more deaths for the same information they could get from a phone call? I figured they'd get someone important, perhaps the Surgeon General or the President, to talk to you and carefully slip in questions about Schober's equipment and condition. Or they might have remembered enough from their last visit, they wouldn't need to bother you at all." Scott shook his head. "Apparently, they figured you wouldn't talk without a direct threat. They still wanted you dead, so they figured they'd kill two birds with one stone." He winced. "Pardon the pun."

Jewett considered. "Why do they want me dead? I haven't done anything." She imagined living on the run, taking a new identity in an unfamiliar location. She thought of rebuilding her life step by cautious step, afraid to settle down or involve friends and relatives because the next knock on the door might come from a killer with a machine gun.

Scott squeezed Jewett's fingers reassuringly. "They're apparently worried you might still identify the murderer. You see him once too often on television, and it's all over. Once we've caught him, they have no reason to go after you any more."

Jewett felt as if the conversation was turning in circles. "You mean our plan is still on? You don't think they'll give up?"

Elaine answered. "You haven't been watching the news, have you, dear?"

Jewett glanced at the Schobers, too curious to respond with the sarcasm the question merited. "Of course not. Why? What's happening?"

Elaine and Scott exchanged knowing glances, and Jewett suspected they shared a secret beyond the explanation they were about to divulge. *My role in this deadly game is obvious. I wonder what Elaine is supposed to do.*

Scott smiled, his eyes as wide and bright as an excited child's. "President Nash is on his way."

"To present some sort of medal of honor to Stan," Elaine added. "The hypocrite."

No doubt any more. If the President would postpone his trip to Washington, he's involved in this murder. Jewett felt it was her turn to speak, but she had so many questions she could not decide which to ask first.

Scott saved her from the need. "If I could have predicted what you just went through, I would have prevented it. You believe that, don't you?" He met her gaze, his pale eyes pleading for her understanding.

Jewett knew Scott told the truth and saw no need to make him suffer. "Of course."

"But one good thing did come out of it."

"What?" It was an exclamation of startlement, but Scott responded as if to a query.

"Since your abductor planned to kill you after he got the information he needed, he didn't mislead you. He asked the essential information and nothing more." Scott picked at a piece of dirt on the radio at his hip. "If you can remember the questions he asked and the answers you gave, we should be able to piece together how the President plans to kill Dr. Schober."

The President plans to kill Dr. Schober. The words sounded strange to Jewett, as if someone had spliced together lines from two unrelated, but familiar, songs.

"Now," Scott continued. "Put yourself in their place. If you wanted to kill him . . ." He gestured toward the bed, and the constant gentle heart beeps became audible over the pause. ". . . how would you do it?"

Jewett considered, the idea of taking a life so beyond her nature she could scarcely conceive a method. "I'd pull out the ventilator hose. Or break the machine."

Scott shook his head. "Too obvious. He'll have three witnesses in the room, and he'll need to be subtle. Besides, he's seen the machines. If he planned to sabotage them, he wouldn't have needed to risk his men, or mine, questioning you. Think."

Jewett forced her mind back to the incident in her car. "He asked about Stan's condition, competency to testify, and exactly what he had witnessed."

"All appropriate to deciding whether they need to kill him." Scott tapped at the radio. "What else?"

"They asked about his medications." Jewett studied

Schober again where he lay quietly beneath his covers. The brain wave screen continued to light in a waking pattern. The heart monitor showed steady, augmented beats. The ventilator hummed as it delivered each breath. On a pole above Schober's head, the bag of liquid nutrition hung, a tan stream through a transparent tube leading into the catheter in his heart. *Anything lethal would need to be injected through the intravenous line. An intramuscular shot would leave tell-tale signs of trauma on autopsy. Oral medications would leave traces in the gut, especially in a patient injured less than a week ago. The accident would have slowed his intestinal transit time.*

"Okay." Scott rose. "Now, can you come up with some drug that might interact with one he's on? Something untraceable on autopsy." He paced toward Schober. "It's got to look like the doctor just drifted into permanent coma. If the coroner calls it murder, the only four suspects are going to be the patient's wife, his doctor, the police lieutenant on the case, and the President of the United States. None of us makes a good suspect. I don't think he'll take that kind of chance."

Jewett scooted her chair around to face the Schobers and Scott. "Nowadays, there's not much we can't trace, by enzyme activity if not the drug itself." The answer blossomed in her mind with such conviction, it seemed like the only intelligent possibility. *"Unless it's something the pathologist is expecting to find anyway!"*

Scott whirled, apparently intrigued by the excitement in Jewett's voice. "What do you mean?"

The words tried to tumble out together, and Jewett carefully arranged her sentences before speaking. "If they give him an overdose of a drug he's already on, it would pass right by the pathologist."

"So now all we have to do is figure out which drug," Elaine supplied.

Jewett shook her head. "That's the easy part. The standard medications we use on chronic care patients are mostly inert. We use them for months or years. We could quadruple the dose of his antibiotic without causing a problem. The anticonvulsant, pikobarbital, is the only logical choice." She recalled the effects of overdosage from years of experience with the medication. "It's a great drug. Works fast. It's metabolized quickly and easily, even in patients who don't have much renal or hepatic function. Hits every seizure known to man. In small doses it's completely safe. In large doses, it knocks out the cardiorespiratory system, which isn't a problem for a patient on an electrostim. Unfortunately, it also poisons the electrical conduction system of the heart and requires frequent dosing. That's why we get patients onto something safer and easier, like barobid, as early as possible. Oh, and it has no antagonist."

Scott exchanged a glance with Elaine, then looked back at Jewett, "Any chance you could repeat that in English?"

"I'm sorry." Realizing she had overused medical terminology in her fervor, Jewett half-stood, keeping one leg bent on the chair. "A single overdose of pikobarbital could kill Dr. Schober despite the machines. Once injected, there's no antidote."

"And the pathologist would expect to find pikobarbital," Scott finished. "Especially since you admitted in the newspaper article that Schober received too much of the drug, which is what supposedly put him into this coma."

"Right," Jewett confirmed. "It also means we're going to have to watch carefully and be ready to move instantly. We can't let the killer actually inject the pikobarb. If he does, whoever gets to Stan first will have to pinch off the I.V. line before the drug gets into the heart catheter."

"I'll stay right by his head," Scott promised. "You—"

A blast of static over the hand radio cut off Scott's next comment. A voice followed, "Scotty, Security reports the President's limo just pulled up outside the building. The lobby's stuffed full with reporters and cameras. What do you want us to do?"

Jewett knew Scott had not told his subordinates his suspicions about the President. To them, President Nash's visit was merely an annoying interruption to their attempt to corner Krystal Fantella's killer.

Scott pulled the radio from his belt and held it to his mouth. "Escort them to the chronic care ward. All of them."

"Uh, Scotty." A different voice replaced the first. "There's about a hundred newspeople. It'll be chaos."

"Good," Scott said, ignoring his subordinate's obvious reluctance. "The more the better. No one comes in this room. No one. I'm going to send Dr. Schober's wife out to get the award." He glanced at Elaine for confirmation.

Elaine nodded.

Jewett relaxed. *So, that's her part.*

Scott turned his attention back to the radio. "If the President gets insistent, call me again. And Jackson?"

The answer sounded hesitant. "Yes, sir?" It was obvious Jackson did not agree with Scott's plan and equally apparent he trusted Scott enough to obey without questioning.

"Don't let them bully you into anything. You answer to me. Ten-four?"

"Ten-four." Jackson went silent.

Scott poked a button on the side and refastened the

radio. He pointed to the door.

Elaine crossed the room, opened the door, and slipped between the guards. The door clicked shut behind her.

Scott's plan made little sense to Jewett either. *If he doesn't let Nash in the room, how can we catch him? I can't believe we're trying to pin a crime on the President of the United States.* Hoping to hear the exchanges in the hallway, and not wanting to distract the guards in the corridor with unnecessary noise, Jewett turned off the television sound, leaving only the hum and blips of the machines. "Where should I stand?"

"Out of the way." Scott's voice gained a sharp, commanding tone he had not used with his men. "Let me handle Schober and the President. We've taken enough risks with you. If I didn't think you were safer here, I'd send you home."

Safer in the lion's den than the sheep fold. It seemed ludicrous to Jewett, yet she knew Scott was right.

A rumble of sound started from the hallway, like distant thunder. The volume rose rapidly into a wild storm of conversation, occasionally pierced by a cry of "Mr. President!" or a growled "Get back!"

Scott pulled the chairs against the wall and returned to his post at Schober's head. Jewett took a position near the door where she could listen to the commotion on the main ward. The flash of cameras lit the crack beneath the door repeatedly.

The crowd went suddenly silent, apparently in response to some signal from Benjamin Nash. Despite microphone enhancement, the President's voice sounded soft after the mixed shouts of the throng, and Jewett had to strain to hear him.

"Fellow Americans! Friends! As you know, the President's Proponents for Life Award is an honor bestowed upon those people who exemplify and further the cause of eliminating death in our great nation. Dr. Stanley Schober has earned this award by showing that people dependent on medical technology are a viable and important segment of our society. His coming forth as a witness to murder will force the courts and our society to acknowledge that these people exist and are an up and coming force in our population."

An outpouring of applause followed. The camera flashes became almost continuous.

"For reasons of security, Dr. Schober cannot have guests. But we are fortunate to have Mrs. Elaine Schober, the doctor's wife and loyal companion for the last forty-five years. We would like you to accept Dr. Schober's President's Proponents for Life Award on behalf of the other chronic care patients on whom some segments of society would have us turn our backs."

The applause started slowly and spiraled to a constant clamor of sharp sound. There was a short pause during which Elaine spoke a few words too low for Jewett to discern, then the applause resumed.

President Nash spoke over the noise, apparently addressing a police guard near the door. "I would like to pay my respects to Dr. Schober before I leave."

Jewett glanced at Scott. The lieutenant stood with his head cocked and his hand raised, trying to listen to the reply through the door.

"I'm afraid that's impossible, sir," the policeman said. "Only Lieutenant Scott, Dr. Jewett, and Mrs. Schober have permission to enter the room."

An authoritative voice, apparently one of the President's entourage, challenged the guard. "That's the goddamned

President of the United States!" Threat colored the voice. "You're out of line. Now, let us through."

Jewett glanced at Scott. The lieutenant stared at the door, holding his breath. His obvious concern touched Jewett, and the importance of the moment struck her. *Does Scotty command enough respect from his men to drive them to disobey the President of the United States?* Jewett bit her lip, doubting the possibility. *He hasn't even told them he suspects the President of foul play. They would have to follow his commands with the same blind loyalty as the Secret Service men have shown Nash.*

The officer's momentary hesitation seemed to stretch into an hour. "I'm sorry, sir. You'll have to talk to my superior, Lieutenant Scott."

Jewett could almost feel the hostility that filled the following pause. Then, Nash's man spoke in a sharp, but diplomatic, tone. "Fine, bring this gentleman, Scott, out here."

"Good job, Mesner," Scott whispered beneath a congratulatory smile. He freed the radio, preparing for the call.

Jewett admired Scott's method of inspiring loyalty. Clearly, he had earned his subordinates' deference by handling dangerous and messy problems in the past, and he encouraged them to dump responsibility for odd requests on him. It made Jones' system of shouting and punishment, and the cowering irreverent obedience it inspired, seem petty.

Static crackled before Mesner's voice wafted over Scott's radio receiver. "Scotty?"

"I'm here."

"President Nash would like to pay his respects to Dr. Schober."

"The President himself?" Scott winked at Jewett, who smiled.

"Yes, sir."

"All right. We'll make an exception for the President. But he has to come alone. The entourage stays out."

Now, Scott's plan became clear to Jewett. *He can't let any Secret Service agents in. Otherwise, they'll attempt the killing, and we'll be back where we started. By refusing entrance to anyone, allowing Nash in alone seems like a compromise.*

The spokesman's voice sounded nearly as loud through the door as over the radio. "Give me that thing!" White noise crackled as the man apparently snatched the radio from Officer Mesner. "Lieutenant, you can't do that. The President doesn't go anywhere without his bodyguards."

Scott remained calm, and his soft reply made the spokesman sound rabid. "Who am I speaking with, please?"

"*General* David Claiborn, United States Army, retired. Director of Internal Security for the President of the United States." He emphasized his title, although it was military and bore no relation to Scott's civilian rank.

Scott placed a foot casually on one locked wheel of Schober's bed. He seemed to enjoy the confrontation. "General Claiborn, we have a comatose patient, a doctor, and a police lieutenant here. There're no windows and a bajillion police outside the door. The President will be in no danger. On the other hand, Dr. Jewett informs me Dr. Schober should have as little excitement and as few visitors as possible. This is my investigation. In my opinion, the President's entourage comprises a threat to Dr. Schober's health."

"Who the hell do you think you are?" Claiborn shouted, and the hubbub faded around him. "I'm going to have you fired! Forget fired, this is treason. I'm going to have you shot!"

Jewett's muscles knotted. She stared at Scott, but the threat seemed to leave him unaffected.

"I'm sorry you feel that way, General," Scott said. "In the meantime, I'm still in charge of this operation. The President comes in alone or not at all."

Jewett decided to press the matter. "Look, Scotty! The brain wave pattern. I think he's waking up."

General Claiborn disconnected with a snap of finality.

Scott carefully thumbed off his own radio. "Nice touch."

Jewett replied with a nervous nod.

The noise in the hallway intensified until Jewett could scarcely hear the steady buzz of the ventilator or the musical beats of the heart monitor.

After several seconds of presumed private conversation, Claiborn's voice again wafted over the receiver. "Lieutenant, prepare for the arrival of President Benjamin Nash. His safety is in your hands."

"I'm honored, General." Scott managed to keep mockery from his reply. "Please send Mrs. Schober in with him."

Jewett nodded approval. *She's safer here than out with the President's security force.*

Scott motioned Jewett away from the door, and she drifted toward the corner. The panel edged open. Jackson's somber, brown face poked through the gap. "Scotty?"

"Let him in." Scott turned Jackson a reassuring smile.

The officer pushed the door open. Jewett caught a glimpse of a wild crowd of news reporters, police officers, and plainclothes men before President Nash entered with Elaine, and the door swung closed behind them.

Nash acknowledged Scott with a nod. "Lieutenant." He turned toward Jewett. "Dr. Jewett, good to see you again."

"Hello, Mr. President." Jewett tried to sound casual, but her voice emerged as a pinched squeak.

Elaine Schober stood just behind and to Jewett's right,

her attention locked on the President.

Nash headed toward the bed. "Dr. Schober, I am certain you can hear me in the name of His Almighty. I just want to speak to you for a moment on behalf of the people you served."

Schober remained still, his eyes closed.

"You may not know how much good has come from your attempt to communicate with us. Your courage will result in the removal of a vile murderer from the streets of Des Moines, but you will do good even beyond your own knowledge. Your testimony will force the legal system of this great United States to recognize chronic care patients from across the nation as viable members of society." Nash rested his fingers on the side rail. "We must not allow the rights of the technologically dependent to be violated any longer by those who seek to prey on those in a weaker condition. On behalf of the men and women I have attempted to champion throughout my tenure as President and my life as a whole, I would like to personally thank you and express my deepest regrets that I could not present the President's Proponents for Life Award to you in person giving you the recognition you so richly deserve . . ." President Nash leaned closer to Schober.

Jewett could feel her heart pounding, half again as fast as the continuous blips of Schober's monitor. She recalled the last time Nash had stood over that same bed, attempting to heal a "seizure." She remembered Schober's eyes widening in what she had mistaken for awe but which she now knew must have been fear and outrage that the man he knew as a murderer would dare to touch him. *Scotty, watch him. Oh, please, watch him closely.* She tried to send a mental message.

". . . but you can rest, secure in the knowledge that your wife has done you much honor in accepting the award for you." Nash drew a handkerchief from his pocket, wiped his brow liberally, and returned it. He kept his right hand clenched. "There is no greater honor that can be received by a man than knowing he has done his fellow citizens so great a service."

Jewett noticed Scott's gaze on Nash's hands. The lieutenant looked bored, but Jewett knew it was an act.

The President continued. "Dr. Schober, I'm not sure what your religion is, but I'm certain that whatever it is, a prayer to the Almighty right now would not be misplaced. Folks . . ." Nash glanced at every person in the room. ". . . I would like you to join me and bow your heads in a moment of silence. With His healing power, I will attempt to do for you all that I may." Nash reached out to place his hands on Schober's chest.

Holy God! He's not going to inject into the I.V. line. He's going directly for the heart catheter! Before Jewett could shout a warning, Elaine gasped in agony. One hand clutched at her breast. The other gouged into Jewett's shoulder. She collapsed, dragging Jewett with her to the floor.

Heart attack! Jewett disengaged from Elaine's desperate grasp. The woman sucked for air in a wild frenzy. Her hands clawed at Jewett.

Scott spoke with quiet authority. "Mr. President, please open your hands."

Jewett groped past Elaine's flailing arms, and, to her surprise, found a hearty pulse throbbing in her neck.

The President glared at Scott. "What manner of mistreatment is this when we're offering a prayer for a man who has tried to do so much of a service . . . ?"

"Mr. President, open your hands now." Scott wrested his gun from its holster. "Mr. President, open your hands."

Did Nash inject yet, or not? Jewett pinned Elaine's arms.

"Hold still, please. Where does it hurt?"

Benjamin Nash lowered his hand, and Jewett heard the sound of plastic striking the tile floor. Elaine went still, eyes open, and her breathing returned to normal.

"Mr. President, back up against the wall!"

Nash shouted, "Rudy! Jeremy! Bruce! The man has a gun. He is pointing it at me."

Scott jabbed his pistol back into its holster, ripped free a handkerchief, and plucked something from the floor. As he rose, arms raised, shouts sounded from the hallway. Someone screamed. Jewett grabbed Elaine's armpits, hauling her from the path of the door just as several men crashed through it. Most wore suits, undoubtedly Nash's security force. Three jammed between Scott and the President, hustling Nash against the wall. Another four trained guns on Scott. Others wore the Des Moines police uniforms, also with pistols, but they seemed uncertain where to aim. Reporters pressed in behind, a veritable sea of curious faces.

They'll kill Scotty. Jewett screamed.

Scott hollered, his voice distinct above the noise, "Fellow officers, I have material evidence: a slapshot with the President's fingerprints. The President of the United States has just attempted murder on Dr. Stanley Schober. Make sure this gets to police headquarters and is enlisted as evidence. I want this public!" Cameras flared.

Jewett cringed, realizing Scott's tenuous position. Without the newsmen and the police officers, the Secret Service agents would simply have shot Scott and destroyed the evidence. *Elaine and I would have been discovered dead in the morning.* "I saw it, too!" Jewett added. It was a lie, but it might erase the temptation of the Secret Service men to kill Scott if they knew they had another witness. Even in front of the reporters, Scott's death might be considered a defense of the President. Hers could only be murder.

"And me." Elaine sat up as if nothing had happened. Ignoring the guns, she ran to her husband and locked him into an embrace.

"Put away the guns," Scott said. "No one's shooting anyone. Mr. President, you're under arrest for the attempted murder of Dr. Stanley Schober. You have the right to remain silent . . ."

"Get me out of here!" Nash screamed. The Secret Service men shoved through the crowd, elbowing people aside like weeds. Within seconds, they had the President halfway down the hall.

"Scotty, what now?" Jackson seemed eager to help, but a shoot-out between police officers would serve no one.

"Let them go." Scott lowered his hands and drifted back to the bedside. "They'll be easy enough to find. We've got evidence and witnesses, and we can add resisting arrest for the President. Obstruction of justice and aiding and abetting for his security force."

The immediate danger past, the Schobers' conspiracy with Scott became vividly clear to Jewett. *Elaine faked that heart attack so I couldn't stop the President from killing her husband.* Jewett saw the brilliance of the plan. *The Schobers got what they wanted. The police may never pin Krystal's murder on the President, but they've got him for Dr. Schober's.* She rushed to Elaine's side, sifting through the noise for the slowing beeps of the heart monitor.

Schober blinked rapidly several times.

Scott placed a hand on Schober's arm. "You're welcome," he said.

The heart monitor went flatline.

Epilogue

The following day, Patricia Jewett sat in her office, studying the growing stack of unread brain wave scans on her desk. Occasionally, she paused to tap her pen on the table and glance out the single window at the perfect rows of flowers on the hospital lawn. With time, her staring periods became longer, her work time shorter, until, at length, she perched on the edge of the desk watching each breeze bow the petals in a line of color.

A knock interrupted her procrastination.

"Who is it?"

"Pat, it's Kaign."

Jewett turned toward the door. "Come in, Kaign."

Jones opened the door, stepped across the threshold, and closed it behind him. He appeared the same as always, his features chiseled to classic American perfection, his dark curls shadowing soft, brown eyes. He looked beautiful, and yet, to Jewett, his stare seemed empty. It reminded her of the time she had returned to her childhood hideaway, an abandoned castle in a jungle harboring all the lions, tigers, and deer her imagination could create. But, at twenty-four, it had become just a broken-down shack in a dirty, wooded lot. The magic had disappeared.

"Pat, I want to talk about the wedding."

Jewett met Jones' gaze without flinching. "Don't bother talking about it. I thought about it a lot. I don't want to marry you."

Jones' face folded into shocked creases. Redness blossomed

in the center of each cheek and spread across his features like a rash. "You just got done talking to Scotty, didn't you?"

"Well, yeah."

"I told you not to listen to anything he said. You believed his story, didn't you?"

"And what story was that, Kaign?" Jewett kept her voice strong and level.

"Don't play dumb with me. I know he told you he caught me cheating with a nurse in an examination room."

Jewett wanted to feel angry and betrayed, but she felt nothing, just a hollow oblivion devoid of emotion. *I should have known.* "What nurse was that, Kaign?"

"Don't do this, Pat. You know damned well he told you he caught me cheating with Karla in the examination room."

Jewett shook her head, not daring to believe Jones had convicted himself. "Well, he didn't, Kaign. But you just did."

The blush faded from Jones' face. "You conniving bitch!"

"Kaign, I don't want to marry you." Jewett felt tears forming, and she blinked them away. "I don't ever want to see you again."

Jones looked incredulous. "You're dumping me for some stupid, ugly, little cop?"

"No." Jewett lowered her head, no longer able to hide the tears. "I'm not dumping you for anyone." She met his gaze directly, despite her tears. "I'm just dumping you."

Jewett drove home. As if to spite her, the radio blared the song she and Jones had considered their own, igniting a painful string of memories. *There's so much good in Kaign.* She recalled the quiet sessions clasped in his loving arms in front of the television or a movie screen, picnics by the river, his willingness to come to her defense at the slightest provocation, gentle sessions of love-making, and the familiarity nine years brings. But, she remembered, too, his loud, opinionated ways and the suffocating jealousy his own indiscretions turned disgustingly ironic. *I'm stronger now. I don't need his protection. I guess I've just outgrown him.*

By the time Jewett pulled into her driveway, her eyes hurt and dried tears had caked on her cheeks. Leaving the car, she walked to the porch, unlocked her front door, and entered. It seemed so different, like a stranger's house. The odor of coffee, the stench of gunpowder, and the less unpleasant smell of perspiration shrouded the more familiar odors of her customary cleaners. She closed and locked the door. Bullet holes scarred the walls and ceiling, and a patch of Winterstein's blood remained by the door. *Nothing is the same.*

Jewett crossed the room and pried the board from her window, letting the warm April air diffuse inside. *There are few enough things in this world to depend on.* She thought about how the man she had loved had cheated, and it did not seem to matter. She thought about how safe she had always felt in a house that had been violated twice in the same day, and it seemed impossible. She thought about the President of the United States, the man in whom the country placed its trust, a murderer. *I need a drink.* Jewett had not imbibed to the point of intoxication in years, yet the need to become numb, to disappear into a quiet void, beyond reality grew irresistible.

From the kitchen, Jewett retrieved a glass and a bottle of wine, purchased months ago on her alcohol allotment. Returning to the living room, she sat on the couch, in the wash of air from the window, filled the glass, and set bottle and glass on the coffee table. Finding the remote control on the arm of the couch she punched up the video. Selecting her and Jones' song, she watched the jazz dancers caper across the screen with the musicians. And cried.

The doorbell peeled.

A Time to Die

Jewett sighed, snapped off the picture and came to the peephole. "Who is it?"

A man in a white delivery costume stood on the porch, clutching a basket of multi-colored flowers. "I've got a delivery for a Pat Jewett. From 'Flowers Are Us.'"

Jewett's heart pounded. She knew it was probably Jones' way of apologizing, but the similarity to yesterday's shooting made her cautious. "Can I see some identification?"

The delivery man set down the basket. He reached into his back pocket, pulled out his wallet, and flashed a driver's license with his picture. Then, he showed her the card reading "Flowers Are Us."

Jewett shivered. "Thank you. Leave them on the doorstep. I'll get them later."

The delivery man hesitated. "I need a signature."

"Leave them on the god-damned porch!"

"All right." The delivery man backed away defensively.

Jewett slipped to the kitchen window and watched him climb into a truck in her driveway. She listened to the hum of the starter, then the vehicle glided onto the main street. She saw the side panel reading "Flowers Are Us" before it disappeared.

Jewett returned to the front door. She edged it open carefully and glanced out. Seeing no one, she grabbed the handle, jerked in the basket, closed and relocked the door.

Ignoring the brilliant array of petals, she pulled out the card. It read:

> *"Secret Diagnosis, 18:30 tonight.*
> *You have the right to remain silent . . ."*

Jewett crumpled the card into her fist. Gradually, a smile formed on her lips. *Gotta start somewhere.*

Jewett poured the glass of wine back into the bottle.

Author Bio

Mickey Zucker Reichert is the best-selling author of more than twenty novels and thirty-five short stories, including the Renshai trilogy, the Renshai chronicles, the Bifrost Guardians series, *The Legend of Nightfall*, *The Unknown Soldier*, *Flightless Falcon*, *The Books of Barakhai*, and *Spirit Fox* (with Jennifer Wingert). A pediatrician, Reichert lives on a forty-acre farm and divides time between a zillion animals, family (including three kids who only seem like a zillion), and "real-life research" for the novels and stories. Claims to fame: Both parents are rocket scientists, and having performed real brain surgery.